Mirrored Souls

Second Edition

Ella Shawn

Previously published in 2020 under
Mirrored Souls: Âmes en Miroire

Copyright

DEDICATION

For the little girl still gripped in guilt and shame who's masquerading as a strong, resilient, gracious, Black woman; Forgive yourself. You have nothing to be ashamed of and nothing to feel guilty about. Be kind to yourself and know you're loved.

Trigger Warning

Mirrored Souls is a dark romance. **Strong sexual themes** and **violence**, which may cause emotional and mental triggers for some readers. The **childhood abuse** written about in this novel is **graphic** and **disturbing**, which may also bring about emotional and mental distress for some readers. THIS BOOK IS NOT FOR EVERYONE! Please be advised.

RESOURCES: Found on www.Stopitnow.org

Rape, Abuse, and Incest National Network (RAINN)
 National Sexual Assault Hotline - 1.800.656.HOPE
SAMHSA Mental Health Services Locator (Substance Abuse and Mental Health Services Administration (SAMHSA))
 Resource directory to locate mental health services across the US.
 1in6.org
 Resources and help for men who have had unwanted or abusive sexual experiences in childhood.
 Male Survivor: Support, Treatment, and Advocacy (Male Survivor)
 Support, treatment, and advocacy for male survivors of abuse.
 Survivors of Incest Anonymous
 Provides support and resources for anyone who has been affected by child sexual abuse.
 survive
 An online forum and support resource for survivors learning to thrive.
 Partners of Adults Sexually Abused as Children
 Peer support for partners of adults sexually abused as children.
 Support for Partners
 Support and information for partners of an adult survivor of child sex abuse.
 Recovery and Support for Adult Survivors and Their Families: Book List (Child Molestation Research and Prevention Institute)
 Book list on healing and recovery for adults sexually abused as children
 Survivor Manual
 Resources on healing and recovery.

Part One

"Gazing into the Internal Mirror"

From time to time, we all must go into a landscape—be it inner or outer landscape—where there are no hiding places. Allowing the stark awe and silence to aid us in both communing and confronting the depth of ourselves. We fear emptiness because we know that within those places of nothingness we will come face to face with who we are the gaze into the internal mirror. But what is the alternative? Shall we go our entire life with hearing our own voice... without ever having met who we are when isolated from all?

Prologue

We never live the lives we deserve, not really, do we? We immolate our hopes and dreams as food to feed the childish monsters who live under our beds. Or sleep in the other bedrooms with our mothers. I learned early my dreams were only meant to choke me as I was forced to watch them fester, stink, and crust over like some kind of sore, rotten, sweet. There was no concern for the way my mouth stretched... or how I gagged on wretchedness I was being forced to digest— because what the hell else are we supposed to survive on?

My childhood was a joke, but I never got the punchline. Probably because... I was too busy getting punched to ever fall in the line that would have secured the benefits of my sacrifice.

My life is a hodge-podge of what-ifs, I-thought-I-understoods, and what-the-fuck-just-happened?! I don't know how I expected to hold on to the love of such an accomplished man, when I knew there were too many parts missing in myself to mirror his wholeness.

On most days, I only knew half of what was really going on and none of it was enough to make up an entire life. Moreover, I was too chicken shit to do anything about it... so. I let it go. I was good at letting shit go, it was the only way for me to survive. Put it in a jar, stick it on a shelf and give no fucks what happens after that.

It had always been that way. Ever since I could remember, and I only remember back to when I was sixteen. Anything happening before that is lost to me. I can't remember having a mother or anything other than pain. Pain. And more motherfucking pain.

I found the most real version of myself when I found my heart beating in the chest of a god, my soul soaring on the breath of an angel who knew I needed his dominance as much as I needed his unconditional love and

acceptance. Who or what I was before meeting my solace and despair didn't matter; not to him and not to me.

Maybe it should have because who and what I was before him is the reason we are starting where we are instead of continuing from where we were. If we knew back in 1993 what we later discovered after we continued to build a life propped-up on fear, hurt, and I-O-Us; we would be in a happier place.

***

The soft warm veil protecting peace from chaos, morphs into sharp, pointy edges, which threatened to impale my senses and draw me back into the promise of darkness. My eyelids open and I feel my entire face fold and blench, as I endeavor to accept the sights, smells, and truth of my morning. I'm back home in South Carolina. In bed with my husband. It's December. Time to embrace the ruined audacity of my reality.

~1~

It's been six months since John and I got back from The Caves Resort in Jamaica. Six months since the last time John and I were in the room downstairs in the basement. The room with a lock that wasn't there before. Some things about that night are clear as the Waterford Mondovi carafe pair sitting on the shelf in his office, others… not so much. I'm not sure I want to remember it all. Just like I can't remember the last six months— well, not in its entirety. I recall bits and pieces or some days, but most of it feels like I've been asleep and dreaming. *Lucid dreaming…yeah, that's what it feels like. An extremely fucked-up lucid dream.*

Six months, three weeks, and fourteen days since John cracked my mind, and infected me with the destructive shards of his love; leaving a parasite to feast off what remains of my broken soul. Searching the recesses of my mind for a reason to get up and be. Hosting this uninvited guest, has left me little room for breath, thought, or patience. So, I knew for certain, there wasn't enough room for me and whoever the hell else was lurking behind my eyes; waiting for me to slip away, opening the door to allow them to peak out and live this life. *Wait! Where the hell did that thought come from?*

The large warm hand protectively cradling my belly tightens as I move to disentangle myself from its possessive, yet gentle hold. *When was the last time I slept in here with him anyway?* I watch the sheet slide from my shoulders and continue its soft glide below my waist. It pools around my hips like some kind of virginal shroud. My heavy breasts are barely contained in the gray and black leopard-print cami, trimmed with black lace and cups big enough to carry two cantaloupes. But apparently, not big enough to carry these elephantine breasts I have now. *What the actual*

12

fuck? Why can't I remember when a whole damn baby crawled into my body and made me look like this?

My gray sleep shorts hug my toned thighs and it's enough to remind me what's happening to my waistline is not permanent and won't be my forever. Pregnant because my husband is a goddamned animal masquerading as a southern gentleman. A demon with the keys to heaven and no remorse what-so-ever in using them. *I remember how this baby was made. For that reason alone, I know it will be difficult to love it...at least the way I'm supposed to.*

Out of nowhere, my head starts pounding in the front, above my eyes like my last thought is too vile to stay inside my brain and needs to escape. The pain is slightly familiar. I've dealt with headaches like this my entire life, but this feels more urgent. More acute...what is happening? I try to reach back to wake John, when I hear a voice coming from inside my mind that doesn't sound anything like my own.

Probably why yo stupid bitch of a mama ain't never stuck 'round to see if you was gonna be alright. I mean fuck, who in their ever-motha-fuckin-right-mind could love a baby that got pushed into their pussy through their asshole? The laughter following the vile words rolled around in a tin-can filled with gravel being pulled by a string on the barely paved roads of my youth. The voice was raspy and heavy with sunup to sundown field work. And walking on dirt roads with dirty, dry, cracked bare feet. And having too many men take what wasn't offered, ruining any sense of self.

She sounds nothing like me and yet, she sounds like everything I left behind when I ran from my father. Defiance. Shame. Denial. Fear. Hope; the most dangerous forgotten part I left behind... She sounds just like hope.

***

13

I know I've been away in Washington state in some high-end psychiatric treatment facility; that's where I was when I finally came to a couple of days ago. John and the doctors explained my missing time as a psychotic break but were delighted to hear my voice.

"Lovely, I've missed your summer sunshine eyes and that full bottom lip being sucked into your mouth when you're feeling shy. Where the hell have you been for the last six months?"

"I don't know what—what you're talking about, John. Are we on vacation? Why aren't I sore in my bottom and what's going on with my belly... Do I have cancer?"

His eyes looked so sad and worried when he finally realized I had no idea what was going on or what had happened. His lips fell heavily on my forehead and then he was rushing from the room to get the doctors. I knew then, I was truly fucked and not just because John had a hard-on for my ass.

***

I realize the hand I try to shove away from my swollen belly is attached to the long, heavily muscled arm belonging to my husband. The reality and carnal nightmare form one big clusterfuck of riotous beating in my chest; when a sleep-roughened voice mumbles something that sounds a lot like *lovely,* and then I feel one of his long legs slide over both of mine. *There was a time I willingly got on my knees to worship this man as my god and savior. His cock my alter and his dominant commands my living bible.*

I shove against his arm where he is holding onto my belly like he knows if he doesn't protect this baby growing in my body, I would destroy myself to destroy it. As I push up to a seated position and prepare to leave the French country slay bed that feels more like a coffin than the luxurious centerpiece in our bedroom; I can't help but notice the beautiful, burnished

wood with its intricate inlay of darker more exotic African Blackwood, it only serve to further imprison me in this designer life I now find myself loathing.

I loved this custom-built home when John and I worked with an up and coming architect firm two years ago, but now the four walls don't feel like home. It's only a house I share with a husband. Not *my* husband, just *a* husband. The house I kept clean and immaculate for *a* husband. The house in which *a* husband destroyed every part of *his* wife he could. And I knew he would, didn't I? I can't blame him for being and doing who and what I knew he would? If I didn't recognize the darkness in him, I would never have given him those prophetic IOUs, but I did see it swirling in the chocolate depths of his eyes.

Every time he looked at me like I was his air. Every time he touched me like I was living water. Every time he fucked me like I was his only source of sustenance. I saw it, felt it, and craved it. I have to move past this if we're going to get through this mess. And I will—as soon as he turns in the I.O.U. I hoped he would never cash in, but always knew would be the first to be redeemed.

"John, don't you need to get up? You're going to be late…" *I had no idea if he was going to be late or not, I was just saying what I always said in the mornings when I woke up before him.* I rest my hand on John's right shoulder and gently nudge him into this world and away from the one where all men want to be him, and all women want to be with him. *Fuck if his dream world isn't the same as his real one.*

"Wake up. John." My voice is a little stronger and my nudge a little less gentle. He rolls over with a huge grin on his beautiful face and tries to pull me closer, so I'm lying across his flat stomach. I resist. There's nothing

sexy about being a fat ass when your husband looks like a damn porn star ready for his next scene in *Pregnant Pussy Stretcher, Inc.*

"Good morning, lovely. I remember when you used to wake me up with your beautiful lips wrapped around my dick. What happen to those mornings, huh? I miss them." His words come out in short staccato burst with soft notes of both laughter and regret playing accompaniment, Purcell's *Dido's Lament*. The minty smell of his morning breath makes me wonder how he always seems to have freshly brushed teeth. I wrinkle my nose to stop the automatic smile trying to kiss my lips and turn away from him as I shed warmed-over suffering from my soul and walk toward our en suite. I toss a mumbled thought across my shoulder, hoping the words would fall on fertile soil and flower soon. "Get your beautiful ass up and start your day."

"I love you too, lovely. So fucking much." I felt him watching me as I went from my dresser to my closet to the bathroom to get showered and dressed. God, I hated the distance and anger simmering between us, but until he redeems the I.O.U. he cashed in, I know I won't be able to move pass what happened six months ago. He has been so perfect. Doting on me and this damn parasite. *I want things to be better between us and I need him to do more than say he's sorry. Sorry doesn't mean he's ready to take responsibility for his actions…as if horrible didn't happened.*

"I love you, John. I miss us more than I can tell you." The words are spoken for my ears only. I make my way into the bathroom and locked the door behind me. My back presses against the cool wood and my head pounds with the pressure of the blood rushing through my body. I hope against all hope he hadn't heard my parting words, while simultaneously praying to every god out there that maybe he did. *I want my husband back and maybe I'll learn to love this baby inside me.* It's only been a few days

since I've returned from wherever the hell I've been, but he's been dropping hints about how much he misses us and what we were, but he doesn't mention what caused us to become what we are.

***

This is my favorite part of the morning. Standing under the spray of the rain shower head while the more than warm water sluices over my body. *At least I remember it being my favorite part of the day before... just before.* From the back, I don't look pregnant at all. *I have no idea what I've been doing to stay so trim and fit, whatever it is seems to be working.*

I'm pretty much done bathing, but the water feels so good and if I'm being honest; I need to come. I love the detachable shower head with its fourteen settings. I know I don't want John to touch me in a sexual way, but I need relief from the constant throbbing against my ever-swollen labia and pounding clit. I guess what some women shared with me months ago about being pregnant and horny was true. *Since I've come back all I think about is fucking. I'm so swollen, I came while sitting in the airplane for the five hours it took to fly back home. There was nothing else happening, just multiple, tiny orgasms shooting pleasure and confusion through my throbbing clit up into my womb.*

Using the shower head, I position it exactly where I need it the most and close my eyes, place my right foot on the shower bench and let my head fall back as the water pulses over my engorged clit. I know it won't take long for me to come but I want to draw it out. Make myself wait for it like John used to do. My imagination takes me down a dark tunnel and at the end, I find my sadistic, sexy-as-hell husband and I turn myself over to his transcendent touch. I'm so lost to the images floating through my head, I almost drop the sprayer.

His hands on my breast. Strong, masculine fingers pinching and pulling my nipples making them hard and sore... *so damn perfect*. His tongue slides up my spine until he gets to the area where my neck and shoulder meet. He mouths the skin gently, just before he bites down... hard. Holding me the way he wants to as he slides his perfect dick against my slit until he's completely coated in my arousal.

His thumb rubs my back entrance and I rotate my hips, encouraging him to plunge that digit deep inside. Instead of his finger, he pulls back and pushes my back until I'm bending over for him and I feel the smooth rounded head of his dick pushing against the back pucker of my asshole and with a deep breath, I push out against him and let him slide inside of me. Where he loves to lay savage claim to my body. To my very soul.

The orgasm steels over me and has me screaming silently into the water and hating myself for wanting what he forced me to love and crave in the basement of debauchery. Hating him for making me the slut my father said I was. Hating the fact I can't make myself come without fantasizing about him pushing through the sensitive tissues I hoped would never be used again.

After a useless orgasm and a quick towel dry, I put my panties and bra on, grab my whipped cocoa/shea butter and walk out into our bedroom. A pair of maternity jeans lay across the freshly made bed along with a white long-sleeve tee shirt and my favorite color, dove gray, cowlneck sweater. John had even placed some thick woolen socks and comfy shoes out for me. It's easy to recognize his efforts to show me his love and attentiveness. *Was he the one who shopped for my maternity clothes?*

Who else would be so wonderful and thoughtful to you? Of course, John went shopping for you. He only ever wants you to look and be your

best, yeah? It's time you let all this hurt go, Vivian and forgive him his trespasses, yeah?

What I don't easily recognize is yet another voice in my head. One that's trying to coax me into forgiving John for his *trespasses*? *Who the hell is she? And why does she sound like an old Black, Baptist church lady?*

Shaking my head to clear the voice and the ache behind my left ear, I walk to the door and stick my head out into the hall to look for John. I don't see him, and I need him to help me rub this butter on my skin, as well as help me get dressed.

"John?! Can you please come up here…I need help with my—" The words died on my tongue when something catches my attention on the bed. I look closely at the piece of paper that was placed unassumingly on my pillow. *If it had been a snake, it would've bitten me.*

I knew exactly what it was. I felt the burn of tears on my lower eyelids and parts of my broken soul start to fuse back together. The worn piece of paper feels like it's been handled over and over again. Like a worry doll, rubbed to ease the weary mind. My hands tremble when I bring it up closer to my face. It smells of whisky, iron, and John. *How nervous was John when he placed this notice that it still trembles when I pick it up?*

2

"Babe, you're o—" His steps falter and come to a halt before he enters the room, his breath saws from his mouth and nose as he looks at me holding the I.O.U in my unsteady hand.

His teddy-bear brown irises move over my face leaving warmth and comfort in their wake. He focuses on the wrinkled piece of paper with the large, red letters stamped across my handwriting from seven years ago, and then back up to the drops of forgiveness dribbling down my cheeks. His breath is caught somewhere between hope and oh, shit. He knows our future is suspended between my tears and my acceptance of what this piece of paper means for us.

"Vivian, you're all right." Not a question because he already knows the answer. I'm afraid to lift my eyes and allow him to see the questions and possibilities scorching the summer-sunshine and blue skies in my eyes. The bold, red letters read; REDEEMED.

"John? What is this?" I'm fully aware of what I'm holding in my hands, but I need to hear him say the words. I need to hear him take responsibility for what he did to me. To us, six months ago.

"You know what it is. I was planning to go to my safe when it happened, Viv. Cut *that* I.O.U. out and give it to you the next morning. But so much happened after you asked me for help." His eyes are seeing something from six month ago, and I can only imagine the horror of the moment he saw me crack. He continues in a broken voice. "I went to you, tried to wash you. Make you clean, again. You were *you* for about five— maybe ten minutes and then." His voice breaks further and his face cracks down the middle as memories of that sickening night play on repeat.

"Then what, John? What did I do that has you looking so… abandoned?" He turns his face toward my whispered words. I'm

expecting to see the broken pain of minutes ago, instead I'm faced with...what is this, anger?

"Then—you. You fucking left me, lovely." His control dissipates right in front of me and I ached to kiss the pain cascading down the sculpted beauty of his face as he endeavors to explain to me what happened.

"... and we've been dealing with the pregnancy and me without *you* and... I just—I didn't know how to give it—if you would still accept it after. Just after you chose to leave me behind."

I didn't give him a chance to finish whatever he wanted to say. It didn't matter anymore. I had what I needed from him. The rest we will figure out together. I wrapped my arms around his neck and sealed my lips over his before he could wrap his arms around my expanding middle. I push my tongue into his mouth as our tears mixed and bleed into the sloppiest, wettest kiss we've ever shared. He did it...he redeemed the I.O.U. *I can love us again.*

I clutch the paper in my hand as I ravish his mouth. I have him back. I'm ready to move past that night, fall back in love with my soulmate.

"I love you, so damn much. I needed. I needed to know you knew what you did—what you took from me. From us when y—you did that." The heaviness that had been draped across my shoulders like a death shroud was gone. Wings. It felt like wings grew from my shoulder blades and spread out behind me in beautiful iridescent colors.

He pulls the I.O.U from my weak upturned hand; I don't know where he places it and I don't care.

"You are the most important human being in my world, lovely. Of course, I knew what I did to you. To us. I died in that shower after I left you on the floor in the basement. I tried to convince myself that all you needed was some aftercare, some soft words, and me. But I knew, lovely. I

goddamned knew I'd raped and sodomized the other half of me." His voice sounds like hard whiskey over smooth sea glass and I want to be his safe space. I know it killed him to redeem this, but knowing he *knew*, helps me appreciate the sacrifice I made in giving him the I.O.U. in the first place.

We're older and know so much more about each other than we did when I gave him the poem seven years ago, but in so many ways we're still learning who the other is. Who each of us is.

***

Without a word, I lift the I.O.U. from the bed where John placed it and walked over to the desk, still in my underwear, pull out my favorite writing pen, turn the paper over, and sign my name to the back and write ES IST VOLLBRACHT (IT IS DONE) under my signature. *There! It's over. I'm done with it all. He has more I.O.U.s but this was the one I feared the most. But it's done and I'm mostly intact. I think.*

"Do we need to talk about this anymore? Lovely?" The tears had dried up, but uncertainty coated his skin and turned his face into a cast-iron frying pan just emptied of hot grease. I wanted to wipe the slickness from him, he was too beautiful to be anointed in the unholy oil of guilt.

My body moved towards him without my permission. I missed his skin against my own. The scent of love, pine trees, and domination. Mostly, I missed knowing I had the right to touch him. So, in that moment when my feet stood almost touching the steal toes of his boots, my right hand reached for that mouth I knew better than my own and my thumb ran from left to right on the top of his full lips as my lips brushed across his left cheek.

"No, John. There's nothing to talk about except what there is to talk about." He knew exactly what I was referring to and neither of us wanted

to confront the broken jars that still lay on the cold floor of my soul, but we only had about three months before a baby would be in the mix and we had work to do to get my jars put to rights.

"Can you rub this whipped coco butter on my body; paying close attention to my belly? I have a hard time bending over anymore." He looked like I'd just asked him to cash a check for a million dollars and by all the pussy he wanted with it. And then it hit me like a wet rag to the face. "You haven't touched me since… that night." I stated the fact. His head moved from left to right a couple of times and he reached a shaking hand out to touch my belly.

"God Vivian." His broken voiced almost breaks me, *again*. I watch as his knees give out and he crashes like breaking waves upon the shore before me, both of his strong hands on either side of my belly. His touch is reverent. I feel a knot in my heart untie itself and reconfigure into a bond between John, our baby, and me.

I lift his face to mine, and I rub his soft, black hair with my free hand. His eyes undo me, and I apologize for keeping our pregnancy away from him, but he cuts my words short with his own tearful ones.

"No, lovely. I apologize. I'm the one who needs to apologize, baby. I did this to us, to you. Oh my God. I never knew I could hurt you and when I did—I just," He continued caressing my belly and whispering his apologies.

"It's over. I knew you would do this, but it's over. I had no right to keep you from being a part of our pregnancy. No matter how this child was conceived, she is ours. Even when we fuck like animals, it's in love. I forgot. I'm sorry, John."

He stood and his eyes dropped to my mouth and back to my eyes, asking permission to kiss me. My head swept up in answer and he kissed

me like my mouth was his personal baptismal pool and only my tongue, lips, and saliva could make him clean again. Worthy of my love. My forgiveness. Worthy to father this unborn child who may have been conceived when he fucked my ass. *You know good an damn-well this fuckin' thing was fucked into your shitty-asshole, bitch. Where the hell else would a demon be made?*

I pull instantly away from his touch, and the look on his face is just this side of what-the-fuck-are-you-doing and is-everything-all right? I have to tell him about this ignorant woman's voice rattling inside my head.

"John. We have a lot to talk about, but right now I just want to make up for the last six months of missing you. I need you." A smile creased my plump lips and I notice the growing bulge in his pants and just like that, my panties are ruined and I'm throbbing for him. The voice is forgotten, and my sex-flooded mind can only think about what it will be like to have him inside me again.

"Lovely, I haven't fucked you in six months. I wouldn't give myself permission to jack off because I didn't deserve it. You're pregnant and I have a mini Louisville Slugger pressing against my left thigh." I couldn't help myself; I had to look and verify what he said. And sure enough. It looked like the fat part of a mini bat lodged against his thigh. Not quite 18", but at least 8" if memory serves me right. His gruff voice brings me back to the moment. "…I don't want to hurt you. How do we do this?"

His trepidation was endearing, but he really didn't have to worry. Well maybe he should be a *little* worried…because I hadn't fucked him in six months either. Hell, as far as I know, this morning in the shower was the first orgasm I've had since everything went to shit downstairs.

"We'll figure it out."

John's eyes hold mine for an epoch. the look on his face was one I had never seen before. It wasn't fear as much as self-doubt. I know I didn't want the dominant man who broke me, but I also knew I didn't want the unsure man standing before me either.

"John—I don't know how to do this. We have so much to get through and over…"

"We'll figure it out." He tosses my words back to me as he opened the jar of body butter to rub my belly.

"Yes, I guess we will."

3

We were both dressed in our jeans and sweaters. I looked around the downstairs area and noticed we had done absolutely no decorating for the holidays. It's as if we've been existing in some type of post-trauma fugue. Honestly, this is the first morning it feels as if I'm truly awake. I don't even remember the last six months. I know I've been keeping my appointments with an OB-GYN; I know I've been seeing a psychiatrist three days a week, but honestly, I can't tell you what happened in those visits. I can't even recall the names of the doctors I saw. *What the hell has been going on in these last six months and why can't I remember any of it?*

I look up and realize I've been standing at the bottom of the ornate staircase staring off into space while John has already started breakfast. I get my shit together and waddle towards our country-French inspired kitchen and see my husband standing at the god-sized THOR range making what smells like French toast and turkey bacon. He looks so comfortable and relaxed. *Has he looked like this for the last six months or has he been carrying around as much tension as the knots in my neck tell me I have?*

"John?" I hate the question in my voice as much as I hate the confusion floating in my brain like some kind of dead cold fish. I'm standing behind one of the large marble islands with my hands spread shoulder width on the cool cream stone with hues of gold and obsidian running roughshod like veins in an addict's arms. He looks over his shoulder to acknowledge me and the smile adorning his usually austere face makes my heart hurt. I lift my right hand to the center of my chest to rub the ache out. *He's so goddammed beautiful.*

"Hey lovely. Are you all right?" He's turned back to face the stove, the muscles in his back roll like thunder under the soft skin and Tarheel

blue cashmere sweater covering them. He's effortlessly masculine and sensuous, and he owns himself and me, thank God.

"Yes. I think so. I don't know. Why don't we have the Christmas decorations up? What did we do for Thanksgiving? Have you been going to work during the week?" My questions are rapid-fire bullets landing in all that lupine-like muscle in his back, but I can't stop them from firing from my mouth. I know he's staring at me now and still I continue to ask because I can't stop myself.

"Have we been seeing someone to help us with what happened... I mean, are we in couples therapy or something? Did the police get involved with the... *rape?*" I wince when the word drops from my lips like a cannonball. No explosion, just a word, but it weighs my soul down. I lift my head but keep my eyes down as I continue to question him. "Did you get me medical help after everything happened or did you just give me aftercare? How did we find out I was pregnant; didn't the OB-GYN think I was in bad shape when she—wait, is my doctor male or female? Is it Dr. Renick?" Each inquiry is shredding the cashmere material of his sweater; tearing his flesh from the bones keeping his 6'5" frame standing erect. When I raise my eyes from the basket I've weaved my hands into, and watch his tortured face, I know something is wrong. Not just wrong but fucked-up-beyond-all-recognition-wrong.

"Lovely?" He has no idea what else to say. His face is play-dough sitting on the table waiting for a child's small innocent hands to come and make something interesting with it. I hate I put that look on his face. I don't even know why he's looking so ashen and lumpy about his mouth and eyes and forehead. *Am I supposed to know the answers to these questions? He looks like I just stabbed him in the back with his own favorite knife."*

27

"Baby. I'm going to come over to you, okay? Don't be afraid, I'm not going to hurt you. I promise." His coaxing voice is grating on some nerve I didn't know I had, and my confusion is quickly morphing into a blue flame of anger. *He must think I'm fuckin crazy. Oh, now he wants to come and treat me like some fuckin patient. I got his mothafuckin patient.* I realize I'm not the one feeling the rage, but I *do* feel it, too.

He moves his big body away from the range and glides over to me. His arms swing loose beside him, in a non-threatening manner as his eyes lock onto mine… like he's trying to see into my brain and figure out what the hell is going on in there. *Hell, I hope he can figure it out because frankly, I have no idea what is happening inside here.* Standing beside me, the front of his body is pressed against the entire length of my left side. I can feel the deep rise and fall of his chest as he tries to take in enough oxygen to feed his brain and his muscles. Large hands encase me. His left-hand spans across my belly and his right hand spans the width of my lower back. Up until this point, I didn't realize how badly I was shaking.

What this mothafucka need to do is back the fuck up from my baby. No rights. He ain't got no rights where this goddamned baby and me is fuckin concerned. Move the fuck on, Jonny. Move yo country-wanna-be-white-ass. Mothafucka!

I feel myself slipping away, but I don't want to leave John with this crazy woman yelling in my head. She's strong and wants out to hurt John. His voice pulls me back from wherever I was sliding into and I'm surrounded by pine trees, warmth, and some scent that only belongs to John.

"Don't be scared, Vivian. I know you are confused about what's been going on and why the house isn't ready for the holidays. You may be confused about a lot more, but I have so much to tell you. So much to clear

up for you." John's hands are firm on my belly. His breathing is deep and even as he starts to rub small circles on my back. It feels so good and I'm reminded of his promise to always protect and care for me.

"Babe? There's this w-woman's voice in my head. Sh-she doesn't sound like me at all, but she's..." My voice trails off and my breathing matches his now and I can feel myself slowly calming down. He doesn't say anything to me, just keeps rubbing and breathing. Eventually, I look up into his chocolate eyes with tiny pieces of gold foil dropped inside, and I see his pain, his fear, but mostly...I see his love. It was mostly his love melting and dripping from his eyes onto his slanted, high cheekbones.

Don't let this lying fuck bullshit you! He don't love you. He ain't never love nobody. If he love you, he woudna fuck you up like he did? Viv! Don't be a stupid ass ho. This mothafucka don't know how to love a used-up bitch like you. Girl, how the fuck could a man like him love a nothin piece of shit-cake like you? Fuck! You less than a nothin, you ain't even part of a goddamned whole. I'm callin bullshit. Game over, bitch. Let's leave his corny ass. C'mon, bitch.

"She won't stop screaming, John. I don't...can you hear her, too. John? She's so angry and *ignorant.* She's screaming about how you can't love me, can't really love me because you love to hurt me, love to break me. She hates you; she wants me to hate you."

"Come with me Vivian, I want to show you something and I hope this helps you understand what's happening with you. I'll answer every question you asked, just come with me into my office and we'll talk, okay?" His right hand was now entwined with my left one and I felt the slight tug on my arm as he led me to his office. I was both curious and afraid to see whatever it was he wanted to show me, but I knew I trusted him and it would have to be enough.

He led me to the teal-blue, leather Chesterfield in front of the wall of bookcases filled with every kind of book; from first editions to caches of comics. I perch on the edge of the supple leather, not sure if I want to see what he's going to show me, but I know I need to. As he rummages around in his desk looking for god only knows what, my heart is running a race with Marcus Green, as I watch his eyes scan over papers and folders and all sorts of other shit.

Finally, he stands with both his hands clutching what looks like a file-folder full of—I have no idea what could be in there, but he's walking toward me with pinched eyes and flat lips. *I'm scared. I don't know what he has, and I know I'm not going to like whatever it is just from the line of his shoulders.*

"Okay, Viv. This is going to be a lot for you to take in, but I'm proud as fuck of you for taking this step. I can't imagine how hard it's been for you, and I need you to know how much I love and respect you for the hard work you've done and will continue to do." He takes a deep breath and places the heavy folder on the wood-stump coffee table in front of us. With his large hands on top of the pile of folders, I can't help but to notice how long and thick his fingers are and some part of me remembers how he used those fingers to fuck me to orgasm, but I'm probably not supposed to let my mind go there.

"Do you remember what happened last June in the playroom?" He sounds like some kind of detached lawyer asking his client about the facts for the case.

"Yes." My eyes are downcast because I'm ashamed of what happened to me. Embarrassed because John fucked my ass and saw me bleed. Before he continues to ask his questions, I feel his index finger and thumb grip my

chin. He forces my eyes up to meet his; shame and hurt collide with sorrow and regret.

"This shame is not yours, lovely. It belongs to me. I am the one who's carrying this shame. Don't ever let me see your head lowered about that night. It was not your fault. You did nothing wrong... not a goddamned thing. Let me know you understand and accept what I'm saying." He was so solemn. I knew he hated what happened, knew how he beat himself up over what he did to me, but still I couldn't help taking the shame as my own. *It's what I what I was created to do.* Wait, where did that thought come from?

"I know, and I hear what you're saying, John. But I—" Large, warm hands wrap around my face; thumbs rubbing my temple to soothe me; I melt into his touch, into his love. "I love you." I don't know why I say it, I just need him to know how much I love him... even after June.

"I know you do, lovely. And I'm so goddamned grateful for *your* love. Even though I know I don't deserve it, I'm selfish and I won't refuse what you so willingly give." He clears his throat and looks at my lips and back to my eyes. I know this look. He wants to kiss me, but he needs my permission to do so. With a quick nod of my head, I watch as he lowers his sinful mouth to my own. This kiss is soft and gentle. His full lips fit over mine like a hermetic seal; airtight and leakproof. I want to open to him, but I know that isn't what he wants this kiss to be. This kiss is an apology, a way for him to show me how much he values and appreciates me. I let him press his closed mouth to my own and the drag back and forth between us is a sweet, tortuous friction that has me doing kegel exercises to stop the viscous liquid drenching my panties.

"I need you to understand what is happening with you. What's been going on over the last six months. Okay, lovely?" He whispers all these

31

words against my lips and gives me one last gentle touch before turning his attention to the folder on the table. I pull my eyes from the banked golden heat raging just beneath the deep brown color of his irises and take a deep breath to force myself to pay attention.

You always been a stupid bitch for this charcoal colored son-of-a-bitch. Why? What the hell's so fuckin special 'bout him, anyway? He black as tar, his lips are thicka than your pussy-lips, and okay... I'll give him credit for height, body, and his long-as-fuck, juicy-ass dick, but really...

"Why doesn't she like you, John?" His head snaps up and his eyes regard me with a mixture of fear and wonder. I don't think he's going to answer me when he surprises me when a huge self-deprecating grin stretches across his beautiful face. That's when I notice some of the tension leave my neck and shoulders.

"She has good reason to hate me. Fuck, I hate me for the same reasons she does." The smile fades as he says the last part and I know he's thinking about more than what I'm starting to call *Ass-Gate*.

"Wait, you know *her*? I mean, is there really a *her* to know?"

"She's made herself known for a long time, Viv. At first, I didn't know what the hell was happening with you, but almost from the beginning of our relationship, she's been lurking behind your beautiful summer-sunshine-eyes."

"Really? I—I don't understand. What are you saying? You. You talk about *her* like she's someone different from *me*... like she's *apart* from me, not *a part* of me."

I'm staring at John like he's been the mental patient for the last six months. My eyes lose their focus and I feel like I'm going to tip right the hell over but I don't, and he wouldn't let me if I did. I look in my lap and realize I'm holding what looks like medical forms… lots of medical forms. The date on the first page is June of this year. The letterhead is navy blue, with bars of shamrock and emerald green. A calming ribbon of white with macaroni and cheese orange running over, under and through it put me at ease, somewhat. The name was simple; The Center. Located in Edmond, Washington on the Pacific Northwest coast.

"I know you told me we've been in Washington state for the last six months, but I can't remember one second of it. And you know how much I love Seattle; wouldn't I remember being so close to my favorite city in the world?" My eyes flip from the pages to his face as my right-hand flicks page after page of medical records. I don't know what to think or how I should feel because right now, I don't feel anything. I'm an abscessed gum shot through with too much Novocain.

"After I—" His face pinches in on itself as he tries to own his actions, but it is the pain leaking from his eyes and dotting his top lip that makes me shake my head in understanding. Hoping he will just move on from the incident and get to the explanation. I want to spare him the self-loathing and hurt seeming to crush his soul. He shakes his head, clears his throat, and continues to tell me what he started to.

"After I raped and sodomized you. After you came back to yourself and told me you were afraid. I tried to give you aftercare, but nothing I did seemed to help you. Not physically. Not mentally. Your body was shutting down right along with your mind. I was scared shitless, lovely." John has always been so self-composed and confident; watching him wringing his

hands and pacing back and forth in front of me… occasionally running his capable hand from the front of his forehead all the way to his strong neck. Squeezing the taunt muscles for a few seconds before starting the process all over again. This was disconcerting to say the least.

"Did you take me to the hospital?"

"Yes. I had to. I couldn't stop the bleeding and you were." He pauses as if he's searching his brain for the right words or the right way to say the right words. *Oh, John, I forgive you. I already told you I forgive you.* "…disconsolate."

"Did the people at the hospital try to arrest you?"

"Yes, they did."

"Why didn't they If they had done a rape-kit, wouldn't they have found your semen?"

"Yes. But they didn't do a rape-kit. They didn't have to. I told them exactly what happened. Every disgusting detail and they asked you if you wanted to press charges…"

"Did you tell them I was out of my mind? In no condition to answer questions?"

"Yes. I told them. I asked to be given time to find a suitable treatment facility for you and then I would turn myself in. Passion is no defense for rape."

"How are you not in jail right now, John? N-not that I want you in jail. I mean. I don't *think* I want you in jail. Did I want you in jail?" *Sweet baby Jesus! I sound bat-shit-crazy. Why am I even allowed to be out of the loony bin?*

"*You* didn't. No. Lovely, you didn't want me in jail, but *she* did, and I can't believe how much I agreed with her."

"She. Who the hell is this *she*?" John. Stop talking in riddles and tell me what's going on!" I felt myself getting agitated and obviously, the baby didn't like any of it. She moved her body around inside my body; kicking me in the ribs and sitting her little rump on my bladder. *Jesus H Christ on a donkey! What the hell is going in on there. This baby is going to push my bladder right out my vagina.*

I wrap my hand around the bottom of my belly as my faced screws up in pain.

"Viv! What's wrong… is it the baby?" John squats in front of me with both hands wrapped around my lopsided belly with concern sifting through his eyes like pregnant rain clouds.

"She kicked me in the ribs and sat her tiny ass down on my bladder! The little booger. She must not like me fussing at her daddy." *She's not even outside my body and she's already a daddy's girl,* I was still complaining, but I felt her move into a more comfortable position. I could take a breath and it gave me some clarity. One more deep breath through my nose and slowly out through dry lips. "I'm ready to hear the rest…I think."

You think you ready to hear the rest of this fucked up story? You won't ready when I showed him me… if you can't keep it together and I get my ass outta here… Let's just say you ain't gonna see the light of day. Not ever again!

"I'm going to get you some water and a light snack; she's probably hungry. Then we'll talk about what's been going on with you." He kisses me on my temple and runs his thumb across my cheek before turning to stride toward the door to leave his office. Just as he crosses the threshold, he turns around and pins me with an unreadable look and tells me, "Sit back, put your feet up here…" Making his way back over to me, mumbling

about something under his breath and then he says to me, "Let me help you." He gently placed my feet on a pillow he placed on the coffee table and gave each of my socked feet a kiss on the top before leaving to get my water.

I use the time to calmly look through the medical records—my medical records in the folder while actively ignoring the grating voice yelling in my head. Page after page of assessments, observations, and prescription authorizations. The words jumping from the page are typed in all caps at the top of each page in a rectangular box labeled 'Diagnosis'. Apparently, I have been diagnosed with Dissociative Identity Disorder. (DID)

My eyes sweep up towards the door as John walks in with a glass of water and bowl of fresh fruit. The moment he sees my face, he knows. He knows I now know just how crazy and fucked up I am. His feet have stopped moving. The right foot, the one he leads with is in front of his left one; which only has the toe on the floor while the heel is lifted.

"Lovely." In just one word, he asks thousands of questions and conveys even more answers. I don't think he's ever called my name like that before. Each letter drips in guilt and shame. Every syllable caressed with apologies and regret. He believes he's culpable in my dissociation. He's taking full responsibility for it because it's what he does. It's who he is.

"John, how long have I been home?"

"I brought you home yesterday. lovely."

"Have I been in the treatment center all this time? Spending my pregnancy there instead of here. Why don't I remember being there?"

"The entire time we were there, she was in charge. We couldn't reach you, so the doctors felt it best to deal with her. To work through her in hopes of getting you to come back."

"But, it didn't… it couldn't have worked. Because I don't remember anything after *ass-gate*. I don't know what's happening." My head is covered in heavy wet blankets of tommyrot. I can't seem to lift them as they get heavier and heavier. I feel my shoulders slump as my neck gives under the pressure and weight of dread and misunderstanding and hatred and need.

You are the weakest bitch. I'm over this bullshit. You don't even deserve to have this body, this man, this life. Every time somethin comes up that scares you or hurts your goddamned feelins… you cry for me to come and take care of shit.

I don't need you to take care of this. I need to know who or what you are. I need to know why you hate me so much and what rights you think you have to my body, my husband, and my life.

You wanna know who I am. What I am?! You cock-sucking-cum-whore-slut. You crack me the fuck up. I'm the new and improved version of you. The you who can handle shit… any shit that come my way. I don't take nothin' from nobody and I'm always about my business. My money and my pleasure. I'm the you, you wish you could be.

What's your story? Do you know everything about me? You know what I know? It doesn't sound like it. Did you graduate from Carolina? Do you know what happened to me before my father sent me to college?

"Vivian." John's voice yanks my mind back to the present. My eyes open and the light is like sharp daggers piercing my brain through my eye sockets. The pounding in my head is so severe I expect to feel blood leaking from my ears, nose, and mouth.

"John, she hates me. She hates I have you, and *my* body and our life. She wants it for herself." I realize I sound completely insane. Because I am

completely insane. *Why would the doctors send me home if they hadn't fixed me, yet?*

I feel John's warm hand rubbing my ankles as he sits beside my feet on the table. My eyes are still closed, but behind my lids images of places, people, and experiences I don't remember flash like little square images from a child's View-Master. Watered down pictures framed in fuzzy-white edges that seem to warble in and out of focus. None of them look familiar, but John appears in a few of them. Some shatter my heart with a hurt unlike any I've ever known.

Why are you showing me these lies mixed with some version of the truth?

Because you need to know what happened when I owned this body. There are no lies between us. What you seein is exactly what happened over the last six months. John likes it dirty and he likes it painful. I gave him what yo sorry ass can't, and he took it. You think them damn doctors wanted to send yo crazy ass home with the man who raped and butt-fucked you?

He wouldn't choose to keep me sick to have what he wants sexually. He wouldn't even touch me this morning, he didn't want to hurt me. He hasn't even jacked off... I know he hasn't been with you and certainly not in that way. This is my body; I don't care whose mind controls it. THIS. IS. MY. FUCKING. BODY. And my husband would not use my body like that.

Wouldn't he? Didn't he already? You think the little bullshit I.O.U means somethin to him... Please? Stop kiddin yo'self. You married a mothafuckin' monster. You and every other woman he so-called loved has been destroyed. He's the only fucker left standin' in all of this. You want to live; you want to survive John? You need to trust nobody but you and

well—I'm just another, stronger, tougher part of you. So, trust me and yourself and we can get what we need to from this bastard.

Wait a minute. I need to think, and I need to at least look like I'm not losing my mind. Give me some time to weigh my options. Let me get through this day without you shouting in my head and then when we are alone, we can talk.

Whatever. Don't be fooled by his foot rubs and sweet talkin. Don't let him fuck you and don't let him know anythin else about me and you. Vivian, I been protectin you for the last six months; who the fuck else are you gonna trust. And remember, it ain't just you no more. There's a girl-baby growin inside and we have to do for her what nobody did for us.

I know...I think I know. Give me today and then we will talk. Um...I don't know what to call you—I don't know your name.

Call me Valery or Val. My name is Valery Denyle.

6

"Baby, are you all right? Your eyes have been going a mile a minute for some time now. Are you asleep?" John's voice is a balm for my splintered soul, but seeds of doubt have been planted and I'm left with fear and suspicions about my own husband and my life. He's now sitting beside me on the Chesterfield, my shaky, left hand is sandwiched between his.

His hands are cool and dry, no nerves or anxiety. Just quiet, calm comfort. His shoulder, rounded with hard muscle, lends heat to my left arm; making me languid and pliant. Everything he's doing seems so innocuous, but my mind is making him a villain; someone out to get me; to use and destroy me. But a bigger part; the part connecting my gut with my cells, knows he's not the person Valery says he is. My soul knows he's not evil. *Broken*? Yes. But not evil. His soul mirrors my own, and I'm not evil.

"No, I'm not asleep. I'm just waiting to hear from your mouth, in your words what all this means." I take a cool sip of water and place it on the glass coasters with the letter *E* emblazoned in the center. "I'm ready to know what's been happening in my life for the last six months?"

A rumble rolls through his chest and washes over me like pumice stone, sluffing the rough and worn parts away and leaving me smooth and polished.

"Okay?" He considers me like he's trying to figure out if I'm me or if I'm her. Or maybe, I'm just reading too much into him because of what Valery showed me. Either way, I listen as he tells me about the last six months. "I found The Center after an exhaustive search with help from a team of doctors across the country. I wanted the best for you, and this treatment facility in Edmond is the best." John's thumb continually rubs across the knuckles of my hand, further soothing and calming me. His face is an open book, every word clearly written for me to read and decipher.

She must be trying to manipulate me. I'll be sure to keep my thoughts about my husband to myself. I have to figure out her endgame.

"How long did it take to get me admitted into The Center?"

"Not long. Money talks; bullshit walks." A rueful smile creases his lip, but it doesn't reach his eyes. His eyes look like ruined chocolate; flat and dull with an ashy overlay. They made me sad and protective.

"How long is not long?"

"You were released from the hospital two days after the incident, heavily medicated, but able to walk on your own. We boarded a charted private plane and were in Washington five and a half hours later."

"You chartered a plane to get me there?" I heard the incredulity slither through my words, but I was kind of shocked.

"Well, yes. I sure as fuck couldn't take you on a commercial flight. You were a mess." His angry words are thrown at me, but the heat of his ire burns up his nose and sets his eyes on fire.

"Why are you so angry? If you don't want to talk about this, then don't. I can read these papers and figure it out for myself; what happened to me— y…" My words freeze in my throat when my ears register the strangled sound of a rusty trumpet being blown by an asthmatic, no-talent-having, tone deaf child falling from John's full lips. It was pitiful and weak and triumphant all at the same time.

"I'm not angry—I—I'm just so damned sorry and ashamed of myself for how I treated you." His hands are shaking, and I know he's hurting. I want to absolve him of his guilt, but I also know he needs to feel it. To experience it as it happens because not allowing him to go through it, will only make his actions acceptable later on.

"I get you feel shitty about what happened, and you damn-well should, but right now; I need you to pull it together and catch me up on my life." I

41

keep my voice implacable. I don't need him to know how I'm hurting for him and how much I want to wrap my arms around his shoulders and comfort him. I can't for more reasons than needing him to feel like shit about his behavior. Valery is watching and listening. I feel her fingernails scratching under my skin. Her dark, whiskey-colored irises roll under my caramel-dipped blue-skies; looking at John. She's right there; waiting and hoping I slip up. *Not this time, sis. Not ever again.*

"You're right. Okay. Once I got you to The Center and admitted, I met with the team of doctors who would be working with you for your stay. I explained the nature of our sexual relationship and how I took our play much too far. I tried to share with them how you may have had some sexual trauma in your past, but you had yet to divulge it to me; therefore, I wasn't sure if what I forced on you caused the break or if it was the combination of old and current trauma."

He looks at me, then. Eyes so intense, I'm sure my skin is going to slide right off my face if he doesn't stop staring at me like he is. I incline my head as if asking what he wants to know, but he doesn't say anything to me. Just watches me for an age and looks away as if he's satisfied with whatever he found.

"I'm listening."

"Right. Anyway, after talking with the doctors and giving them all the information, I could about you, me, and us; I checked on you and was told not to return for three weeks. That's how long it would take for them to fully evaluate and assess you and hopefully come up with a diagnosis and treatment plan." He extricated his hands from mine and stood. John could never stay still for very long. His long legs eat up the length of his office. Back and forth. Back and forth. Hands in the pockets of his jeans, head held at the aristocratic tilt that drives me crazy, and his bottom lip pulled

under his bright, white top teeth. It was like watching a black lion pace the grasslands. Mythical and untouchable, but so damned necessary, you wish you could find, tame, and love one.

Finally, he was ready to continue. He took a breath and I watched his chest expand and hold for one, two, three heartbeats before he expelled a rush of cool air from his warm, lush mouth.

"I wasn't comfortable leaving you, lovely. You are *mine* to protect and take care of. The idea of leaving your care completely in the hands of strangers didn't sit well with me. But what the hell else could I do?" Exasperation hangs on his shoulders like a *Sisyphean* weight he never wanted to carry. "It almost broke me. Leaving you there with them when you were so, vulnerable. But I did because it was the best course of action. I flew home…"

My face must have registered the shock that stole my breath momentarily because before I could ask, John stood in front of me and poured hot chocolate apologies into my soul as he rushed to explain himself.

"There was no point in staying in Washington. The Center has a strict no visiting policy during the first three weeks and if I had stayed; knowing you were within my reach and I couldn't get to you, lovely. No one wanted to know what would've happened if I'd stayed near you, so I came back home to get things in order for the both of us. I made sure, Tamie knew you would be out indefinitely and I would keep her posted on your progress. Then I had to speak with my partners to let them know I would not be available for any reason for the foreseeable future—I…"

"John? Are you telling me you haven't been to work in six months? I know how important your company is to you and what did Tamie say

43

when you told her about me? Does she know what happened between you and I or just thinks I cracked up?"

"First of all, no. How am I supposed to work while we're dealing with *this*? I mean not a goddamned thing in this world means more to me than you do, lovely. And secondly, why the fuck would I tell your assistant what happened between you and me? And last of all, you did not crack up... *I broke you.* That's two completely different things, don't you think?"

Could this mothafucka be anymore a narcissistic sociopath?! How the hell does he make every damned thin all about his cocky ass? Vivian, you need to really be payin attention. He's sayin all the right shit, but I promise you; he talkin out both sides of his mouth with this bullshit. Trust me.

I asked you for some time to think things through. How do you expect me to trust you when you can't even honor my wishes? Please, give me some time to feel this out.

John sits down next to me and the gentle brush of the back of his fingers down my left cheek feels like white puffy dandelions blowing against my skin on a warm spring day. I turn my eyes toward him and didn't see any of the puffed-up cockiness Valery tried to force my mind to conjure.

7

I leaned into his touch and it became a balm for every ache and hurt living in my body. John has gentled, and I missed the entire process. More than anything, I was pissed about that fact. I wanted to see how his horrendous actions affected him. I wanted to bear witness to his growth and watch as he transformed into the man; some secret ancient part of me knew he could.

But Valery was the one to reap the benefit of my greatest sacrifice. I had to know what happened over the past six-months and why I couldn't remember any of it. *If I can't remember any of it, then why am I home. Shouldn't I still be locked up somewhere getting treated?*

"You have that look on your face, like your mind is filling in the blanks with either a version of the truth or a million questions. What's going through that brilliant complicated mind, Viv?" His voice brings me from my bird-walk and helps me focus on him alone. I noticed he didn't look concerned or worried, just calm, and self-composed and patient. There is still a dominant and unmistakable energy pouring from him, but it somehow seems to simmer just below the surface. It is... he is so confident and sure of himself and everything in his world; I want to belong in his world with him, again. I want to know I still fit in the puzzle that is Jonathan R. Ellis. *What if I don't and he's just keeping me around long enough to give birth and then he'll throw me back in the keep-my-batshit-crazy-wife-away-from-us-center?*

"I don't understand why the last six months are not a part of my memory. I don't understand what's wrong with me, not really and you're kind of dancing around the nuts and bolts of it all, John. I'm a big girl, I can handle whatever it is you need to tell me." At this, I stood with my glass of water in my hand. My hips were hurting, and I needed to move;

hoping that walking around would get this baby back off my bladder and sciatic nerve. As I lifted the water to my lips, I noticed a picture on the shelf adjacent to John's desk, I didn't remember it being there before.

Waddling closer to the faded image in the balsa wood frame, I realized I had no idea who that woman was, but something about her looked painfully familiar and made me rub my chest where an ache bigger than any I'd ever felt in my life bloomed like blood after a gunshot. "John, who is this woman in this picture?" I held the frame up for him to see as I turned to the left to face him and realized too late, that he was standing right behind me. Close enough for my preggers-breasts to brush against his solid chest. My nipples puckered, painfully and a not so silent exhale fled my mouth. John reached for the picture his eyes going soft with a look I don't think I've ever seen on him. Certainly not for me. But for the woman in the picture? It looks like he just found the reason for his entire existence. *What the actual fuck is going on here?*

"This is Auntie, or Violet as I came to call her." He stepped around me and placed the frame back in its spot and looks at it for a second longer than I feel is necessary before guiding me by my elbow to the couch. "I had some time on my hands during the three weeks you were inaccessible to me, so I hired a private investigator to look into Aunties past." This is one of the few pictures he was able to find of her. It's from years before I ever knew her, but not much had changed as far as her looks went.

She was a ridiculously beautiful woman when that picture was taken and when I had the honor and pleasure of knowing and lov—" John realized I had stopped my forward momentum and stood rigidly in front of him when his word vomit stopped spewing from the cave of his mouth; falling like volcanic ash around my feet. Burning away the confidence I had in our love.

"What, John? What were you going to say… when you had the pleasure of knowing and *loving* her?" I'm looking at my husband with astonished eyes for probably the first time since I met him. I do a quick mental check to ensure these are my own thoughts and not the manipulation of Valery…they are. They are all mine. "So, let me get this straight. While I was away at an I-fucked-my-wife-up-so-bad-with-my-angry-dick-I-broke-her-fucking-mind institution in Washington, my husband—that's you, just in case you think I'm talking about someone else—was reliving his time with a fucking pedophile and looking for pictures of her to what… jack off to? Am I correct in my assessment of the situation?" *I can't fucking believe this.*

I attempt to step away and leave, but John was having none of it and snatched me around until my pregnant front collided with his stone-like chest and rigid abs. *Damn him for being so god-awful fit.* I slam my eyes closed to block him from my view and to keep the oil-slick hurt from leaking down my cheeks. It didn't help. I saw his furious hurt face behind my eyelids and my own hurt would not be contained. *Fuck him for making me feel so inadequate and forgotten.* I pull myself up to my full five feet eleven inches and square my shoulders in preparation to let him have it, but before I can fix my mouth to chew him out; his lips part and hell, fire, and damnation rain down me.

"Have you? Oh yeah, you have obviously lost y-your. Your whole fucked-up-goddamn-gone-out-to-pasture mind." Whenever John was well and truly pissed, Georgetown came from him in the most unholy of ways.

Well shit. You done went and pulled the fuckin tiger by the goddamned tale now, and what you think gonna happen when you let it go? I swear, you bout the dumbest slut-pig I ever seen in my life. Fuckin idiot.

I asked you to please give me some time to sort everything out. Please leave me alone, I don't need you yelling in my head about my short comings. I tune back in just as John is ramping up for round two.

"Obviously! The fuck is wrong with you? How could you even?" He was so angry and hurt, he couldn't string words together into complete thoughts, and I had done that to him because of my insecurities and the crazy woman's voice in my head. He continued or at least he tried to. "…I mean, really? How could you think something—so fucking foul—like that?"

His voice is a bullet shot through a silencer; leaving no time to avoid the impact that shreds my insides. I feel something like warm water running down the back of my head. I look up to see if there was a leak in the ceiling but found nothing. The warm water continued to drip onto my neck; it was distracting and somewhat soothing, too. Someone is calling my name but it sounds like it's from somewhere far away, but as I looked around to see who might be calling me, my eyelids closed, and my world is blissfully quiet, and I can finally take a breath.

Valery

"John, I knew you'd show your true colors and scare poor-fucked up-little Vivian back into her jar. Why the hell did you take her from that fancy ass center? You know she ain't hardly right in the head and now she here… all kinds of fucked up, and you have no idea what the fuck she needs. You gonna keep right on and be stuck with my surly ass for the rest of your days." I slide a sexy as fuck smile his way while I look at him like he fuckin hung the moon and stars or some shit like that. We did shit I goddamn know won't legal in most states. John is dirty. Filthy as they come.

His beautiful ass is standin there looking like the avengin dark fallen angel he wants to be, at least he tries to be that for *her*. "There is a reason you only show up when Vivian feels threatened or afraid. You do understand what your purpose is, don't you." John looks like he's bout ready to chokeslam me and I don't want nothin but to egg him on. I put my hand on my hips, I stare two fingers of whisky into those sexy ass chocolate eyes and mix a little of my attitude in for a delicious old fashion with a twist. "Fuck you and the horse you rode in on." His face is blank. *I Can't believe he tried that psycho-babble bullshit on me. I don't give a fuck.*

"Do you know what I hate more than your silly ass?" I ask as I walk around this overdone room.

"I'm sure you'll tell me regardless, so do go on." *Asshole.*

"I hate a weak ass woman. A weak ass woman who don't know her worth and don't know she's supposed to have the whole mothafuckin' world, but she settle for a goddamn last name, a pretty mcmansion she got to keep clean, and some man's dick in her ass." He ain't got shit to say. Standin there lookin like he suckin on lemons and his fuckin pride. This sorry ass excuse for a man needs to learn his place. *Shit, he don't need no map, I'm just the bitch to give him directions. John, make a right on your-dick-don't-mean-shit lane and keep goin til you see, my-pussy-is-a-tunnel-of-life boulevard.*

"You want Vivian to stick her head out and play house with you? Let me tell you a few secrets, *Jonathan*." I hold up my left hand, which is the one I use the most; I don't know how the hell Vivian uses her right hand to do everythin. I flip my pointin finger at him before I start tellin shit I know. "Secret number one: Vivian needs me when you scare her cause you a coward who sufferin from I-got a dick-and you owe me-bullshit thinkin.

49

You think because you have a dick and a wife you have a right to fuck her any way you see fit. You so confused and wrong. Remember she chose to be your wife, not your fuckin slave. Secret number two," I make sure to flip him the bird before I finish. "You and your when-animals-attack tomfoolery didn't make me. I been with Viv, she just never knew, and I never cared to make myself know to her stupid ass. Truth is, after leavin home, she ain't been scared of nobody but you."

I'm watchin him so close I can see when his left eye starts to twitch. This fucker so worked up right now, he probably gonna do somethin painful. *God, I hope he do somethin painful. I need it so bad.* "So, either you like havin me around…" I raise my right brow and cock my head to the left and just for shits and giggles, I flash my look-at-my-pretty-white-teeth-smile at him. I can feel my locs fall over my left shoulder settlin in this big ass collar on the sweater but I know he love wrappin them around his fist when he fuck my ass and pussy with the help of a toy, so I make sure he notice them when they move. John's eyes follow the movement and then his eyes slide to my lips. *Poor bastard, he just can't help his fool ass self.* "…or, you more sadistic than you thought. Which one is it, Jonny? You wanna another go with the woman who let you fuck her ass with anythin you can fit into it? Because you know good and damn well Vivian ain't ever gonna let you fuck her like that again." I watch his eyes narrow and that plump bottom lip disappears behind his teeth as his tongue slides out to moisten the flesh of his top lip. His nostrils flare and I swear right the fuck now, he look like a wild animal and my underwear are wet as fuck with wantin him to fuck all that aggression; all that passion and guilt and hurt and shame right the fuck into my soppin pussy.

He steps closer to me. So close, the tips of his big, booted feet touch the tips of my much smaller ones and I have to let my head fall back to meet

his disgusted glare. I want to step back, but I won't let this son of a bitch know he got me so damn hot right now, if he blow on my neck... I'm comin. Hard. He ain't never gonna know how much he scare the livin shit outta me. How the hell am I supposed to protect Vivian from the boogieman when I don't wanna do nothin but fuck his brains out and let him... beg him to do some nasty shit to me? I feel his words against my ear more than I hear them.

"Knowing I had a hand in bringing you out, is the exact reason I knew I would be the only one to help Vivian get control of you. I knew the night I broke my wife; that I'd be the one to put her back together again. The Center was to keep up appearances. To show all interested parties the length I was willing to go through to take care of my wife. Do you think anyone knows her better than me?" The grindin of his big, white teeth that could be a smile, does nothin to make me feel at ease. But I don't give anythin away. I just listen to him and realize one important thin. Vivian don't need protection from him. I do.

With this understandin, I rattle a few jars on Vivian's shelf and one of them looks vaguely familiar, but I can't place her. I search until I find the one Vivian is hidin in and I unscrew the top and dump her feeble ass out, so I can climb in. In passin I say, "He want you back. Don't goddamn dip out on me without me sayin you can, all right? You said you need time to figure shit out. Do it and then we can fuckin talk."

~8~

The water trickles down my neck and my back feels soaked with warmth, but I realize it's not water warming my back; it's John's warm hand rubbing me from my shoulder blades to the small of my back. The pain behind my eyes is severe and I don't want to open them, but I have to see him and know I'm home and not somewhere unfamiliar.

My heart is beating some ancient tribal rhythm and I swear the baby is dancing a jig. I force my eyes open but close them just as soon as the light touches them. Now all I see behind my lids are painful shades of greens and blues and black. Deep breaths to center me. I peel them open, more slowly this time and I see him. His eyes are soft pools of melted heaven and I want to fall into them and swim with chocolate dolphins until I feel safe and whole again.

"John?" Why is his name a question like I don't expect him to be himself?

"Lovely?" He doesn't expect me to be myself either. *What happened?*

"John, what's going on. I feel like I'm missing something. Like I took a nap, but kept right on having a conversation with you, but it wasn't me. I mean, it was me but not the me I am right now…" His smile is the only reason I didn't lose my shit. He looks almost happy about my confusion and that fact alone throws me off. My hand instinctively goes to my belly as I look into him. Looking for answers. For clarity. For a reason to be calm because right now I feel like my skin is too tight for me and my chest too small to contain the wild thing trying to claw itself out."

"Lovely, you don't know how amazing it is to hear you say those words." I look at him with what I can only assume is a confused and worried expression on my face. *Why is he so happy about this?*

"You're happy? That I'm slipping further down the rabbit hole?"

"No. I'm happy you're finding it."

"Explain, please."

"Come and sit with me. There is so much to tell you. So much I've learned about you, about us."

We walk back to the blue Chesterfield and sit beside each other. We're so close, our thighs press together. He takes my hand and absently rubs his roughened pad of his thumb across my knuckles. The little wild thing in my chest is trying to come to heel, but it's slow going.

"Okay. What were we talking about before something weird happened? Was it? Did it have something to do with the woman who left you her money and her houses?" I remember him yelling at me. Flashes of his hard eyes skitter across my mind and a shiver runs up my spine. My heart rate is increasing. Tiny earthquakes rack my entire body. *What the hell is happening?*

"Vivian! Viv, baby. Lovely…" I hear his voice through the fugue, and it tugs me away from the dark place inside myself. That place is familiar and warm and makes me feel safe, but I come back to him because he has words and information and I need to hear the words, know the information.

"I'm here."

"Where did you go, lovely?"

"I don't know. You yelled at me, you *scared* me. Your eyes, they looked so cold, like you would do something horrible to me if I—I continued to question you about her. There was a dark, warm, and safe place and I went there to get away from—y . To get away from you, I think I went there to get away from you, John." A single tear dropped from the corner of my left eye and anoints our joined hands. He watches it and then he lifts our hands to his full mouth and licks the tear away. Placing a soft

kiss where the tear had fallen as if he were kissing away the hurt that caused it. It was… powerful and moving and it made the hurt more painful.

"I'm, the reason that dark, safe place exist, well partially. Partially, I'm the reason it exists, but you have other dark places inside you. The night of, what was it you called it—*ass-gate*?" he lifts his eyes and a small smile plays about his full mouth. I return it with one of my own. We stay in this peaceful moment until John clears his throat and breaks it. "You called them *jars* and at the time, I had no idea what you were talking about, but when you were in the bathtub, after the incident…the r-rape. You didn't look like you anymore and you didn't sound like you. Everything about you was different, but it was still you, you know?"

His thumb is a little rough against my knuckles and his eyes are begging me to know what he means and I know he's trying to make me understand what he was saying, but I don't. I want to understand because he looked so happy before, and there is always going to be a part of me that longs to please him. To make him proud and happy he chose me. *Once a submissive, always a submissive.*

"I really want to know, but what you're saying doesn't make sense. You said I didn't look like me or sound like me." Then I remember the crazy lady, Valery! "John! Oh my God. Valery! Is that who was in the tub. She almost sounds like me if I were angry, uneducated, and cursed like a sailor. If I was hateful and mean…full of piss and vinegar. If I smoked and drank and raged against everyone and everything."

Some of the tension in his square jaw eases a bit and his eyes linger a little too long on my eyes; like he's looking for the owner of the voice I just described to him. Like he knew her and had business with her. The kind of business a man doesn't want his wife to know he has with another woman. Was she telling the truth, was there something going on with John

and this woman in my head who was really me, but not me? And if there is or was something going on, does that count as cheating? *Oh God, I'm a fucking headcase.* John squeezes my hand to bring my focus back to him and releases it as he stands to walk over to his desk to retrieve his laptop. When he sits back down beside me, he flips it open and tap something on the keyboard, then turns the screen towards me.

The screen is full of information and as much as I want to make sense of it, my mind refuses to process the black letters floating ominously in the blue light of the monitor.

I see lots of letters and bold print, links, but none of it is registering as something I should understand. John's voice slices through the buzzing in my ears and he pulls my face toward the center of his chest. He tucks me into the spicy, citrus redolence that says it's okay to let go and fall into the warmth of his chest and the hint of possession as his fingers lay heavily across the back of my neck; keeping me present in this moment. In this second of knowing and succumbing and acquiescence. *I am really and truly fucked.*

"Lovely, are you still with me?

"Yes."

"Are you ready to look over this site with me?"

"No, but I'm ready to know what's happening with me and who the voice in my head belongs to."

"Always so brave and eager to learn something new. Sit up, take a drink of water and let's get to this." I notice he's using his Dom voice; I don't know if he realizes it but it makes me feel so safe and cared for. *I didn't know how much I missed him like this before now.*

I couldn't get started until after going to pee. I almost asked permission to go and use the restroom, but remembered we were not that couple anymore and hadn't been since our first anniversary. Upon my return, John had several journals laid out on the coffee table beside the computer and had refilled his tumbler with a smoky finger of Macallan.

"Okay, let's start at the beginning. Do you remember our first house in the Shandon area in Columbia?" John takes a small sip from his heavy lead crystal tumbler while he waits for me to answer him.

"Yes. I loved that house." I smile broadly because I really did love that house. It was the first time we ever decorated a Christmas tree together. The smile falls from my face, because it was also where I prophetically gifted him with the IOU poem. He doesn't notice my change in mood, so I school my features before he looks back up.

"Me too. We had some good times there, didn't we, lovely? We had a lot of passionate arguments in that house, as well. One of those arguments was about you meeting some cocksucker to do a fucking project and you were supposed to wear a body suit and let him wrap you up in plaster." John was back in the kitchen in our small house, his eyes not seeing me or

where we are right now. His anger is riding him like a jockey. *He cannot still be angry about that. Can he? Of course he is.*

"I remember that. I remember how I destroyed our bed—*I can't believe I did that*. That I smeared ...*feces* all over the covers and peed..." I can't even finish. I was disgusted with myself and even more so because I had no memory of doing it. "You know John, I didn't remember. I still can't remember squatting, defecating in my hands, rubbing my feces all over that beautiful Sferra Milos bedding; I would never do anything so appalling. So abhorrent." There's no way in hell it couldn't have been me. And then it hits me. "It wasn't me... who did that, was it? I wouldn't do that to our home; I know I wouldn't, right?"

"You remember telling me how you thought something was wrong with you... how you had been blacking out." His eyes are completely focused on me. He's not asking as much as confirming.

"Yes, of course. I was scared out of my mind, literally but you fixed me. In the *playroom*, you fixed me, and I was fine after that. I didn't have the moments of missing time and lost memories. *You* fixed me."

"Right. How did I fix you, Vivian?" He knows all of this, why he wants me to rehash it is making me nervous.

"You took me to the playroom and twenty-nine and half minutes later, *it* was gone. I was myself again." My voice is so far away, I'm worried I'm not in the room with him anymore. I feel his hand on my lower back anchoring me to this moment; to him. This second of knowing. Of succumbing—submitting—to my new reality. I have Dissociative Identity Disorder.

9

John is as patient as he's always been with me and in this moment, I'm grateful he's as impassive as he is and for the silent control he exerts over me. My chest rises and falls with the slow rhythm of my breath, I needed to calm down and allow myself to listen and try to understand what John's telling me.

"Do you understand what this website is saying?"

"It's saying I'm all kinds of crazy and should probably be locked away...why? Why did you bring me home, John?"

"No, lovely. This site is saying you have experienced serious *childhood* trauma and at some point, in your early years. Like before or around the age of five, your mind developed in the only way it could—to protect you from whatever that trauma was."

"This makes no sense. I don't remember any type of childhood *trauma*." The word trauma tastes like I'm eating live bait worms and not being allowed to chew them before they get to slither down my throat. I try to swallow the bile and ick burning up my esophagus as I continue to explain my memories,

"I lived with my father and..." I trail off as an olfactory memory catches my breath and then stops it altogether. *The slow-moving rise of a single ribbon of burnt plastic and clean floors wrap around my neck and without malice, squeezes the tender muscles of my throat. There are hands. Rough and mean, grabbing at my arms and legs. I still can't find where my breath skirted off to, but the hands are dark and dirty with thick fingers and jagged fingernails. They leave a film of filth and shame and guilt and ruin on my slender arms. I watch a tear fall like acid rain on that squandered space between the thumb and the accusing finger. And then a thick, pink and white-coated tongue; slimy with a film of sour milk. And the*

bruises around a horrible mouth. The web of crawling black sugar ants,
crisscrossing the sun toughened leather-like flesh separating his
decapitated thumb and his pointing finger.

"John." My voice is too afraid to actually make a sound louder than
sigh; the non-man hand has scared it away, but I refuse to allow it into a
jar. I need to face and understand what this means.

"Where did you go, lovely? You've been staring at your hands for the
last twenty minutes." There is no accusation or even concern, only a
statement of fact with hope of gaining insight.

"I don't know if what I just saw, *remembered*? I don't know if any of it
really happened or if I read about something like it in a book or saw it on
the news. But the smell of burning plastic and feeling nasty hands and my
salty tears. It was me. Someone touching me, but not this *me*. Not my adult
self, the me when I was younger. When I was all long arms and legs and
knobby knees. Tiny breast and—I was a *child*. Maybe twelve?"

I lift my face to his and I see the most unexpected thing. Awe and
wonder. He looks as if I've just given him my whole heart for the first
time. It confuses me, but the submissive in me is pleased as punch that he
is happy with something I've done. Even if I don't know what it is.

"God, you truly are the most amazing woman I've ever known. How
you could think I could ever love someone else, half as much as I love and
worship you. That someone else could pull my attention away from you is
absurd." I know he is referencing the time he went looking for information
about *Auntie*, and it does so much to ease my hurt feelings. *Damn*
pregnancy hormones. Like I'm not crazy enough on my own…

"For six fucking months, those stupid doctors had you in that place.
You refused to surface; *you* wouldn't talk to them. Only if we were alone
did you come forward. I thought I'd never see you again, never feel the

caress of your beautiful summer-sunshine eyes." He is so ferocious in his need and love for me. I hate I hurt him. Hate I left him here to deal with the aftermath of what happened and the subsequent pregnancy and the obvious break.

"I don't understand what you mean when you say *I* wouldn't come out. Where was I?"

"Lovely. Your mind developed what the psychiatrist calls, alters. They help you cope with various traumas and other difficult situations that were and *are* too difficult for you to deal with on your own. Somethings happened in your early childhood. Something your mind was not ready to handle or felt you needed protection from. Once the first alter appeared to protect you, Viv." Whatever he was going to say was lost with his exhale.

"The doctors at The Center encountered three different alters or distinct personalities. *You* only came out for me. You never shared yourself with anyone, but me."

I'm trying not to throw myself onto the floor, kicking and screaming like the bat-shit crazy woman I obviously am. *How in the hell are there three—what did he call them—alters living inside me.* John is still speaking calmly and doesn't look the least bit concerned about any of this. Either he's crazier than I am or he's just trying to keep me placated until I have this baby and then he'll lock me up for good and my child will never know me. *Just like I never knew my mother.* And then he'll be the one reading the wretched bedtime stories to our daughter. Making her earn her milk and cookies. *Wait, where the hell did that thought come from?*

"Why are you so okay with all of this?"

"Vivian, I've had six months to come to terms with what's been happening with you. That night, six months ago—I" His words abruptly stop and a darkness creeps across his face. Like he's reliving every horrible

moment that followed the rape. I watch him as his eyes blink like the shutter of a camera lens and I want to go to him. Go to him and take away his sudden bout of melancholy.

"John?"

"I'm so fucking sorry, Viv. I knew I had broken you. I never wanted to do anything but build you up. Make you the very best version of yourself and I didn't. I was no better to you than that fucker, *Earl* was to my mom. No better than that cocksucker we saw in that shitty ass club in Paris. You chose to be my wife and I turned you into my *slave*." His voice is whisper soft and filled with his silent anger. Melted dark chocolate with tiny flecks of gold dripped onto his naturally sculpted cheeks and in his repentance, he was the most beautiful thing I'd ever seen.

"I forgive you, John. A thousand times. I forgive you. I won't forget that night and I don't want to. That night, what you did. It created this baby growing inside me. Our baby. From a dark and terrible act, the best parts of me and the best parts of you clung to each other. They wouldn't let go and in their holding on, we made this life.

I forgive because who am I without us, John? Who are you?" I didn't realize we were both standing or that his arms were around me. His right hand cradling the back of my head and the left rubbing circles on my lower back. His tears drip onto my neck where he'd buried his face as he sobbed. "I love you and I forgive you." I hope my words baptized him, making him new and shiny, and clean. "I forgive you. I love all of every part of you."

After an emotional morning, I was no closer to learning about my alters. I knew who Valery was… well, I at least knew her voice and a little bit about her but the others had not made themselves known to me. I don't know what caused the initial break, but most of me is happy John is not the trauma that broke the first jar. For some reason, knowing this makes it

easier to deal with. Knowing his love wasn't what destroyed me, gives me just enough hope in our relationship to keep fighting and learn how to live with my *selves* and him.

10

Lunch was a small salad with pan-seared scallops and lemon water. I settled on the oyster shell grey, linen Chesterfield in the family room with a cashmere throw in a few shades darker than the sofa. John is in his office, catching up on work and I'm trying to find a comfortable position because I'm exhausted and just want to take a nap. I notice a pair of eyes looking at me as if I'm the reason for the pain robbing the beauty from the russet colored irises. There's so much hurt and shame. I want to take it from her. Help her. Show those eyes how to smile and shine. They look as if they deserve to smile but never had a reason to do so. *Who are you? What's your name, sweetie?*

My body is no longer able to fight the lethargy weighing down on it and as I wonder whose eyes are staring at me, she whispers in the voice of a child,

"I'm Valeria Anne Bruno." Darkness envelopes me and I welcome the sweet, velvety heaviness like my favorite blanket.

This feels like a dream, but I know I'm not dreaming because I'm not aware in my dreams. Right now, I'm fully aware of the fact that I'm in my subconscious mind and there is a little girl sitting in the corner. Large cinnamon- golden-brown- curls form a huge afro around her heart-shaped, nut-brown face. The little copper freckles kissing her nose and cheeks makes me want to squeeze them. She is such a beautiful child, but something about her vacant stare caused my chest to ache and my breathing to falter within my lungs. She's so familiar to me, but why?

I don't make a move towards her because something tells me she would just go away. I make my voice sound the way I wanted my mother to speak to me. *If I'd had a mother to speak to me.* I think about warm, fresh-baked chocolate chip cookies and ice-cold glasses of milk sitting on the table

after school. I wrap the smells and tastes of love and affection around my words when I finally speak to her.

"Hi, I'm Vivian, are you—" I give her a minute to recognize the warm cookie dough in my voice before I continue. I watch her wandering gaze narrow as she tries to see me better, but she's too afraid to come closer.

Keeping the warmth of fresh-baked cookies in my voice, I say her name. "—Valeria Anne?" Her name tastes like heavy hands and thick fingers, too large and demanding for a child's mouth to hold. I wince as the thought wafts through my mind like snow drifting on warm cement sidewalks. She cracks her full berry-colored lips into something close to a smile; if smiling hurt every muscle in your face and made you think about decomposing bodies pressing down upon you—then, I guess she was smiling at me.

Her head falls forward and back up again like someone was pulling a string to make her move. Her floppy afro falls onto her forehead and she raises long, piano-playing fingers to push the clutch of curls away from her face. She parts her lips to speak, but then shakes her head like the thought is too big and gets stuck somewhere between her brain and her mouth.

"I'm Valeria Anne and I was born August 5, 1975 to Regina and Robert Bruno. My mother named me Valeria Anne, after my two grandmas. I'm an only child so, most of the time I played by myself or with my daddy."

Valeria paused to part her hair in the middle and places rubber bands around each large section of her russet curls, forming two perfectly round afro-puffs on either side of her childish face. Once she was done, she stepped a little further out of the shadows and sat crisscross applesauce on the floor, weaving an intricate basket with her fingers as she looks up at me.

"So. My parents worked a lot. I don't know what my mom's job was; I just know she was always gone. My mother didn't really want to talk to me and when she did, she just cried and told me how sorry she was for bringing me into the world. How the only thing I would ever know is pain and more pain on the 'count of me being born with a pussy instead of a dick.*"

Valeria's words fall like molasses dripping from a clogged spout. I watched her weaving her little finger basket and felt a connection to this child. She was so matter of fact when she spoke about her mother. No emotion, just saying how things were. I wanted to be closer to her so, I moved into what I now realize is an open room with comfortable floor pillows and plants and fountains. *Wait, I know this room. I've been here before.*

"I don't ever remember her saying she loved me, playing tea party with me, or even tucking me in with bedtime stories. She just didn't want anything to do with me.*" Her voice is every dried-up dream buried under years of lost hope and too many regrets. I want to snatch her up and squirrel her away. The compulsion is so strong to protect her, it's all I can do to stay seated on the large multi-colored pillow just in front of her. Instead of following this incessant need, I just sit and listen. Giving my full attention to this little soul whose brokenness somehow mirrors my own.

"My father adored me, though and maybe that's why I wanted to do whatever I could. Just so he would always love me." Valeria lifts lids so heavily lashed it causes a small breeze to travel across the space between us. Eyes the color of expensive whiskey crashed into my own. I'm drunk on their beauty. Wasted on the defiant fire burning in their depths.

She wanted to believe she'd survived; that she had overcome whatever had wrenched the spirit out of the whiskey in her eyes. I smiled at her,

hoping to reassure her of her survival, that I am proof she came through on the other side of whatever happened to her and it must have worked because she cleared her throat and continued to tell me about her childhood. *And maybe about my childhood, too.*

"When I was about 5 years old, my daddy started doing story time at night. He said that story time would be our very special daughter/daddy time. I loved that he gave me special attention. I guess he was making me a daddy's girl and I loved it. " Valeria went on like this for some time before she got sleepy and said she would come out to talk with me later. With a shy wave of her elegant fingers, she faded back into the corner and I sat there in silent horror at the horrendous life this poor child had endured. *Who is she and what does she have to do with my broken soul?*

Something was tugging me away from Valeria and as hard as I tried, I couldn't fight the draw back to the light shining down into my tired eyes. With reluctance, I said goodbye and allowed the pressure of strong fingers rubbing me from my left shoulder down to my hand—pausing on my wedding rings and making the journey back up to my shoulder again—to coax me back to consciousness.

"Viv? Hey lovely, are you in there?" John's voice was about as sure as Bambi standing up for the first time in the middle of the forest. Shaking and wobbling, but still trying to do what's expected. I know this uncertainty is costing him. He's a man who's always in control of himself and usually, everyone else who's allowed to exist in his orbit. The next time he ghosts over my rings, I entwine my fingers with his, to let him know I'm here. Clearing my throat, I use his arm as a fulcrum to help me sit up and get myself together. I'm not sure if I'm going to share what happened during my nap or if I want to keep Valeria a secret, at least for a

little while. I felt as if she has so much more to teach me, and I want to know as much as I can about her before I share her with John.

"Hmmmmmm. The sound is a lament to the horrors I've just heard, but they have an arousing effect on the man leaning over me. I watch as a shutter moves through his broad shoulders. My eyes fall down to his crotch where his dick is thick and long behind the confining zipper of his jeans. I'm immediately wet and achy and swollen for him. *Don't see them together. Don't see them together… damn!* But I can't put it out of my mind and just like that—my pussy dries up and that peaceful feeling evaporates.

I'm sure my face has already told him the story that's played out in my mind because he kneels down in front of me, his right index finger follows the line from my ear to my chin and then down the front of my throat where he wraps his entire hand around my neck to give it a little squeeze. Not enough to make me nervous, just enough to make me aware of where I am and who I'm with. *Damn, I miss the edge of his handling me. The total control that kept me grounded in the present and kept everything locked away where it couldn't harm me.*

***

I was almost certain I would never be able to look John in the face again and not tell him the horrors I discovered while walking through my mind with Valeria. *Does he know about her? He said the alters showed themselves during my stay at The Center.*

"John, I would like to see the journals." My voice was a mixture of submission and accusation. I was only just able to restrain from saying, *Sir* at the end of my statement. His arched right eyebrow told me he heard the unspoken word, but I couldn't read his expression otherwise.

"Of course. Do you need use the bathroom or would you like to freshen up before we delve back into it, lovely?" There it was. Just a little bit of the voice that held my entire world together years ago. I allowed it to flow over and through me before I answered him. It felt like the familiar caress of a lovers warm breath over my pulse point, but I dismissed it. I knew he would never allow that part of our relationship back into our lives but I wished like hell that he would.

"Yes—um. I'll need a minute, are we back in your office or can we stay here where I'm comfortable?" The question followed me as I duck-walked out of the room toward the guest bathroom. I heard his answer only in his movement toward the office and the gathering of things.

"I cut you up some fresh veggies and made you a cup of feng shui tea. Where do you want to sit? Lovely?"

"Thanks. You always take such amazing care of me. Anticipating my needs before I even know I have them. I'll take the chaise lounge; I'm developing elephantiasis of the feet and ankles. The look he shoots me makes a laugh bubble up from my belly and fall raucously from my opened mouth. It was a familiar nameless sound. I lift my face and our eyes lock, just as I wrap my right hand around my belly; I feel the tiniest smile kiss the corners of my mouth. It felt so strange and so good to laugh with him.

"Your baby girl must be having a giggle-fit in here. She's all over the place. Give me your hand, hurry up John." I grab his large warm hand and place it at the bottom right-hand side of my belly and just as his fingers curved in possessively around my taut skin, she kicks the hell out of me and his eyes fly up to mine with a look I've never seen on his face before. A look I didn't know could even breach the austerity of his proud and knowing eyes. And then he did what I've been seeing him do more often. He smiles and the softness in his eyes spill down his cheeks.

"Jesus Christ on a skate board!" John's eyes look like the 4th of July and Christmas and every birthday all rolled into one glorious holiday. "That's our baby—I can't believe I just felt her tiny, little feet kicking. Did you feel how strong she is?" His hands were moving all over my belly now, chasing the little and not so little movements of his daughter. His joy and excitement was palpable; it bounced from him to me right inside my womb to touch his baby girl. I was as giddy as he was, but something was tugging me from the inside. I didn't want to miss this moment. I wanted to stay and enjoy my time with John and my baby, but the pull was too strong.

"John, my head is pound—I..." My words faded to nothing as my world fades to black. *Why can't I stay when he's happy?*

~11~

I look up into the face of a man who is kind of familiar, but not really. I rub my eyes with both my fists and blink up at him trying to figure out if he was a good man or a bad man. He didn't move towards me and I wasn't feeling afraid or nervous, so maybe he's not a bad man, but I don't know him so that makes him just another man with a dick.

Valeria

"Hello Valeria. How have you been?" My mouth falls open and I scoot farther back into the couch and grab a pillow to cover my front with. If he can't see my boobs, then he won't want to touch them or lick them or hurt them. "It's okay to talk to me. We met several times when you were in The Center. I'm John, Vivian's husband." He still didn't try to move towards me, and I relaxed a little bit. I didn't really know who Vivian was, but I think she may have been the lady with the Bob Marley hair I was talking to before I got sleepy. His voice sounded like I'd heard it before, but I didn't trust him because he still had a dick and he could hurt me.

"I don't know who Vivian is and I don't know who you are, either. Where's Vera? I know who she is, but I haven't seen her in a long time, and I miss her. I don't know if she's all right. Did you do something to her? Are you one of the men Vera's daddy brought home?" His face was darker than it was before, and he looked like I'd asked him a really hard algebra question. He squatted down in front of me and held both his hands up like I had a gun pointed at his chest and I kind of wish I did have a gun pointed at his chest. I guess he wants me to think he won't hurt me, but they all hurt me. *My mom at least told me the truth about men and their dicks.*

"Valeria, I'm John. I know who you are because you are a part of my wife. Do you remember talking about the dark place you sometimes go

when everything is calm?" He sat down on his bottom, crisscross applesauce with his hands linking together in front of him. They dangled in the triangle between his legs.

His face was like a nice man's face. No mean lines or red peeling lips with thick white spit in the corners. He had smooth skin the color of the dark chocolate candy bars Daddy sometimes gave Vera. And his eyes were bright. Like someone was shining a flashlight through a hole in the back of his head or something. He looked like a picture on the cover of a magazine… not real, but I couldn't let his looks fool me. *Not all bedtime stories have happy endings.*

"How do you know about the dark place? I didn't know what that white man meant when he said I was only a part of Vivian, not a whole person… that makes no kind of sense to me. I don't even know who this Vivian is. Are you going to hurt me with your dick, mister?" I don't know what I was expecting from him, but it wasn't what I got. He was on his feet so fast; I didn't realize he had left the room until I looked around for him when he didn't answer my question.

I waited a minute and noticed all the nice furniture and stuff. This house is so fancy, whoever this John is, he must be rich. My mom said that rich men were the nastiest men in the world. Because they had so much money, they could do anything they wanted and that made them want to do more and more nasty stuff. She said don't ever get caught up with no rich man, his dick will hurt me the worse of all the dicks in the whole wide world.

He comes back to the room holding some kind of book in his hand. He looked like he had sucked on the most sour jawbreaker in the world and it was no way he was ever gonna get his lips to come from inside his mouth again. That made me smile and giggle a little, cause what would a grown man be doing sucking on sour jawbreakers for, anyway?

He stood in the middle of the room and stretched out his arm to me. I guess he wanted me to look at the book he was holding. I took it but didn't open it. Not at first. I didn't do anything but listen to his rough sounding voice.

"Valeria, when we were at The Center, you came out quite a few times. You had a lot to share with us about your life and how you helped someone named Vera. The doctor asked you to keep a journal and write down things you wanted the other alters to know, this is your journal. All of the alters have read it, except for Vivian. Would you like to see what you shared with us?" His hands were in his pocket and he stayed a good ways away from me while I turned the journal all around making sure nothing on the outside of it could hurt me. I sit back in the fancy chair with no arms and put my feet under my butt while I pull the softest blanket in the world over my skinny legs. All the way up to my neck. I opened it to the first page and saw my handwriting.

THE * CENTER

September 2000 8:00 A.M.
Alter Name: Valeria(12)

<u>Session Notes</u>: Speaking about how father's abuse started around age 5 years

In the beginning, he would come in with two cookies and a glass of warm milk and read me my story. After a while, he changed. my father started to change the way he did things. The first change was how many cookies I got up front. He showed me both cookies, but only gave me one cookie and told me to drink only half of my milk. After he read me the story, he said I had to earn my other cookie and the other half of my milk

He told me that I had to give him a kiss...on the lips with my mouth opened. He said that way he'd know I had room for the other cookie. The first time I kissed my daddy with my mouth opened, he put his tongue in my mouth and licked around my teeth. I was missing my two front teeth and I he rubbed his tongue on my gum where the teeth had come out. It made my stomach hurt, I wanted him to not do that to me, but it was the only way to get my cookies and milk.

My daddy's stories didn't really make sense. He told me stories about little red riding hood meeting her daddy in the woods for a picnic and how they played special games like peel the banana and pet the kitten.

by the time I was seven daddy had hurt me with his dick. He took more and more of my cookies and milk and made me do more stuff to get them back. Every night he read me a story. he set up the video camera and taped him reading his story. Kissing me. Petting my kitten. Me peeling his banana. Him making banana pudding. Me taking my two cookies and warm milk. I HATE BANANA PUDDING. I HATE COOKIES. I HATE MILK I HATE KITTENS. I HATE BEDTIME STORIES.

"You know I wrote this. It's my handwriting. You know what he did and you…what? I don't get it. I want to know what's going on, but I don't."

73

My voice is too soft and not like I want it to be. The mom used to say it was important to never let people with dicks see or hear your fear or questions in your voice, but I couldn't help it. I was scared, and I didn't know what was happening. I just wanted to go back to the dark place where it's quiet. That's where I'm safe. *There're no dicks in the dark place.*

"It's all right. You don't have to be afraid. Vivian doesn't know you yet, but she will. I'm going to show her your journals and she'll understand who you are to her and then she'll be able to share what she knows with you?" He's trying to make me feel better, but nothing could. I'm not ever going to feel better. I just want him to leave me alone and let me go back to the dark place. It's always so warm there and nothing can hurt me when I'm covered in darkness. No dicks. No cookies and nasty milk. No kittens or pudding or bananas or daddies.

"I don't want to be here anymore, mister. I—I'm going back. I hope you get your lady, Vivian back. Thank you for keeping your dick in your pants, *John.* You the first man who didn't hurt me with it." I toss the journal down on the floor and try to get up, but I can't find my balance. I just flopped around until I landed on my butt on the armless couch. I saw him lunge for me. By the time his large hands and arms wrap around me, I was in the safety of darkness.

~12~

I came to with a pounding headache and a feeling of monachopsis. I had no idea where I was or who was with me; I just knew I didn't feel like I belonged.

"Lovely. Hi, it's good to have you back. We were enjoying feeling our daughter move around inside your belly and one of the alters pushed through. She must have been curious about what was happening." His voice is what drew me into my present. John was talking to me as if what he said made sense. Like what he just said to me wasn't the craziest thing he'd ever said to me in our life. I look up at his too handsome face and give him my best what-the-fu*k* look and he just cracks a smile that makes my panties wet, again. *It seems everything is making my panties wet. When was the last time John and I made love?*

"I know you're confused, but it's all right. We *are* going to get through this. The doctors at The Center thought they knew what was best for you but Viv, I've always been the only one who knew what was best for you. Once you get your head around what's happening with you—w" I cut him off as I scanned the journal I'd picked up from the floor in front of the sofa. I didn't recognize the handwriting, but I knew the name and the story. Well, at least part of the story.

"What is this? Where did this come from and how did you get it?" I held the journal up to him like it was a writhing snake; ready to pierce my skin and inject me with venom capable of ending my life. I was scared in a way I couldn't explain, but even in my fear; I had to know everything John knew about Valeria. Had to know how he had her journal. And why she was at The Center at the same time I was. Taking a couple of deep breaths, I willed my heart to slow down and my hand to stop shaking. I waited for him to tell me something that would make this make sense.

There ain't nothin about this fucked up situation to make sense of. How the hell you gonna make sense of a cracked-up brain that don't work normal? You think John goofy ass can help you? Me? Any of us? I don't know if he been fuckin that little girl or the fat cow bitch, too but he surely fucked every whole I had on offer. We got to figure this shit out for our own mothafuckin selves or John is just gonna get to live out all his filthy goddamned fantasies with four different women. Well, three different women and a twelve-year-old girl.

"Vivian." My name is a command to present myself to him and show him what was rightfully his. I immediately felt a pain of remembrance and my body wanted to kneel on the floor at his feet and hold myself still until he told me what to do. I set up straight and placed the journal on my lap; my hands folding around my belly. I was silent and waiting. Trying my best to unhear the bullshit Valery kept whisper-yelling in my mind. She's so persistent in her accusations against John. I'm wondering if they are true or if she's just trying to make me doubt him.

Ask him, stupid. I motha-double-fuckin-dog-goddamn-dare you to ask him if he fucked my ass. If he fucked my face. Throat. Mouth. My pussy. Ask if he fucked my titties and then shot his thick sticky cum all over my face. Dumb bitch, you don't really want to know, do you? Nah. Didn't think so.

That's enough with you, Valery. I don't want you lurking around in my head. I've asked you for time and you said you would give it to me. As soon as I figure out a way to block you; you can rest assured, you won't have access to another thought in my mind. Now leave me alone and let me figure shit out for myself.

"Lovely?" I feel John rubbing my shoulders in a circular motion and his breath warming the side of my neck where he's whispering my name to

pull me from this madhouse that is my mind. Thank god! I could never deny him when he called my name like this. In that voice.

"I'm here, John. Valery is going to be a problem. I don't know what her problem is with me but she's so angry and vengeful. The things she says…"

"I know. But right now we need to talk about this journal. I promise we'll get to Valery but if we give her the attention she seeks right now, she'll never allow you to get to know the others. And Vivian. Believe me, you really want to get to know the other two alters." He says this with the biggest, brightest smile on his face. And I wonder why he's smiling like that about these other two alters. Maybe Valery is right. No. I can't think like her. She's crazy.

"Does the name, Valeria sound familiar to you…have you ever heard it before?" Again, his voice was the soft commanding one that could coax me into doing and saying anything if it meant he would fuck me.

"Yes, S—I mean. Yes. I've heard the name, I dreamed about a little girl, well she wasn't so little. Maybe twelve or thirteen. Why do you know her?" I see the way his eyes flare when I almost answered him as I used to when I was submissive. *Fuck, I want that feeling. I need it and he looks like he misses it, too.*

"Tell me what you know about her." Not a question.

"Um—she's tall for her age but seems to be really lonely and she doesn't trust men. In my dream… wait, was I dreaming, John?"

"No. It's called internal communication between alters. Your doctors worked hard with the others. They were more than willing to talk with you, but you never came out to talk with them. They all seem to have mastered the art of internal communication, which usually is not easy to do.

"Valeria is thought to be the first alter created. She is what is called a primary protector. Her role is to help protect you from whatever type of trauma you experienced initially to cause the break." John's voice is strong and solid. He makes the fact I have a serious mental illness sound so normal and even fixable.

I'm looking at him like he's lost his goddamned mind because I think maybe I'm not the only crazy one in this house. *Oh, Lord! This poor baby has two looney-toons for parents.* The thought makes me giggle, for some reason. John looks at me like I may actually be breaking again, and it only makes me laugh harder. I'm laughing so hard my eyes are watering. Hot streams of liquid sanity running down my face, scalding my cheeks and burning into my sweater. My hands cover my face and my howling laughter becomes low and sorrowful wails and then I'm crying in earnest. I can't seem to stop the body racking sobs cracking me into pieces.

Strong hands on my shoulders don't make a difference. I know nothing will make a difference until it does. The hands tighten on my flesh and a voice like smoke, death, sex, and life rolls over me quieting my mind and my soul at once.

"Vivian. You are all right and you will stop this laughing/crying bullshit right now." He didn't yell or raise his voice, he simply spoke. Spoke in *that* voice.

That voice which left no room to argue or be contrary. The voice I haven't heard since our first wedding anniversary. *Oh my God, I need that voice and the promises that come with it.*

"Answer me. And don't forget your manners, lovely." A sense of calm washes over me and my breathing evens out, my shoulders relax under his firm grip, and he becomes my latibule. The safest place I've ever known. I let my eyelids fall and my face is soft and open, just the way he likes it.

"Yes, Sir. I am all right. Thank you, Sir." A breath I'd been holding for three years and six months whooshes out of my mouth with great suspiration; filling my lungs with a lightness that gives me permission to breathe again.

"Good girl. I knew my instincts were right. I knew what you needed the moment Valery showed up. I failed you, Vivian. I took the one thing keeping you together away from you because I was selfish and short-sighted. You know what I'm talking about."

"Yes, Sir."

"Tell me. In your own words, lovely?"

"On our first anniversary, you made me choose between being your wife or being your slave, Sir."

"Why did you choose to be my wife?"

"Because as your slave, I had no safe word. There was nothing you couldn't do to me. You would own me, and I would have nothing of myself left over, Sir."

"Were you not happy as my wife, lovely? I need the truth from you."

"I—I was. I wasn't not happy, I just needed more from us—from you. And from me, too. Sir."

"Were you happy as my wife, Vivian?"

"No, Sir. I wasn't. I felt trapped and alone and most of all; I just felt lonely, Sir."

"Why didn't you tell me you were feeling like that?"

"I—I tried to in my own way, but I kept missing time, and my headaches were so bad and coming more and more frequently. I—I just lost track of my words and why I needed to say them. Sir." My words are whisper soft and although I'm not a blubbering mess, my eyes didn't get the memo to stop leaking. I feel John's disappointment with my actions

like a branding iron to my soul. He has always known he could trust me to be honest with him. But how could I be honest with him when my truth would have caused him so much self-doubt and confusion?

"You lied to me." John's voice was a cracked plate and no amount of crazy glue would fix it. My need to protect him, caused my mind to break a part and obviously, I'm not the only one suffering a break in our family. *God, what the hell are we going to do?*

"I didn't lie, Sir. I just didn't tell you everything. I—"

"A fucking lie of omission is still a fucking lie, Vivian. So, yes. You did FUCKING LIE to me. Don't try and clean it up and make it pretty. If you smear a twenty-five dollar tube of lipstick on a goddamned pig, it's still a goddamned pig, right?" I have no words. He's is so angry right now. He acts like all of this is my fault. I feel Valery pushing against my mind, she doesn't think I can handle this. She wants to come out, but I don't think she wants to help me. I push her back down and decide to deal with this myself.

"Sir, your anger isn't going to help the situation right now. Valery is pushing to get out and I'm not strong enough to keep pushing her down. I need your strength and control, Sir. I need it to fight my way back to you." I lift my eyes to show him the melee between summer-sunshine and angry drunken whiskey that's taking place inside me. The melted warmth of his gaze covers me and he breathes in as if he's able to inhale the cacophonous imbalance of my selves.

"I'm sorry. You're right, lovely. Obviously, you've been dealing with so much more than either of us thought you were. Thank you for bringing me back to center." He lifts his hands from my shoulders and a whimper leaves my throat, I don't want him to not touch me. I need him. "I'm not going anywhere, Viv. Come on. Get up. We need to get you moving. How

80

are you feeling?" That voice is gone, and my loving husband is back with me now. I don't know what it all means, but if I know John, and I do know him; he has figured out a way to help me.

"I feel kind of like humpty dumpty. But I don't need all the king's horses or his men... I've got you to put me back together again." As he helps me from the chaise lounge, I shoot a beam of joy and satisfaction at him I didn't even know I still had.

"You're damn right you don't need anyone else. I fucking love every part of you, Vivian. It was horrible and hateful shit that broke you. I'm going to love you into wholeness, and it starts now. Upstairs in our bedroom. Now. I need you naked in bed when I get up there. After I've made you come a couple of times and you've sucked my dick dry, we'll talk about Valeria, Valery, and Vera. You've got three minutes, take the elevator." I turn to leave, and he swats my ass, hard. An unladylike squeak slips through my smiling mouth and I'm too excited to be embarrassed about it. My hips sway left to right with my walk. God, I love this man and he's going to fix me. He's the only one who can.

"Yes, Sir."

When I woke up in this bed this morning, I was angry and hurt and holding on to six months of shame, confusion, and betrayal. Now, as I stand at the foot of our bed, none of those feelings coast through my blood. Heat. That's what's scorching my veins and setting my core on fire as it pools in the tiny bundle of nerves pounding out a rhythm so filled with longing my knees almost buckle. I try to breathe through the craziness runny rampant across my skin, making gooseflesh rise and hairs stand on end. I'm all electricity and light. I'm going to implode if something isn't done to harness the power rising in me.

"I'm sure I told you to be naked in the bed when I got up here. I gave you more than three minutes, considering you are beautifully round with our baby. You are testing me already, lovely." Not a question. A knowing smirk lifts the left side of his mouth and my panties are effectively ruined. I'm shaking with my want for this man, but still my feet and hands are paralyzed and refuse to obey. "Get those clothes off—or." His voice is a soft purr of sex and domination and nothing in me can move, not even my lungs. My breath is stalled in the electric air crackling between us and my eyes are glued to the god I have missed. I want to fall at his feet and worship him, but I can't. I just stare at him. In awe. I'm humbled and relieved to have him near me again.

"I—I wanted to be ready for you, Sir. I—uh"

"You want me to undress you, lovely."

"Please, Sir."

"All you had to do is ask." His elegant fingers skim down the sides of my torso and he lingers on my belly. Cradling our child protectively; his breath gusting over my face is a sweet reminder to me that I am also breathing for our child. My eyes are on his hands as they move to the

bottom of my soft cashmere sweater and his thumbs tease the taut skin of my lower belly. It tickles, but I can't find it in me to smile or laugh in this moment.

John lifts the material from my waist and continues up my body. Trivial amounts of my baby-laden belly is revealed, and I hear him suck in a quick breath as the entirety of my rounded torso is on display.

"Arms up." Simple request. Simple response. John absentmindedly folds my sweater and places it on the bench at the foot of our bed. "Turn around." His nimble fingers unclasp my bra and my heavy breast are freed as he pulls the straps down my shoulders and removes the entire thing from my body. It joins my sweater on the bench and his greedy hands turn me to face him. I can't look at him. I'm afraid he may find displeasure in what he sees. I've never looked like this before. I know he has been watching my body change for the last six months but in my mind, he hasn't seen me naked since *ass-gate*.

"I know what you're thinking, lovely. I have never found you more beautiful than I do now. You are carrying life created in fire and brimstone. That life inside you is what burned away the masks we'd both been wearing. This beautiful baby girl thriving in your womb broke every jar and forced us to face demons and truths only a god could reveal. I want you with a tender brutality which borders on insanity. Don't ever doubt my desire for you, Vivian. You." He lifts my chin with his thumb and forefinger, holding me in place until I'm able to see the umber licks of fire dancing in his eyes. He dips his head and licks a tear from my nipple and sucks the tight bud into his mouth, slashing his tongue back and forth until I'm not sure if I'm still standing. He lifts his mouth from me, and I'm panting like I'm practicing Lamaze.

"You—I desire you. I know Valery indicated I'd been with her sexually in the last six months, and I have." I jerk my chin away from him and cross my arms over my chest. I didn't know it would hurt so much to hear him admit to being with another woman. Even if the other woman was me…I don't know how to process it. She is nothing like me and yet she is still me.

"Vivian." My name snapped in *that voice* calls me to heel immediately. "You will not hide yourself from me. You are my wife. Every part of you belongs to me. I fucked Valery because you wouldn't let me touch you. I fucked her because she provoked me. She's a fucking masochist and she spoke to my monster. I felt horrible at first, but then something occurred to me." How can he make something so repugnant sound like a win for me and us?

He waits for me to respond, to ask him what occurred to him. But I'm sure I don't want to know. In fact, I don't want to hear any more of this bullshit.

"What occurred to you?" I don't recognize my own voice. I'm angry and hurt and scared and it makes my voice sound like I eat glass for all my meals.

"When you and I were actively in the lifestyle, sometimes you would do almost anything to get me to punish you. I was afraid you were becoming a pain-slut." His voice held his power over me, and his hands deftly remove my protective arms away. His fingers move to my jeans, he goes to work undoing them and that damn fire roars back to life in my pussy.

"What does that have to do with anything? It's nothing wrong with enjoying pain, you told me that." I'm defensive and this smug bastard

84

smiles at me. Making me clench my thighs together as he is trying to pull my jeans down my long legs.

"I had no trouble doling out your punishments, lovely. I rather enjoyed punishing you. It fed a need in me, the need to cause you pain—to take you to the edge of your sanity and know I could bring you back. Your love of pain fed my need to have power over you. Lift your right foot, Viv." I do so without thought of stumbling over, he would never let me fall. Once he has the right leg off, I lift my left one without having to be told. I want out of my clothes.

I look into his smoldering eyes as he folds my jeans and places them on the bench. I'm standing before him in my black bikini panties and heavy wool socks. I don't know if I want to take them off, my feet are freezing. Even with them on.

"We'll leave your socks on, your feet are always so cold lately." *How does he do that? Reads my mind, and knows what I need before I tell him?* His thumbs in the sides of my panties, brings me out of my thoughts.

"That's not what I was getting at. I thought Valery was a result of what I did to you Six months ago. But as I think back over our relationship, Vivian. She's been as much a part of our journey as you have. There were times when you were so different sexually. Sometimes you would be so aggressive and other times you would beg me to punish you. I always felt like something was off, but I was young, and you were an addiction."

My panties are scrunched up in his right hand and he casually brings them to his nose and inhales deeply. His eyes close and he looks so blissed out, I could almost believe he just took a hit of something quite potent. A gush of liquid floods my core and I feel it running down my thighs. He looks feral. He spreads my panties open and brings the cotton crotch to his mouth and licks my arousal from the soaked gusset. It's hedonistic and the

most erotic thing I've ever seen him do. *Holy fuck! I'll be mad at him about Valery later. I need him to fuck me right now.* My hands are making their way to my drenched slit, but a firm grip stops them.

"No. You don't have permission to touch what's mine." He folds my panties and places them on the bench. I must make some simpering noise in the back of my throat because a deep knowing chuckle that falls over me like pheromones, tightening my inner walls so much, I worry I might go into early labor. John's hand is rubbing my belly and my hips, my internal muscles are clenching so violently, I'm pretty sure I'm coming.

"Fuck, Viv. You're so damn beautiful. Wait a minute… I know that face you're making. Are you coming right now?" I can't tell if he's mad or turned on, but nothing is going to stop this orgasm and thank fuck for that. I feel more moisture coat my thighs. *What in the hell is this?* I vaguely hear his belt clinking and I discern movement in front of me, but my focus is on what is happening with my own body.

Standing about two feet from John, I push against the bed post for support, my sex is clenching and releasing intuitively. A fine sheen of sweat covers me from head to toe and the throbbing. *Oh, my fucking God.* The throbbing between my legs buckles my weakened knees. Just as I feel myself going down, a muscled arm wraps around my waist and a warm, sticky mess clings to my belly. As the waves start to subside, I look at John's right hand holding the ebony pole between his spread thighs, pumping the last of his release onto my skin. It's the most beautiful thing I've seen in such a long time, my eyes mist over.

"What. The. Actual fuck? How the hell did you do *that*? God, I have missed you. Come, I want to rub my cum into your belly, breast, and

neck. I want you wearing me while I fuck you. We can finish this Valery talk after I've had you."

His breathing is harsh and ragged in his chest and his slightly parted lips tell me he's struggling to maintain control. *When had he taken off all his clothes?* He helps me get comfortable in the bed and then his hands are on my tight belly; it's exquisite. He cups my sex and ladles my liquor into his palm to add to his own essence, he continues to rub us into my skin.

He takes a filthy lick of what's smeared on my belly, just before his tongue claims mine. I taste him. I taste me. I taste us. Together. *This is what created this beautiful baby growing in my belly. Our love. Our pain. Our brokenness.*

His right hand is massaging my belly, his left hand my sensitive clit, and his tongue is in my mouth; I come. Hard. He drinks my ecstasy down and breathes for me.

"Never—I never knew how much I loved you until I thought I'd lost you, Viv." John's voice is crushed glass sliding over the broken hopes of a small child. I pull him to me, as much as my belly will allow me to, and I hold him in the cradle between my thighs. His tears run down my neck and kiss my collar bone so softly, I want to cry with him, but I don't because he needs to redeem himself. I promised I would take his sins when he needed me to. I think this is him—giving them to me, so he can be who and what I need him to be. "I failed you in the worst of ways and took advantage of what you were."

A sob falls from him and the thick, wide head of his dick brushes against my swollen cleft. *I want him inside me, I want to make this better for him.* I lift my hips and rotate them a little to the left and I feel the slick, silky crown of him slide into me. "Fuck, Vivian." He groans and surges

forth. I'm so full. Too full of him, the baby, my emotions, and these damn voices whispering in my head.

Shut the hell up, Valery. I don't care what he did with you, he's with me and I'm who he wants.

You think he thinkin about yo' ass right now while he deep in this wet pussy? No, he thinkin about how I gave him my asshole to fuck whenever he wanted to—d

Valery. Leave them alone. Nobody bothers you when you drive the body, so leave her alone. I like her. She's pretty and nice. I don't want her to go away again. If you don't leave her alone, I'll find Vera and you know she's the only one who can...

It ain't fuckin fair she get to feel his love for her, and he only ever goddamned showed me anger and pain. He fucked me the way he did cause I won't her. I hate that uppity bitch. When the fuck is he gonna say somethin nice to me or cry about the fucked-up shit he done to me?

John doesn't owe you anything, Valery. Please just go away and let me concentrate on what's going on. Write what you need to tell me in a journal, we'll talk later I promise.

Yeah, whateva' bitch. Enjoy his dick in your pussy, he know who to come to when he want to fuck the way he really like to.

"Vivian. Are you with me, lovely?" John's voice calls me from my conversation, and I blink my eyes a few times and find chocolate pools of melted worry gazing at me. He has no idea if he's fucking me or Valery or, God forbid, Valeria. This situation is fucked on so many levels and he wants to stay with me and them? *Maybe John's crazy, too.*

"It's me, babe. I'm sorry, they pulled me away for a minute, I didn't know they could do that." My hands clutch at his shoulders because I need him to anchor me.

88

"Maybe, we should stop and continue going—o" I cut him off by pulling his lush bottom lip between my teeth and biting down hard enough to cause a rumble to crawl up his throat and my chin to vibrate against his own.

I tear my mouth away from his and respond with an upward thrust of my hips, inviting him to sank deeper into me. I'm so wet and slippery, he slides all the way to the hilt and my body sucks him in; enveloping him in what I know he loves almost as much as me.

"I just need you, John. It's me. I'm here with you doing what we do best. Please fuck me, John. I need you. I've missed—y..." He pulls almost all the way out, I'm expecting him to slam back into me, but he doesn't. He creeps into me. One thick inch at a time. Holding my eyes with his. I'm not breathing or moving or thinking. I'm just feeling him. His hips move infinitesimally. There is no back and forth, only the constant and persistent surge forward. He's making me feel him spread my swollen, wet lips a part as he reclaims me as his sub. His Dom has risen in his beautiful eyes and there is no softness left for me. Only his immense, unwavering control and fuck me, but I gladly acquiesce to his demand to take what he gives me. What he allows me to have of him. I don't have the right to ask for more or request less.

"Do you feel that, lovely?" He doesn't need or want an answer. He knows I feel his power. He knows how much it turns me on, my pussy is flowing like Rainbow Falls and his dick is bathing in my juices. He's not halfway in, yet and the stretch and burn is devastating and sustaining at once. *I love it. I love him.* He sits back on his knees, I spread my thighs wider for him; they hang over his spread knees as he continues to push into me. His exacting and restrained penetration is making me crazy with lust. I

know not to move, right now he's reminding me I'm his to use as he wants to.

He's reminding my cunt of her true purpose, to serve him. To make his mouth, dick, fingers and heart happy. Tears make tracks down my temples and moisten my hair. John doesn't smile, he doesn't look sorry. He looks like the savage god he is. He's enjoying my tears. They feed the monster living just under his refined elegant skin. The thick root of him notches just inside my silky entrance and the pain is almost too much. I wince, but don't ask him to move or to stop because I understand he's the only monster terrible enough to soothe the beasts living inside me.

"What's your safe word, lovely?" He doesn't move. I watch as sweat trickles down each grove of his abdominals. Each pocket of muscle quivers every time the air cools the moisture on his defined belly. I want to lick my lips and his stomach, but I do neither. I don't have permission. *Fuck, I'm going to come and he's going to have to punish me. Hell, if I can bring myself to give a fuck right now.*

Breathing through my nose, I force the words out my mouth on puffs of air. "Red, Sir."

"Good. Don't forget it. Use it if you need to but be sure you need it before you let it slip from your sweet lips."

"Yes—s..." I'm panting so hard, I'm close to coming. "Yes, Sir."

~14~

It's intense and I'm sure he feels my covetous inner walls clenching around him. And still he says nothing. His dick, a rigid caveat of his control of himself and my pleasure. He's so powerful when he's like this. And finally, the fragmented parts of me are quiet. They watch through my eyes, all except Valeria. She doesn't want to see any of this, it frightens her. Valery seems to be ambivalent towards what is happening, but I can feel her scratching at my insides; her nails digging into my lungs—stealing my breath from me. Valery doesn't want me to feel pleasure, she wants to be the only one to enjoy sex.

John's eyes bore into mine and I know that he knows. *How does he always know when my mind wanders?* He pulls all the way out of me and takes his arrogant dick in hand and strokes his length while watching the vulgar way my sex is spread open. He doesn't meet my eyes and he won't let me close my legs, so the ache of not having him inside me is only that much more acute. I'm empty and cold and I'm leaking like a broken faucet. Not one-word forms on my tongue because I know he is going to punish me. What I don't know is how.

"You're not going to be able to think about other *shit* while my dick's deep inside your exquisite cunt. Are you, Vivian." It's not a question so I don't answer him. "I am all there when we are together like this. I don't give a fuck who's in your goddamned head talking to you Do you understand me, sub?" John's voice is liquid nitrogen, burning his meaning and his absolute domination into my ear canal with the kiss of an artic freeze. A shiver runs down my spine and I feel the baby shift to a more comfortable position. Her tiny foot stomps on my bladder and my right hand immediately goes to the bottom of my belly to lift her weight and push her over. I expect John to stop the scene, but he doesn't. While his

right hand is still languidly pleasuring his stiff cock, he uses his left hand to massage the lump of baby that has balled up at the bottom of my belly until she relaxes and stretches out again. Proving he not only controls me, but the baby he placed inside me knows to yield to his commands, too. *Well damn, she's not even here and she's already a daddy's girl. For some reason, the notion of that bothers some part of me.*

"I understand, Sir. I'm—I" He leans over me and shuts me up with slow licks of his tongue over my lips. He doesn't want to hear my reasons. None are good enough for my transgressions against my Dom. My mouth waters for him, but he won't kiss me properly. His leaking tip grazes my opening and I almost come, but I don't. Everybody in my head is silent and they are waiting him out. When John is like this, he is the master of his universe and everyone else orbits around him; grateful to be anchored by his gravitational pull; which keeps them from floating up and out into the nothingness of everyday life. *God this man.* I'll be whatever he wants me to be and right now, he wants me to be whole and present. I can do this for him. *Back the fuck up, Valery. This is not your body You don't get to have him like this.*

"You're with me again." A smile tugs at his sexy lips and my heart soars to the twenty-foot ceilings. "I'm always going to give you what you need, Vivian. I'm only going to be with you this way.

"Yes, Sir."

"That's my good girl." He eases back into me, slowly and then he grabs on to my hips and starts a punishing rhythm. My greedy walls are sucking him deeper every time he tries to pull out. My body doesn't want to be without him. His audacious balls are slapping against my ass and there's a fire glowing low in my belly. Sweat and love pour from me and the only thing I want to do is give myself over to him.

"Please, Sir. Please make me yours again." I'm weeping, tears falling into my mouth and snot running from my nose. I am a hot ass mess, but I don't care. I'm breaking in the best possible way and John ingeniously fucks the pieces of me back together again as something new and indestructible.

"Yes, Sir. Thank you. Thank you. Thank you!" My whispers becomes shouts and my shouts become screams. And my screams become a prayer as my body moves from a physical, writhing thing beneath him to something akin to light particles floating through the atmosphere. I hope my baby transformed with me and will be put back together when this is all over as something new and indestructible, too.

"I've got you, lovely. You are my beautiful girl, aren't you? You need me like this and I need you just the way you are right now. I love you so fucking much. Keep coming, milk my cock. Don't you dare stop until there is no cum left in my balls. All for you, Vivian. No. Fucking. Body. Else gets this shit, but you."

With his last word, he pulls out to the tip and slams into my fluttering walls, head thrown back in ecstasy and the sound tearing from his throat silences the crazy in my soul as he comes and comes and comes some more. He is a god among men. *I should have never stopped worshiping him, ever. He is my alter. He is my sacred space. And me? I am his glory.*

"I love you, Sir."

"You are my motherfucking world, Vivian. I will not lose you. Not even to another version of yourself."

"I love you, John."

"Nothing and no one will ever be more than us. You, me, and the children we made will rule this fucking world and we will do it together."

"I love you."

93

"I love you, too." He pulls out and kisses my belly as he whispers what sounds like, *I love you, too baby girl. Sorry for the bad words.* I laugh as he crawls up my body to pull me into his chest where I immediately fall into a dreamless sleep. His lips kiss my temple and he dozes off beside me. I know we have a long way to go, but I have my Dom back and for now, that's all that really matters. He finished breaking me, and now he will be the one to make me whole.

Part Two

"The Mirror Does Not Flatter."

"Whoever looks into the mirror of the water will see first of all his own face. Whoever goes to himself risks a confrontation with himself. The mirror does not flatter, it faithfully shows whatever looks into it, namely; the face we never show to the world because we cover it with the persona, the mask of the actor. But the mirror lies behind the mask and shows the true face."

I wake up alone in bed. For a moment, I'm not sure where or who I am but then the memories of John making love to me flood my brain and I know I'm home and my name is Vivian. Sliding out of bed, I realize I'm sore in all the best places. My body has always had a difficult time accommodating John, he's living proof behind the saying men with big feet have bigger dicks. John wears a size fifteen. I make my way to our bathroom and find myself in an oasis of jasmine and rose petals floating on top of water at the perfect temperature in our soaking tub. Candles are flickering on every surface and two champagne flutes rest on the white marble counter top alongside a wooden platter of crackers, cheese, and fruit. Floating through the speaker is the melodious voice of Whitney Houston, singing "I will Always Love You."

John holds his right hand up to help me into the tub with him, and the look on his face is pure love and awe. I take his hand, only to realize my own is shaking. I'm not scared or nervous, but my emotions are all over the place and what I feel for this man is rocking me to my core. Once I'm in the water; seated with my back to his front, I feel his arms wrap around my belly and we simply sit and listen to music. Holding each other.

"You're so beautiful, Vivian." John breaks the silence with sweet words. I turn my head toward him to offer him my mouth, he takes it in a chaste kiss.

"I remember the first time I saw you walking through the Horseshoe." I can hear the smile in his voice. I smile because he's happy.

"I was trying to get to my class early to get this seat next to this girl before the meathead on the football team did." His chuckle is self-deprecating, and I continue smiling with him. I have no doubt my husband

was a skirt chaser before me. I shake my head at his admission as he continues.

"There I am. Chasing some other girl and I look up from my pager and my fucking heart stops beating. I thought I was having a damned heart attack." I hear the astonished grin in his voice and my face mimics his.

"John, you tell the biggest whoppers. You only noticed me because I'm a klutz and bumped into you." I call him out on his version of our first meeting. His hands continue to rub my belly and I lean further into his warmth.

"Lovely, you really think me bumping into you was your fault. I saw you across the yard. I was coming from Cooper, and you were just walking like you had all goddamn day to do whatever the hell you pleased. I knew I had to meet you, but shit Vivian. My brain was fried. I thought the best way to get near you was to accidently-on-purpose bump into you. I didn't mean to knock your books to the ground, but fuck if I felt bad after seeing you up close."

I twist around in his arm so I'm facing him. He has a shit-eating grin on his beautiful face and I'm sure my face mirrors his. "You are a horrible! I was so flustered and embarrassed. When I looked up and saw you. My god, John. You should've had a warning on your shirt. You ended me. I was wet and swollen and scared half to death. You were just so...so damn dominant."

"I wanted you and nothing was going to keep me from having you. I fell in love with you immediately. I've thought about that day for the last eight years and even when I try to tell myself it was only lust; my heart—no, fuck that. My soul knows it was love. Scared the shit out of me back then, too. Still does. I didn't think God would make someone just for me,

but here you are, and I would die a thousand times over before I give you up."

His passion for me is as endearing as it is frightening. I twist back around in the tub and relax against his broad chest. This is home. He is home and together we'll fight to make sure my soul mirrors his own.

"You know I can't have alcohol, right?"

"Lovely? Do you think I'm crazy? That question is rhetorical, by the way." His laugh is light, and it makes me feel like I'm floating in a cotton candy wonderland made just for me. He chuckles around his next words.

"That's sparkling apple cider. We're not trying to bring some little drunk ass baby into our family." His laughter rumbles through his chest and I clench at the sound of it. I spank his left thigh as it stretches out alongside my own. A slap turns into a rub. I can't help but appreciate the feel of lean muscles and silky hair under my fingertips as I caress him. Soon, his laughter is a growl and I'm wet for a whole other reason. "Lovely, you trying to get fucked in the bath? Let me know and I'll take care of you."

I lift myself onto my knees, turn and straddle his lean hips as I place my lips on his. He stays me with his left hand on my hip and forces me to look into his eyes. I know he's checking to make sure it's me and no one else. I hate this, but I understand. "It's just us, John. Please, help me take you like this. I don't know how much of you I'll be able to accept with—th"

He snatches the words from my mouth with a louder, rougher growl as his hand tightens on my hip. There's going to be a bruise there in the morning. The thought causes a rush of fluids to slick the inside of my thighs.

"Every inch. You will accept all of me. Just as I accept all of you. Are we clear?"

"John, I didn't mean like—t"

"I know what you meant, and you know what I mean, don't you? There is no part of me that your body won't accept. And there is no part of your body I won't give myself to. Are we clear?"

"I can't, John." Tears fall from my eyes and my heart cracks a little because I know he's disappointed with me. I can't even bring myself to look at him.

"You can. You have. And you will again."

"That wasn't me, John! You fucked Valery in the ass, I'm not her. She's a slut and a whore. I'm not her!" My body is vibrating as I lose control of myself. I knew he'd fucked her, but I didn't want to hear him talk about it. *Fuck her and him. Goddamn, this hurts.*

"Vivian. Calm the fuck down! Right fucking now." His voice is so quiet, like cashmere without the warmth. I know that voice and my body responds as it's been trained to do. I sit back on my heels; my hands fold in my lap and my eyes fall to the water. My tears dry up and I take a deep breath and wait for my Dom to tell me what to do. The water laps at my hips and soothes the growing baby, who loves the weightless feeling floating on water must give her.

"There is no *her* separate from *you*. Valery is a part of you. Your mind created her to deal with an uncomfortable situation. A situation your body enjoys, but your mind associates with abuse that took place in your childhood." His voice is laced with love for me, but that love is encased in iron bars meant to hold me together. It's working.

"May I speak freely, Sir?"

His finger strokes down my left cheek and lifts my chin so I'm looking into the gentle turbulence of his eyes, and I fall in love with him again. "I

hope you will, lovely. You need to tell me what it is you're feeling. Your fears, what excites you, and most importantly, what you're thinking."

I nod my head in understanding. This reminds me so much of our time in New York when he first introduced me to myself as a submissive. I had to trust him then, and I have to trust him now. I clear my throat to dislodge the softball size lump of hurt and confusion before I attempt to speak.

"Logically, I understand. I know I'm not these separate people, and I know all of the alters are just parts of me that my mind created to help me cope with. With traumas. But, john. I don't know what traumas they're here to help me deal with. I know there was abuse, but I don't remember it. Those memories belong to the alters. I can't access them. And I don't want to."

"You don't have to access them. They have shared all of them with each other; piecing you together from childhood to right before you left your father's home and came to USC. They carry your scars. But, lovely." He stops talking and waits for my eyes to return to his. They do, and he continues. I notice the music for the first time since Whitney. Now Jewel is sing-yodeling about saving souls and how the world is going to shit. I tune her out and listen to my god.

"You are not the sum of your parts; you are whoever you choose to be. We will face the abuse together. Each of those alters protected you; took what you couldn't, and we owe a debt of gratitude to them. In our gratitude, we are also entitled to ask them to return what they took from you. Do you understand what I'm saying, Viv?"

Confusion clouds my mind as I consider his words. "No, what did they *take* from me, Sir?" My eyes bore into his, I need his guidance and domination to anchor me to the right now. He is the only thing keeping what makes me Vivian, tethered to this body. *Fuck me sideways! I can't*

even claim my body as my own, because it doesn't only belong to me. I
share it with others, it's like three teenage sisters sharing one crappy car.
Well not so crappy, but…

"Hey, are you with me, lovely? You seemed to have zoned out." The
concern in his eyes is not conveyed in the iron of his voice.

"Yes, Sir. I'm with you. I just had a weird thought run through my
mind. May I share it with you?"

"Of course. I love weird thoughts. Especially yours." His lips quirk up
on one side and the tension riding my shoulders become residual drops of
drying water making me shiver.

Retuning his cheeky smile, I speak openly because I know he won't
judge or ridicule me. There is something so comforting in knowing the
man who loves you is able to love all of you. It gives me courage to face
fears. *I've never had this before him.*

"I was just thinking about how this body isn't really mine. I mean. I feel
like it's just a vehicle, you know? Like… anyone of the alters can just
jump in the driver's seat and take it for a spin. Somehow, even though we
all have different keys and need different ignitions; we can all start the
car." I shake my head in frustration as my words playback in my ears, but
in my mind, I see Valeria and Valery shaking their heads in agreement.
Like they feel the same way but haven't been able to articulate it. *I guess it*
pays to be the one who actually went to college and took a shit-ton of
psychology classes.

I return my attention to John and notice he too is nodding his head. Like
this crazy thing I just uttered makes perfect sense and in this moment; I
realize I'm not as fucked up as I thought I was. "Sir? What did they take
from me?"

His lips still hold traces of pride and bemusement from earlier, but now he's all Dom and counselor? His voice, a perfect summer rain, washes over me as he places his powerful hands on my arms and rubs them from shoulder to elbow and back. Over and over, he's comforting and anchoring me in and to this moment. *Thank you, baby. I can do this with you. For you.*

"Your strength. Your will to survive at all cost. Your passion and sexuality. And most importantly, the entirety of your soul."

"I want them back!" My outburst startles me, but I don't cower from it. I do want all of it back, but what about the things I want them to keep?

"…but will I have to take the *memories* back, too? The memories of the abuse, Sir?"

"Yes, lovely. It's all or nothing. One cannot exist without the other. As Rumi said, 'The cure for pain is in the pain.' I'll be here with you. We will go through the pain to cure the pain. You and me. Trust me, I've got you Viv. I've got you."

We get out of the tub, dry off and dress for bed. John takes the untouched snacks downstairs and promises to bring me back Valeria's journals. He wants to get started tomorrow. I don't. I don't know if this will work, but I trust my Dom to know how much I can take and how far to push me. *I wonder if I can safe word? I guess I'll find out because the only way I'm going to be able to do this, is as his sub. There is no other way.*

~16~

Vera

The apartment smelled of fresh paint, pee-pee, and bleach. The carpet looked like lumpy oatmeal after it was out too long. Don't know who thought that yellow walls would be nice. It isn't. None of this felt like home, but it was where my daddy and I set up house after my mama finally sent the papers. She been gone for six years before that. I don't even remember her face.

"It don't smell right, daddy. I don't like this ratty old carpet, either. Why can't we stay in our old house? All my friends live there and now they won't be able to come over here to this old funky ghetto side of town."

My daddy turned his sad eyes on me and quirked his lips to make a smile when nothing was funny. I didn't want to be here, but here and him was all I had. I watched his eyes look me up and down and I knew what was coming. I tried to walk away. To go to my new room and lock the door, but he moved so fast, his hands was already pulling my halter top over my head and pushing me to the floor.

"Daddy done the best he could do for you and now you have to tell me thank yo, yeah?. Show your daddy how grateful you are for him finding this nice apartment for you when your mama didn't care if you had a pot to piss in or a window to throw it out of." His crusty and ashy right hand scraped over my ribs and squeezed hard enough to bring tears to my eyes. But he didn't stop long because at eleven years old, I was already wearing a size 34C bra and stood at 5'6".

His touch was rough and angry. He was mad because I complained about the apartment. I knew not to cry or make a sound when he pulled my nipple between his dirty cigarette-burnt-thumb and his ugly, crooked pointing finger.

*"How're you gone show me how much you 'preciate my hard work?
You not 'bout to be like your high-yella, upidity mama, yeah? Open your
mouth and use it for what it was made for."*

*That's when I felt the nudge at the back of my head. Someone pushing
to get out and trying to pull me in. Her voice was stronger than mine and
she was stronger than me, too. I listened for her and when I could finally
hear her, I took a deep breath and thanked her for coming to help and
rescue me. I went to my special room where it always seemed to be the
most beautiful day and I could look at all my favorite paintings and
sculptures for as long as Valeria wanted to stay out with my daddy.*

Valeria

*"Open your legs for me. Let me see that pretty little pussy you got down
there, yeah?" I open my legs and watched his eyes glaze over as he look
his fill.*

*"What you think I need to do to that pretty little blackberry cobbler you
got between your thighs?" I never answer because he would know I wasn't
her. He would know I was here to help her, and not here for him.*

*"I'm feeling a little hungry after all the heavy lifting. I'm gonna have to
have my dessert before I have my meal, yeah?" His bubblegum lips spread
wide, showing pink in the center and his big teeth stained with yellow,
brown, and bright white patches. He slid his tongue across his lower lip;
leaving a trail of slimy spit as it dragged along the dry, cracked skin. I
didn't want him to look at me or touch me but she can't take him. He broke
her once and I won't let him do it no more. I'm stronger. Older. And I can
deal with it because he's not my dad, so fucking me isn't as bad as when he
used to fuck her.*

*"Why you always so fuckin' quiet when what I want is to hear your
little soft voice telling me how good my dick makes your pussy feel." I*

"Daddy's little girl ready to come, yeah? I feel that pussy of yours getting hotter and wetter and yes—fuck yeah, baby-girl! Come all over this thick, long dick." He shoving himself into me so hard. The carpet burning my butt cheeks and back. It hurt, but I keep moving with him. Pushing my privates against his and moving my hips like I do when I play with my hoola-hoop. That when he really go crazy on my pussy and pound me so hard, my eyes roll back in my head.

"My dick made you and it's the only one gonna ever make you come, yeah?" I guess in a way his dick did make me, but not in the way he think it did. He ain't my daddy and me fucking him ain't wrong. Oh my God! He doing that thing he do when he twist hisself so deep inside me, his balls push against my butthole.

Then he rock his hips and nudge my button with the top of his dick and now I get to see all the pretty clouds. I never know clouds came in so many different colors and tasted like clean sweat and love and dirty words and sickness. I didn't know how much I like the taste until he force it down my throat.

Her daddy must really love her to want to show her these clouds and feed her this flavor like he do. But she don't love him that way and she don't like clouds with all them colors and she won't open her mouth to drank down that salty, sweet milk he shoot from his dick. So, I get so full and fat with it and she can just be his sweet little girl. I'm Valeria and I get to be his sweet little fuck.

***

I'm drenched in sweat and I'm so cold, my teeth are chattering. I look around but still don't quite know where I am. Then a large, warm hand wraps around the back of my neck and squeezes one, two, and a third time—I take a breath and turn to look into the warmth of my husband's

eyes until my heart rate returns to something resembling normal and I'm breathing in time with him. "John, I—Pl…" I throw my hand over my mouth and make for the toilet. I have to remember to be careful because I'm pregnant, but I'm going to be sick and I don't want to be sick in our bed. My head is in the sink—I couldn't make it to the toilet before I'm retching so hard, I know I'll have burst capillaries in my eyes. I can't stop. It keeps coming and coming. My belly hurts. *I'm sorry baby-girl.* I throw up some more. At the thought of calling my baby that name. *I'll never let her be somebody's baby-girl. I'll kill the first motherfucker who tries to call her that.* Not sure where these thoughts are coming from, but I mean it. Every last one of them is my own. Not an alter. Not something outside of me. No. These thoughts belong to Vivian Anne Ellis.

"Lovely, what's wrong with you? Do I need to call the hospital or your doctor? Viv, talk to me." I look over at John as I wash my mouth out and offer a weak smile, trying to assure him I'm okay, but I'm sure I look more deranged than reassuring. The heat from his hand is seeping into the thin material of my top as he rubs my lower back in small, tight circles. It feels so good, a quiet moan slips from my lips and flows into the drain with discarded water from my mouth.

"I had a dream, a maybe a… memory? Or maybe it was a nightmare; it was so real, John and so repulsive. Disgusting. I need to read Valeria's journal. I need to know what her experiences were—are—what they are, and how they relate to me." I accept the towel from his hand and wash my face. His eyes are round and concerned, but he's ready to delve into this with me and that's all I need to see from him right now. "John, if any of what I saw happened to her… to me, oh my God! What kind of sick bastard would do that to his *own* daughter? Why would he do that?" I don't

realize tears are carving a path down my cheeks until I feel his thumb scrub them away and his soft lips kiss the sensitive skin beneath my puffy eye.

"Why don't you take a warm shower and get yourself together. I'll get dressed and head downstairs to make breakfast and then we'll get started." Another kiss on the forehead and then he starts the shower for me. All the while, I'm standing in the middle of our country French bathroom, surrounded by pristine white marble and gray wooden trim. I realize my life before John must have been horrible.

"Vivian. We will get through this. Together. Just like we get through everything else. You trust me."

"Yes. Of course, I trust you. I just can't fathom what I endured before meeting you at USC. Who was I? Why can't I remember what happened to me or what that *man* did to this body?" I look up at him as he peels the sweaty night clothes from my torso. There's nothing sexual in his actions, he's just taking care of me like he always has. I step out of my underwear and shiver when the cool air hits my nipples, but I'm not turned on at all. Just confused and scared about what I'm going to find out when I start digging through these journals.

"Have you read the journals?"

He lifts his head from beneath the seamless white cabinet where he was looking for the unassuming rectangular glass jar of my favorite French bath gel and simply nods his head in the affirmative. I feel the bile rise up my throat again, and I know I'm going to lose it. I don't want him to see how knowing he *knows* what happened to me is affecting me. I want him to see me as strong and able. Swallowing convulsively to push the acidic disgust burning up my throat. I quickly side step him and move into the warm spray of the shower and close the door. If I cry now, the water will hide my tears and drown out my quiet sobs.

"Do not hide from me." His voice commands me to open my eyes and acknowledge the presence of my Dom. The relief I feel at hearing him is almost enough to make my knees buckle with gratitude. *God, I can't do this unless I have no choice.* Thank fuck he knows me well enough to know when I need him to bend me to his will; to invoke his hegemony over me.

"Sir, I'm not hiding."

"Yes. You are hiding. You think I don't know you, Viv? I don't know what you're thinking right now about yourself? What I think about you?" I know he's waiting for an answer, but I can't bring myself to give it to him.

"Answer me." His voice is quiet, but I can still hear the edge in it; even over the fall of water bouncing off my shoulders and my belly. I look at the pumice stone pebbled floor as I contemplate my response, but apparently my time is up because John yanks the door open and is standing there—butt-ass naked—looking like an ebony god of war and destruction.

"I don't know what you know… from the journal Sir, but if what I dreamed or remembered is what you know…" My voice trails off and shame washes over my body and turns my stomach sour for the third time this morning. He doesn't say or do anything. Just stands there, letting all the steam escape and cool air to seep inside. His eyes bore into the top of my head and I know he's not going to let me get away with what I just said to him. I clear my dry throat and swallow past the lump of humiliation and self-loathing, trying to find words—any words, but they won't come.

And now my head starts to pound on the left side and waves of dizziness pummel me until my vision narrows to a pinpoint and I'm not standing in the shower anymore. I'm sitting in a room; it looks like I'm inside of Henry Tanner's "Flight to Egypt" painting. I'm surrounded by warm shades of blue and soft pinks and hints of mossy green and a dim moon with a halo of

109

gray and lilac. It's peaceful here. I can breathe and my head doesn't hurt, and I don't have to have the words John wants me to. I don't know who he's talking to, but I'm thankful they gave me a break. I can't do it all at once. He can't push me like this.

Vera/Vivian

"I don't think we've met before. I'm Jonathan Ellis, Vivian's husband, and the father of the child you're carrying. Who are you? I hear John's voice, I'm aware of what he's saying. I guess I'm sharing consciousness with... wait a minute. John said he met all my alters, why doesn't he know who this is?

"My name is Vera. I know who you are, and I know who Vivian is, too. I don't hardly ever really come out, only a few times, but I never talk or interact with you, yeah? Or her. Or any of them except for Valeria. She's my best friend and she kept me safe from my daddy." Her voice is so soft. Like a child. She knows who I am and who John is, but I have no idea who she is and from the silence; John doesn't know any more than I do about this new alter.

"Well, Vera. It's lovely to meet you. I'm going to shut the shower door and give you some privacy. If Vivian wants to come out, please allow her to do so. We have a lot of work to do and I'm sure she'll want to know about you. Enjoy your shower and it was a pleasure meeting you."

How the hell does he talk to my alters like they're real people. Real and separate from me, yet still a part of me. Why didn't he question her or shower with her? He admitted to fucking Valery, why not take this Vera for a ride? I'm so confused.

"Hi—um, Vera? I'm Vivian. I'd like to come back out now, if you don't mind."

"No Vivian, I don't mind at all. Don't be afraid, I was here before you, yeah? Before any of y'all. I'm the original… the one this body belongs to. Don't worry, yeah? I don't want it back. I like how you live in it, yeah? How you use it and how you take care of it. We'll talk later."

"Oh! I like your room. It's pretty. Like a painting." She speaks just like her daddy. My skin feels dirty and shame is once again climbing up my throat threatening to choke me to death.

17

I find John downstairs in the dining room with two plates of grits, eggs, and turkey sausage placed on the table. Orange juice in my glass, skim milk in his. Toast cut into triangles and a jar of apple butter placed to the side of the heavy blue-speckled stoneware holding our breakfast. I'm unsure if he's my Dom or just my husband. My mind is reeling as I take a seat across from him and now I remember why we decided to do away with this part of our relationship. He scans my face like a copier machine, his gaze feels like the sun if the sun was covered over with a thick cloud.

In the background, the Goo-Goo Dolls belt out their hit, *Iris* on the radio and I can't help but notice how the words of the song express my emotions so perfectly it cracks my chest open. I really just want to know who I am, and I do feel I was made to be broken. I can't seem to find the right glue to put myself back to rights. I thought it was through submission, but that's not going to work, at least not on its own; and now I have to tell John. *Why is he just staring at me like I did him dirty?*

"Good morning. *Viv?*"

"Oh, that's why you're staring holes through me."

"Yes. I met someone else this morning. I've never—s"

I interrupt him by placing my right hand on the top of his and squeeze it.

"I met her, too. Vera. She's different from Valery and Valeria, but not so different from me."

"What do you mean, not so different from you?" His perfect brow arches over his right eye as he levels his question at me. In response, I bite the inside of my cheek and purse my lips together to stop the smile from cracking my face wide open. He's so obvious. I can't even believe he wants to know what this alter looks like—but then again, I can totally

believe he wants to know what she looks like. His own mouth is twitching in an effort to stave off his amusement. I love him when he's like this.

"Vivian, I'm serious. What do you mean? Does she present like you, *physically?*"

The way he says physically is so funny, I burst out laughing at him. *God, he is a nut.* "Well, kind of—I mean. She seems more like me than the others." *I don't know if she is the original or not.*

John's astute examination of my face feeds like someone peeling all the skin and flesh away just to see what my bone structure looks like. I hold my face as impassive as possible. I hate how well he knows me, and that he knows the alters better than me, too. *Do I tell him what she said or not?*

"I'm listening. Lovely? We won't keep secrets from each other and you sure as fuck won't keep secrets from me with your alters." His voice is a peaceful lake, but I know him as well as he knows me and that's enough to know not to pull any shit with him. He's at his most dangerous when he's quiet and thoughtful. I look up into the eyes of a predator. If I don't give him what he wants he will hunt it down and take it from me. A shiver crawls up my back like tiny spiders spinning webs around each of my vertebra.

"Well, Vivian. I'm waiting."

"She said she was the *original* and I was an *alter,* but she doesn't want to control the body because she likes the way I use it. How I take care of it." I move the grits around my plate before bringing a forkful to my mouth. If not to ease the hunger pangs, then at least to give my hands something to do and buy myself some time to find the right words to express what's going through my mind.

After a sip of orange juice, I continue with my train of thought. "And she… she looks like me, but different. Younger. Innocent. My age. No

locs, though. Her hair is like I use to wear it. You remember when my hair was loose. Natural—with all those curls? Like that. That's how she wears her hair." I have no idea what John is thinking. He's just looking through me. No expression or anything. I may as well finish with my word diarrhea and get it over with.

"But John. She's so innocent and trusting. Like she never had anything bad happen to her. And if she's the *original*, then what does that make me? Is that why I don't remember my childhood? Why I never feel like I'm enough? Just a part of something dirty and broken?"

I don't realize I'm crying until I feel John's arms wrap around me while he plucks me up from my chair. His lips brush my ear as he whispers soothing words into my hair, while rubbing circles on my back.

"Lovely, you are who you always were. The woman I love. I don't care if you were first or last, you are the woman I fell in love with. The mother of my child. The beginning and end of my world. You are exactly who the fuck I say you are, are we clear? Repeat."

"I am exactly who John says I am."

Hot rivulets of pain and confusion flow down my cheeks as I gather my breath to repeat after him.

"I—I am." I gulp for a breath. "I am exactly… who." I try to take a deeper breath to calm myself down. "I am exactly who." I close my eyes and remember my life with John and finally, I can breathe. "I'm exactly who, John s-says I am." When I open my eyes, I find my resolve staring at me with nothing but love and devotion. I can finally take a breath without shuttering.

"I don't give a fuck who or what says differently, lovely. You and I are who will survive this situation. I didn't fall in love with Valeria. I sure as fuck didn't fall for Valery. And I don't even know who in the hell this

Vera person is, nor do I have one fuck to give about her ass right now." His obstinate eyes bore into me; leaving absolutely no aspect of who I am untouched. Consecrated by his will that I accept his words as the blessing they are.

"I'm in love with Vivian Anne Bruno Ellis. You are my wife. End of the motherfucking story. Got that, lovely? You and me. That's it; at least until our daughter is born." His shy smile pulls me up out of myself and reminds me why I'd follow him into and out of hell. This man loves me. Without reason or hesitation. He loves me for no other reason than I'm alive. Whatever state my mind is in, he loves me with his entire soul. And if nothing else, it's why I'm ready to fight for the right to continue to love him just as much as he loves me.

"Yes John. Yes, to everything you said. We are going to be the last three standing." He releases me and wipes the tears and snot from my face with a pearl-gray linen napkin. Pulls my chair out, and after he's got me seated again; takes my cold breakfast to the microwave. I hear the door open as he calls out from the kitchen.

"Drink your juice, Vivian. You need the folic acid and the vitamin C." I shake my head and smile. He is who he is, and I love him more than I thought I could. Feeling lighter than minutes before, I decide to give him a cheeky response.

"Yes, Sir. Would you like to watch me swallow, Sir?"

"Vivian. Don't make me spank that gorgeous ass of yours." I hear the smile in his voice and as he opens the microwave and on que, my stomach growls like some kind of wild animal. *Loosing and fighting to keep my mind must make me hungry*

18

Breakfast was eventful, and I honestly just want to go lay down on the sofa, but John has all of Valeria's journals and we are sitting in front of the fireplace getting ready to start with the first one. The hearty food my husband prepared for me is attempting a reenactment of the second coming. I take a sip of ginger ale and place a dry cracker in my mouth to keep the acidic saliva from burning up my throat. It's not really working, but I won't succumb to this nausea or the desire to let an alter come forward and deal with this shit. *I'm stronger than I give myself credit for. I can handle this. I will handle this.*

"Do we have to listen to Tupac while doing this? I have a feeling I didn't grow up with a mother worth writing a whole rap song about." Dear Mama was softly playing through the surround sound speakers. It wasn't up loud, but I still heard Tupac's heavy voice rolling over and through words of appreciation and devotion for the woman who gave him life, raised him, and sent him into the streets. I have no recollection of a mother, but I'm sure she wasn't *in the kitchen trying to fix us a hot plate after work.*

"Stop stalling, lovely. You're going to read some painful shit in Valeria's journals. I want to help prepare you for some of it, but for the most part…you're just going to have to be fucked up with her entries." I could feel the tension rolling off John like fragile ribbons of blue haze cascading down the mountains we visited in Asheville. "I can tell you she is the first alter to develop. She is what's called the primary protector alter, as well as child alter. Valeria has been present for the longest. Her memories start around the age of four or five. She does not age with the body, and she has been somewhat dormant since the body turned the same age as her. She went away for the most part around the time you turned

116

twelve or thirteen." He lifts my chin and gazes into my eyes. I know he's checking to make sure it's me and not an alter. *I fucking hate he has to do this every time.*

John's holding my right hand in his left and rubbing his calloused thumb across my knuckles. I know he's doing it to anchor me to the present and thank god it's working. He takes a breath and the words that fall from his beautiful mouth makes my stomach contract.

"We have journals with memories recording your life from about the age of five until twelve. Then we have journals with memories between ages ten and twelve—different memories from Valeria's—that are some of the most disturbing ones we have. The doctors have no idea who wrote then or when they were written…"

"Vera." I interrupt him with a voice so small, I'm surprised he heard me. I clear my throat and squeeze his hand with clammy fingers.

"Vera is telling me she wrote them when everyone was asleep. She said she wanted people to know she was there, but she didn't want to come forward." Her presence is a sad and heavy syrup lining my throat like post nasal drip. Clogged with emotions that don't belong to me. Tears, thick and oily, roll down my face and I can't figure out how to turn into myself and pull Vera into my arms and comfort her, but I have an overwhelming need to protect her from this sadness. I need to help her. Somehow make her feel better about what's happened.

"Oh, my fucking god." The words escape on a puff of spent air. I'm sure John didn't hear it, but after the air whooshes past my lips, I hear the most stentorian silence I've ever heard in my life. It is absolute and filled with a lifetime of instant camera images of cotton candy pain, cream-spinach colored sodomy, salty-sweet deprivation, graffitied desecration, and rancid desolation unparalleled by anything I've ever known. Except, *I*

117

have known it. I lived it. I took it so that Valeria wouldn't have to. She was only a little girl, I was older...I was fourteen when Valeria cried out for help. And I couldn't leave her alone to take what that repugnant man was going to do to her.

"Vivian. Talk to me, lovely. What the hell is going on. You're scaring me." I feel his hands on my shoulders. Squeezing me tighter than is comfortable, but not enough to bruise. His voice is low, and commanding and it calls to that part of me who lives only to serve and please him. *Thank god she is still here.*

"Sir?" My hands are folded in front of my belly and my chin rest easily on my chest, I am only able to see John's gray woolen socks. I take a deep breath and look at him through my lashes because I know he needs to know it's me who's with him right now.

"I'm not the original. I showed up when Vera was twelve and Valeria couldn't protect her from...from the man. I had to protect Valeria, she needed me and so did Vera." There's an enervating pause between what I've discovered and actually understanding what it really means.

"I'm not the original, John. I'm not real. I'm just some fragmented part of a mind too fucked up to deal with her own shit, so she created all of these separate parts to take what she couldn't. How fucking selfish can one person be. We deal with all her shit! All the rapes! The ass fucking! The dick sucking! All the horrible, nasty, foul bullshit her motherfucking daddy doled out and then all the shit he let that man—dirty, filthy, and unclean man—do to me. I was the one who had to f-fuck th-th-him. I had to bend over and spread my ass..."

A sob tears from my throat and continues to rip me a part. A phantom feeling of thick, warm shit runs down the backs of my thighs; making me squeeze my asshole to try and keep it from spilling from me. I can't

breathe, and I can't stop crying. I need air to cry and air to breathe and I don't have air for any of it. Dizzy.

"John. Please hel—p…" Warm, earth covers me. I rest my head on the subtle lumps and bumps of the ground. I'm moving, but not on my own. I'm floating. The earth is still covering me. I'm warm, and still too cold. What is that blaring noise? Who are the people digging me out from my grave? Leave me here. It's safe and warm and it smells like John.

***

It's cold in here and this doesn't smell like our room. It smells clinical… sterile. *Beep. Beep. Beep. Beep.*

"What the hell is that incessant beeping?" I try to peel my eyelids open but slam them back down as soon as the fluorescent lights try to burn the summer sunshine from my gaze.

"Hey you." I know it's John, but his voice is so heavy; he sounds like he lost his best friend and I know that's not what's causing the dense sadness in his voice because I'm still here. *Oh no… Please God don't let it be true.* My hands fly to my stomach and tears of relief pour from my eyes and saturate the curly edges of my hair.

"Vivian. You're up."

"Yes." I reach for his hand. I go to put it on my belly, but he yanks it away before it makes contact. I'm confused and scared.

"John? What's w-wrong? Why won't you…" I stop talking because I realize I don't feel her moving. She always moves when she hears her daddy's voice.

"Why isn't she moving? John!?"

I realize I'm yelling and screaming at this point, but I can't stop myself. I know. I fucking know she's gone. All these alter bitches, took my baby away. I'm a tornado of broken homes and disfigured limbs. My stuffing is

119

falling out and the leather thread used to stitch me together is snapping. I'm not going to survive this. I want to die with her. I don't want to be here anymore. And then I remember, I don't have to. I'm not the owner of this body. This body does not belong to me. I can leave and never come out.

The Internal House

I don't have to take anymore shit for Vera. Or for Valeria. I'm leaving. Checking out and no one can do anything to me because I don't even really fucking exist! I'm just a secondary personality. I don't have to stay and deal with it.

Vivian, don't you even think of leaving us, yeah? I'm not a person anymore. You have to stay—"

I don't have to do shit, Vera. How dare you tell me I have to stay. You're a selfish bitch. If your daddy was fucking with you, why didn't you tell someone? Why create us and then make us take it up the ass, literally for you?!

The same fuckin reason your scary ass ran and sat in the corner rockin like the demented crazy bitch you are when John slid that big, beautiful dick into your ass. Who the fuck want to deal with shit they don't want to deal with. Get off your fuckin high horse and stop bitchin about this shit cause we got bigger shit to deal with than your hurt feelins.

Fuck you, Valery. You've only been here for a short while, and anything you endured—with pleasure it seems—was done with the man I love and the man who loves and treasures me. It's not the same, is it?

Okay. Vivian, I hate you got your memories back, yeah? But we got to deal with the baby. She was alive and now she isn't. We're not the only ones who was waiting for that baby to come in three months. Vivian, the only person John is…

120

Oh my God. John. He needs me. He was so excited about this baby and even though I wasn't excited in the beginning, the love and joy he derived from knowing he was starting a family with me won me over. Okay. I'll make a deal with you guys.

What kinda mothafuckin deal we gonna make with your selfish ass? You don't think bout no body but your damn self. That baby was more my goddamned baby than yours. I'm the one took John's dick when you checked the fuck out. I was controlling this body when he dumped all that hot, thick cum into my tight pussy. Me, bitch. That baby was mine and John's.

Valery kinda makes a good point. She was the one who got pregnant with John and you can't just think about what the best thing for you will be. I know y'all think I don't know what I'm talking about because I'm young, but I've been in this body longer than the two of you. Fair is fair.

First of all, John didn't impregnate Valery's ignorant ass. The baby belongs to John and me. We are married. I don't care what either of you say. There would be no John if he hadn't met me at Carolina. Secondly, I will do what's best for me and that will be what's best for the rest of you because I've been living this life for the last seven years.

You fuckin wrong about that shit. Vivian, you a uppity bitch and I don't understand why you don't like John fuckin your ass, but you did come back to own your own shit. But if you think for one cotton-pickin minute I'm gonna let you make decisions for me and mine...You can just get the fuck right on back to wherever you go when hidin.

Okaaaaay. Thanks for your nonsensical commentary. Anyway. Here's the deal, I'll maintain control of the body, but we all have to resolve to find a way to make sense of the dysfunctional upbringing Vera had. If we're stuck in here, we have to learn how to live and be functional. Our first

mission is to take care of each other and then secondly, we make sure John is taken care of.

I love this! Finally, I have two big sisters and I'm not the only one holding on to Vera's hand when she's crawling up and down the walls. Oh! Can we have girl time and sleep overs?!

Awe fuck. I didn't sign up for this shit. What the fuck ever. Listen, we gonna look out for each other and somebody gonna have to take care of John. Me and Vivian can do that shit together. Don't goddamn look at me like you gonna say some stupid shit. You not gonna fuckin deal with John when he wanna fuck every hole he can fit his fat dick in. Me? I fuckin love all that ruthless shit he love doin.

I know you all don't believe me, but I appreciate you guys, yeah? I love you and I do want to be a part of this but, it may take me a while. With the loss of the baby, yeah? My heart hurt and I don't deal well with heart pain like this. But thank you.

***

It feels like I've been inside my head for days, but apparently it's only been a few minutes. Valery has some nerve; she thinks I'm going to just turn my husband over to her? Later. I'll deal with them later.

"John, I'm so sorry. I'm sorry I lost her." Tears roll down my swollen cheeks and he uses his large thumb to wipe them away, but they keep falling. I feel his warm, soft lips on my face. Drinking my sorrow and regrets.

"Lovely." Pain is a lump in his throat and my heart clenches. He's trying to be strong for us, but he doesn't know we're here to be strong for him.

"I love you. You didn't lose anything. These things happen, and we will get through it. I saw you trying to check out, what happened?"

122

"I love you. We will get through this. I did try to check out… I didn't want to be here without her." Saying it out loud fills me with shame and self-loathing. *I really am a selfish bitch.*

"You're entitled to feel whatever you feel." I must have been wearing my thoughts on my face. John has always been able to read me so well— too well.

"Yes, feel what I want and need, but not abandon the man I love. The man who fights for me every day. I don't have the right to do that and the others, they called me out on it for trying."

"Have you met all of them now? Can you all talk inside your beautiful mind?"

"Yes. It's strange, but I'm glad I'm not having to deal with everything on my own. We've decided to be there for each other and for you. I know how excited you were for this baby. I can't say I had the same attachment as you did in the beginning, but I wanted her for you." I lift golden eyes to dark chocolate and his sadness feels like a fist lodged my throat. I can't catch my breath because it's running away from the heaviness shrouding the room in sadness. Away from our mirrored brokenness.

"Breathe, Viv. I'm okay. We're okay. Sounds like you guys have a plan. I want to be in on it. You're not doing this shit by yourself. And no, having the others help you is not the same as having help." The tight smile playing around the edges of his gorgeous lips returns my breath to me. *He's going to be alright. He's strong enough for him and me and all the other crazies living in my head.*

19

After three days in the hospital, I was more than ready to go home. John looked no worse for ware, but the slight smudges under his eyes and the slightly turned down tilt of his full lips told the truth of how he was feeling.

The nurse gave me the directions for dealing with the bleeding and assured me it should stop within two are three weeks, reminded me not to insert anything inside my vagina for six weeks or until my doctor gave me permission and then she told me how to make a sitz bath to help with the swelling and soreness caused by delivering the baby—our daughter.

John gathered my bags and all the crap the hospital gave me to take home and left to get his Toyota 4-Runner after kissing me on top of my head and squeezing my shoulders.

"You know if you need counseling, there are a lot of great grief counselors around. It may be helpful for you and your husband to go together, you know… to learn how to deal with this and not blame each other." I know she was just trying to help, and some part of my mind appreciated it, but the last thing I wanted was to sit in some office holding John's hand talking about how I feel after losing his child. I have bigger fish to fry and none of it will get done sitting on the couch in a stuffy office.

"Thanks. I'll keep that in mind, Tracey." She helped me sit in the wheelchair and made sure I was as comfortable as possible before rolling me towards the door. I looked around the room to make sure we hadn't left anything and saw the pre-packed baby bag sitting on the floor by the bed. My breath caught in my chest as something like bubbling acid crawled up my throat, burning all rational thought from my brain.

"Mrs. Ellis? Vivian, are you alright? What can I do to—hel…" I was out of the chair and on the floor before I realized I'd moved a muscle. I

picked the pink and white baby bag up and clutched it to my chest. I prayed it would keep the heart beating out of control safely inside my ribcage. Why the hell would John leave this here.

This is for our daughter... the daughter who's not coming home with us. The daughter who took five breaths and chose to leave before she even had a chance to know us. A daughter who was the product of the worst night of my life. She knew what she was, how she was conceived, and she knew I wouldn't have been able to love her the way a mother needs to love her child. She knew, I would've eventually abandoned her just like my mother abandoned me. She was so much smarter than me. Bless her soul. She chose herself over me and I can't help but love and respect her even more than I already did.

"I'm fine. Just noticed the bag we'd packed for our little girl and I wasn't prepared for it, is all. I think I'd like to leave it here. Maybe donate it to someone who's having a little girl but doesn't have much. Would that be all right to do. Just let me make sure we didn't put anything personal in here." I dig through the sweet-smelling onesies and the tiny mittens and boodies, caressing each piece to say goodbye to the little girl who was smart enough to know this was not a safe place for her. I run my hand across the smallest diapers in the world and remember thinking about how small a butt would have to be to fit them.

The faintest smile graces my lips and it's in that moment I feel her. Her perfect little fist on my left cheek and her tiny little cupid's bow lips on my right. *I love you mommy, but you and daddy have so much to work out and when my brothers and sisters come to you, don't forget to tell them about the daughter who knew better than her parents did.*

"I'm ready to go, now. Could you wheel that chair back over here? Now that the adrenaline has worn off, I don't think I can walk back across the floor."

"Yes, Mrs. Ellis. And I'll be sure to give your gift to someone deserving." I watch as her blond ponytail swings side to side as she comes towards me with the chair and a placid smile on her pink lips. She's so small, I almost feel bad having her push my five-foot, eleven-inch frame out of here.

"Thank you, Tracey. You all have been so kind during our stay. Please make sure the baby bag goes to a Black mother and daughter, thank you." I catch a glimpse of her blush and wide green eyes and could almost see her thoughts as they were spinning in her head. *She'd better do as I asked, if she knows what's good for her.*

"Yes, Mrs. Ellis. Let's get you out of here so you can get home and heal."

John is waiting just inside the door at the pick-up area with an anxious look on his face. As soon as he sees me rolling up, the tension in his shoulders falls away and I watch as his wide chest moves up and down, with what looks like his first real breath in a long while. *God, I love this man. I have no idea how we're going to get through this, but I know as long as we are us—we will.*

"What took so long? I was just getting ready to come back up there and carry your ass down here myself." The irritation is back in his eyes as he walks to where Tracey has parked the chair under the awning. It was warm in the hospital, but outside, the cold air cracks across my face like a whip. It feels like ice is forming on my skin.

John realizes how cold I am and lifts me from the wheelchair and carries me to his truck, new-bride style. He walks to the passenger side of

the truck and tucks me inside. I notice the car seat was no longer in the back and I appreciate him for doing that. With a kiss to my right cheek and solid click of the seatbelt, he shuts the door and waves to the nurse before walking around to get in the driver's side. *We have so much work to do and too many obstacles standing in our way for this to turn out any other way but messed up.*

"You ready, lovely? After I get you home and settled, I'll go to the pharmacy and get the prescriptions filled. Be thinking about anything else you may need me to pick up for you, all right?"

Thank you."

"For what?"

"Loving me the way you do."

"No need to thank me for that, loving you is not an option. I don't have a choice as to whether or not I'll love you and you don't get to choose either."

"No, I guess I don't."

~20~

Settling in was easier than I thought it would be. John didn't let my feet touch the floor one time. He carried me to the bathroom, put me on the toilet after taking my pants and panties off. He carried me to the shower, held me up while he bathed me and doted on me like I was something precious. He carried me from the shower, placed me on the counter over the sink where he proceeded to dry and lotion my body before putting the mini-mattress the hospital sent home in the seat of my lady-days underwear and sliding them up my legs.

He put a nursing bra with pads on and then pulled my favorite Cuddle Duds over my distended belly. He carried me to our bed, gave me something for pain and announced he was going to make me lunch. All the while, his eyes never left mine. He needed to know it was me he was taking care of. With a final kiss on my lips, he walked out the door to make me something to eat.

***

Time moves slower when your body is healing. Luckily, the alters were quiet as they allowed John and I to care for each other throughout the rest of December. We never did put up the Christmas decorations and we didn't exchange one gift. Our first child was born and died on the 21st of December. There was nothing Santa could've left under the tree for either of us to ease the hurt, disappointment, and anger brewing within our broken hearts.

On Christmas morning, John announced he was going for a run around the lake and would be back to help me get ready for breakfast. He didn't fix his mouth to wish me a Merry Christmas and I didn't open my mouth to say good morning. Something was beyond broken in both of us.

He shut me out and shut down. I was waiting for him to rage or cry or lose his shit, but he did none of those things. His response to the loss of our child was simply… nothing. He walks around like everything is fine and I'm recovering from something other than giving birth to our dead daughter.

***

My alters have gone quiet and for the first time in my life, I am truly alone and on my own. I'm not sure I hate this feeling. I realize after I left Vera's father's home, I didn't have much time to figure out who and what I wanted to be. I found and fell in love with John within two months of starting college. I've never had the opportunity to be by myself. To make choices based completely on what I wanted for me.

Maybe my daughter gave me this chance to discover who the hell I am and what the hell I really want for my life. There has to be a reason for so much crazy to happen in such a short period of time. I mean really. What are the odds that John would lose his mind and rape me, get me pregnant, my mind would further fracture alerting us to the fact I was already fucked up, finding out I'm not the original, and then our ill-conceived baby comes three months early—takes sixty breaths—and dies. *What the fuck is the universe or God or whoever the hell is out there, trying to tell us.* Not us…no, someone is trying to tell *me* something and it has nothing to do with John.

***

Four months is a long time to spend with yourself, even if yourself has three other personalities to keep you company. John finally went back to work and seems to be throwing himself into growing and expanding his company. He talked about going back to school to pursue a Ph.D. in

economics or some shit. Our conversations have been going something like:

Me: How was your day?

John: Fine.

Me: What did you do?

John: Same shit I do every day, Vivian. Work.

Me: Oh. So, what do you want for dinner? (it's usually after 11 pm when he gets home now)

John: I already ate. I'm going to shower. I'll be in my office; I have a lot of work to do. Don't wait up for me, okay lovely.

Me: Okay. Oh, I had a good day, too.

John: Good. I'm glad. You deserve good days.

He hasn't touched me since I came home from the hospital and for the most part, I'm okay with that, I guess. I have a large assortment of vibrators, dildoes, and bullets. I miss him and our intimacy, but I'm not going to beg my husband to be my husband.

I went back to my art gallery six weeks after the baby was born. We had to name and bury her because she was considered a live birth. John said to name her whatever I wanted. I chose to call her Gayle because it means a father's joy. It seems when she died, she took her father's joy with her and left me with the husk of what John used to be. I can't be angry with her, she did what she had to do for herself and in doing so, gave me permission to do what I needed to do for me.

I had Gayle Reese Ellis cremated on December 25, 2000. I gave her ashes to a glass artist who exhibited some of his work in my gallery. I told him to make my daughter into something beautiful and permanent. Every time I glance at the exquisite pink and yellow, glass lotus flower with the

brown hand-blown stem, I smile because that's my Gayle in that crystal vase.

***

It's Tuesday, which means I have an evening appointment with my therapist, Dr. Kerrigan. I found him using the pamphlets Tracy packed away in all the shit the hospital gave me. The alters and I have been talking about everything from Vera's upbringing to how to best deal with John and his bullshit. Vera still refuses to come out and talk with us, but she does use the journals and we all cry for her. She's the saddest person I know and that's saying something coming from me. We try not to keep secrets from each other, but Valery is such a twunt.

Although I can't prove it, I know she's been fucking John behind my back because I have control of the body for the most part and I know what it feels like to have John lose control. Every time I ask her about it, she just flounces off to her room and turns up whatever that horrible music is she listens to.

I'm already tired of dealing with her and John. But I need to know why he can be with her but can't even look at me. *Does he blame me for losing Gayle? Is this how he's punishing me*? I don't understand, and he's not talking. Val's not talking, either. It seems I'm the only one who *is* willing to talk, and what the hell do I know?

I place my phone in my purse after turning the ringer off just as Dr. K steps out of his office. He's not hard on the eyes at all and it makes him easy to talk with. He's not like any man who's ever been in my life before. Not like Vera's father. Not like the men he allowed to rape and sodomize me. And certainly not like the man I fell in love with and married. No, Dr. K. is in a class all by himself and sometimes I wonder what it would be like to be his classmate.

131

"Good evening, Vivian. How are you getting on?" His deep voice is only made sexier by his lovely, lilting Irish accent. I'm glad I'm so dark, or he would surely see my blush. I smile as I slip pass him to walk into his office. On Tuesdays, I take extra care with my clothes, makeup, and hair. He never fails to notice.

"I always have to remind myself you're asking how I'm doing when you say that." I chuckle as I sit in my favorite whimsical chair across from his more austere one. The chair I love is so at odds with the six foot-eight-inch man folding himself into the navy blue, Chesterfield wingback chair while taking stock of me as I settle into the off-white inverted turn of hardened plastic.

No softness or padding, but still the most comfortable chair I've ever sat in. It looks like the designer forgot to finish it or decided he didn't like what it was shaping up to be, so he abandoned it. Just walked away from what it was, what it could've become and decided it wasn't worth the effort. I notice the small, feminine, velvet Chesterfield in the same color as his large, leather wingback sitting just off to the left of him at an angle. *Maybe for couple's therapy.*

I find my spot and take a shallow breath before I answer his original question. "I'm doing better than I was last week, but not as well as I will be doing next week." I tip the right side of my full mixed-berry-colored lips up just enough to let him know that I know my answer is total bullshit because it's the same one I give him every week.

The cloudless blue skies of his eyes cover me like a warm spring day, as he looks at me. Really looks at me with something akin to amusement dancing across his lovely face and then he schools his features and dons his I'm-a-professional-medical-doctor-face and I know it's time to get down to business.

"Really?" A slight shift in his chair as he uncrosses and re-crosses his long, muscular legs. *I wonder if he plays soccer or tennis.* How has your week been, Viv?" *I love when he calls me Viv. Okay, I've got to stop crushing on my doctor.* Both he and I deserve better than that.

"I don't know how my week has been. Well, that's not actually true. It's been lonely. Really fucking lonely." I chance a glance in his direction, and I don't see the one thing I don't want to see. Pity. Dr. Kerrigan doesn't pity me at all and for that I'm really grateful.

My hour is almost up, and we've covered a lot of ground. Ground my feet didn't want to tread over, but somehow, found their way across the scorched land.

"So, Vivian we talked a lot about how your husband is probably having sex with your more adventurous alter, Valery and how you feel about it. Do you think we can get Valery out here to chat before you go?" His blue eyes slide over my face, looking for signs of a switch. Sometimes it happens without my permission, usually it's Valeria who has to be heard. She's only twelve, so everything is the most important thing in the world when it affects her.

Valery, I would really like if you came out and spoke with Dr. Kerrigan. I won't listen in, I promise. I just want you to get some clarity about what's happening with you and John. I feel like he may be using you as a substitute for me and that's not fair to you, me, or him. Please, come out and speak with Dr. K.

I don't know what finally convinces her to step forward, but she does. I feel her pushing against my mind and I know she's angry and hurt and mostly confused. I've never understood her dislike of me, and maybe I never will. She doesn't acknowledge me as I walk towards my room, hugging Valeria as I go. I catch her whisky colored eyes with sparks of multi-hued fire dancing through them like a peacock spider trying to attract its mate, but she quickly averts her eyes and pushes through. I find a soft pillow in the corner of my room and sit in the lotus pose to find my center. I've been meditating lately, and it seems to help me figure out what my path is. Before I completely slip away, I vaguely hear Dr. Kerrigan's voice as he acknowledges Valery's presence. *I don't think he likes her very much.*

"Valery. Thank you for choosing to come out and speak with me. How are you? How have you been doing?"

"You can cut the bullshit. I don't really know what that bitch been sayin about me and John, but she need to shut the fuck up about shit she don't know about."

"I'm sure I don't know what you're talking about, Valery. Would you like to share where these hostile feelings are coming from?"

"Oh, you sure you don't know where my *hostile feelins* is comin from, right? How about I tell you then? How about I tell you how much of a cunt your Vivian is. She don't do shit for John and he do every-fuckin-thing he can for her."

"Why does this make you so angry. John and Vivian have a seven-year history of which you're not a part. Why does her treatment of him upset you so?"

"Why you think you need to remind me about that? You think I don't know how fuckin new I am in this relationship? I'm upset with how she fuckin treat him cause she don't fuckin deserve his beautiful ass. That's why! Any more questions, doc?"

"Just one, Valery. Are you and John having sex behind Vivian's back?"

"That ain't none of your or her fuckin business. This body belong to me just like it belong to her simple ass. And that mean John is just as much mine as he is hers. Even more so cause he don't want to fuck her no more. Just me. He only want to fuck me because I let him do anythin he want to do to me and I don't cry and scream and run to hide in the corner like some little-baby-girl-bitch like that lyin cunt, Vivian."

"I was under the impression you and the rest of the alters, including Vivian, agreed to no secrets amongst you all. Why are you all of a sudden keeping secrets from your co-alters?"

"I know what we said, but John—h—he need me, and I like bein needed by him."

"It was also my understanding you and the rest of the alters were working together to understand what fractured the original's mind and that Vivian would maintain control of the body unless all alters agreed upon something different. When are you taking over without Vivian's, Valeria's, and/or Vera's consent?"

"It ain't even like that, Dr. K. I know it look all kinda fucked up from where you sittin in that big ass blue chair—why is your chair so fuckin big, anyway?"

"We don't have time for deflection, Valery. Answer my questions. Vivian is worried about you. She thinks John may be using you to deal with the pain and disappointment of losing Gayle. And if he is, it makes him no better than the men who abused this body and created the need for Vera's mind to fracture originally."

"First of all. He not usin me and she not fuckin worried about me. If she is, she only worried my pussy so good she not gonna be able to get him back."

"You do understand that your pussy and her pussy are the same pussy, right? And yes, Vivian is concerned for you. You were created as a result of John's rape and sodomy of Vivian. If he continues to use you for that specific purpose, he is continuing to violate his wife. Do you see how that behavior is not okay? How it is not healthy for him, you, or the other alters?"

136

"I—I know w-what it look l-like when you standin on the goddamned outside lookin in, but what John and me have is somethin deeper than what he thought he had with Vivian."

"Really? Does John talk with you about his day at the office? Does he share his fears, concerns, and dreams with you when you're lying post coitus in his arms?"

"What. The. Fuck is you talkin about? John and I don't use words to talk, we talk with our bodies. He like to use his tongue, but not for talkin. I don't lay in his arms when we done fuckin… we just fuck and then he tells me what to do to make sure when Vivian wakes up—s-she. Won't. B-Be in any pain. He says, he don't want her to feel no more pain than she already felt."

"What's wrong, Valery? What are you thinking?"

"He don't ask me nothin about me. He want to know how Vivian is spendin her day, how she acts with other people. He don't ever ask me if I'm enjoyin the sex we have or if he's bein too rough. He usin me."

"Here, Valery. Take a few tissues, wipe your nose and eyes. I'm sorry to have been the one to help you realize what's been happening, but you stopped talking with the other alters. When you alienate yourself from your pack, you make yourself vulnerable for outside forces to pray upon. You need them as much as they need you to function as a whole."

"Why I'm not as important to him as she is?"

"Because he's in love with Vivian. Because he loves her completely with his entire soul."

"But I'm her, ain't I?"

"No, Valery. You are not her. You are you and that makes you part of a whole. Do you have a childhood memory, memories before John raped Vivian?"

"No. I ain't never been a child. How can I remember somethin I never was? I'm just Valery. I love to fuck and party and drink and get high."

"Has John been getting you high, Valery?"

"Fuck no! John would kill me dead if I fucked up and did drugs. He so batshit about it, he make me take a fuckin drug test every time before we fuck. He told me if I let somebody else fuck me, he would find a way to kill me."

"Valery, the hour is almost up. I would like to see you and Vivian back here on next Tuesday. If you're willing to be co-conscious with her, I would really appreciate it. And until then, I advise you to stop sleeping with John. He's not doing any of you any favors. He's hurting, and he doesn't know how to deal with his pain."

"We'll see, doc. I can't make no mothafuckin promises about the co-mind-thing and I don't know if I'll be able to tell him no if he wanna fuck me."

"I hope for your sake you can do both. I'd like to say a few words to Vivian before the appointment is up. And no, I see the way you're looking at me. Our appointments are confidential. Vivian won't know what you say to me and you won't know what she says either; that is unless she grants me permission to share it with you and vice versa. It was lovely speaking with you again, Valery."

"Yeah, okay doc. You gave me a lotta shit to think about. I'll go get Vivian and I guess… whatever. Fuck it.

***

There's a light knock at my door. I turn my head over my shoulder and see Val standing in the doorway, framed by the light spilling in from the hallway. She looks so sad and distressed. I don't know what was shared

between her and Dr. Kerrigan, but whatever it was, seems to have really messed her up.

"Hey." I don't think I've ever heard her sound so despondent. My heart aches for her, but I know there's nothing I can do for her until she decides to do something for herself. She lifts her broken bottle eyes to look at me before she continues with what she came to tell me. "He want to see you before it's time to end the appointment."

"Hi Valery." I smile and push myself to standing. My legs are stiff from sitting and meditating, but my mind feels more focused and I feel as if I'm moving towards some sort of precipice. "Thanks for talking with him. I hope it was helpful."

"It was. I got a lotta shit to think about. Sorry for bein such a ragin bitch lately. My head is fucked up on some old bullshit. Talk later?"

I want to go to her and hug her, but Valery isn't a hugger. I settle for a clasping of hands as I walk by her and pull the door to my room closed. She squeezes my hand back for a brief moment and I know then Dr. Kerrigan has worked his Irish Mojo on my girl.

"Yeah, we can talk later. Hey, can you check in with Valeria, she's been moping around the house lately. I don't know what's going on with her, but she won't talk to me. Maybe she'll talk with you about whatever it is that's eating at her. She smiles with her lips and eyes and my heart skips a beat.

"Whateva, bitch. I can check on the little shit and see what the fuck is goin on with her strange ass."

A couple of hard blinks and a dull pain in the back of my head and I'm back in the uncomfortable refuge of the forgotten chair. I'm finally able to focus my eyes on the good-looking doctor and notice the way his thumb and forefinger are pulling at his plump bottom lip as he studies me. For

some reason, it makes me want to squeeze my thighs together, but I don't. Surely, he's just fascinated with treating someone as crazy as I am.

"Welcome back, Viv. Nice to see the lighter, golden color of your eyes again. Every time I witness a switch with you, I'm amazed at the difference in the eye color. Do you know what color Valeria's eyes are?" He doesn't wait for me to answer before he reveals that the color is gray. He goes on to say how they look like rain clouds on the stormiest day, and how the ring of gold surrounding them is the only ray of sun shining in her eyes.

His observation makes my skin pucker up all over like it wants to kiss the air coming from his lungs. He looks so intensely at me; my legs try to move me toward him of their own will. If I don't give them some sense of mobility, I'll be embarrassed when they kick out from under me like I have no control over my own limbs. He blinks a few times and his expression clears of its fervor and reverts back to the serious doctor face he wears for his patients.

"Anyway." He clears his throat, his voice lower and huskier than earlier. It's late in the evening. I can't imagine how many people he talks with during the day. His voice calls me back to the conversation at hand. "… as I was saying, thank you for getting Valery to come out and speak with me. She was worried I would share our session with you. I—" I cut him off and lean forward so he knows how serious I am about what I'm getting ready to say to him.

"Please tell me you assured her that was not the case. I need her to feel comfortable talking with you. She's on some kind of self-destructive path and I may have to share this body with her, but I am not going to allow her to destroy it or the life I have worked so hard to build."

"Relax, Viv. Of course, I confirmed for her the conversations she has with me or confidential; as are yours. However, I did ask her to join us

next Tuesday for a co-conscious session, I hope you're all right with that. If not, we can do it like we did tonight. Whatever works best for the two of you."

I take a deep breath and remind myself I'm seeing one of the best doctors in the country and he knows how to take care of me and all my head partners. With a smile, I stand and extend my right hand to him as I express my complete faith in his competence and bid him good evening.

Before I clear the threshold of his office, he places his right hand on my left elbow staying my forward motion. I stop, looking over my left shoulder and realize I'm looking at his broad chest covered in a crisp white, tailored shirt. His large, manicured hand radiates heat into my joints. His suddenly penetrative blue eyes, the color of my favorite little gift box that comes wrapped in a white bow, pin me where I'm standing. My breath catches as we stare at each other for seconds or minutes or years.

"Yes, Dr. Kerrigan?"

"I just wanted to know if you drove here and if so, I would prefer to walk you to your car. It's late and dark out. Our session ran a little long."

Just as I'm about to answer him, a shadow falls over his face. The hairs on the back of my neck stand at attention and my skin feels too small to cover the muscles, bones, veins, and organs keeping me alive. Without even looking away from my doctor, I already know who is standing in front of me, with thermonuclear anger pouring from every part of him.

"No. She does not need you to fucking walk her to her motherfucking car. Dr. Kerrigan. She has a husband who is more than capable of making sure she gets where she needs to be safe and sound." He yanks my elbow away from Dr. K's warm hand and I immediately feel the cold seep into my bones. There will be hell to pay, I just don't know who's going to be signing the check.

141

~22~

The air is a chilly hand grazing my cheeks as John steers me away from my psychiatrist's office and towards the parking lot. His fingers dig into my upper right arm as he tugs me along with him. I'm not so much as walking as being dragged behind a very angry man. He can't or won't look at me. Even when I call his name repeatedly. His chocolate eyes are so dark, the soft gold is lost in the depths of the blown pupils. I've seen him like this before, and that poor Frenchman had to pick his ass up and carry it out with him from the sex club. *I don't know what the hell he has to be angry about. I'm not the one having depraved sex with someone else behind his back.*

"John, I drove here. Let me go and we can discuss this—whatever this is—when we get to the house." I tried digging my heels in, but he's having none of it. He doesn't even spare me a glance, a grunt, or any kind of acknowledgement. He merely ensures there'll be bruises on my arm tomorrow.

"Why the hell are you so angry? I told you I was seeing someone, and you told me it was fine and to do what I needed to do to feel better about things." My voice is a high-pitched whistle blowing in the ears of a deaf man because John doesn't care what I have to say. He only cares about his own agenda and what that is... who the hell knows?

Upon reaching my car, he clicks the key fob and the lights blink on and off, indicating the doors were unlocked. He marches us to the passenger side of the sleek, red Lexus crossover and opens the door, slams my ass into the seat, buckles my seatbelt, and then acrimoniously slams the door. When he slides into the driver's seat and adjust everything to his liking, he cranks the car and proceeds to drive and brood all the way to Lake Murray. The longest 30 minutes of my life. Not a sound. No radio, no heavy

breathing; not one damn sound in the car. All of his antics but I had no idea what had him so riled up. But I imagine I'll find out when we get home.

John brings the car to a smooth stop in our three-car garage and quiets the engine. Deep breath in through his nose and a long, slow exhale through angry lips. Long fingers wrap around the steering wheel, so tightly the inside of his hands are white with the effort. I glance to my left and notice the consistent ticking in his jaw and the way his chest heaves up and down as if he's just run a marathon. *What's got him so mad he could drown puppies?*

I turn to get out the car and his right-hand clasps around my left thigh so fast, I almost thought it'd been placed there the entire ride home. He squeezes my thigh as roughly as he had gripped the steering wheel and somewhere in my sick and sex-deprived mind, I realized this was the first time he's touched me in almost four months. My body responds immediately. Breast are heavy with firm, erect nipples. My sex starts throbbing, swelling, and dripping with want—just for him. Always for him. It pisses me off; his effect on me. It isn't fair he can shut me out and still my body craves him more than anything or anyone. My anger rides the razor's edge of my arousal; leaving a powder keg of I'm-not-taking-this-bullshit-anymore, ready to blow up in John's too perfect face.

"What the hell is your problem, John? For the last four months, you haven't had two words to say to me. You don't even come home from work and you haven't made love with me in—since you've been fucking Valery." I didn't even know I was going to call him on it, but I knew what was happening and it hurt. It hurt so bad, I wanted to make him hurt just as much as he was hurting me.

His body stiffens. Not enough for someone who doesn't know him to notice, but I know him, and I notice everything about him. He was a coiled

viper, waiting for the perfect moment to strike his unwilling victim. In a moderated tone, barely moving his supple lips when he spoke to me, but I hear him loud and clear.

"The fuck did you just say, Viv?"

"I didn't stutter, John. You heard me and I'm no longer in the habit of repeating myself. Not for you. Not for anyone else, either."

"Ooooooooh." John drew out the word like he was pulling back his muscled arm preparing to throw the mother of all punches. Turning ever-so-slightly to face me in the passenger seat, his lips turned down in a hard frown, his arrogant right brow ticks up… and he simply stares at me. Stares at me as if he's never seen me before this very moment. I notice his head bobbing up and down like he is confirming something for himself with his careful perusal of my facial features.

"Well?! Aren't you going to say something in response to what I just said to you? That is the way communication works or do you not remember how to talk with your *wife*—you know, the woman you married right after we graduated college—*Vivian*?"

"Oh, I don't need a reminder of who you are, Viv. I'm thinking maybe…" I watch as his nostrils flare and the subtle changes slide over him and I know it's too late. His lips form a sexy as hell smirk before he continues with whatever he's going to say.

"… just maybe, you're in need of a reminder of the motherfucker I can be! That I am."

I've obviously lost my mind because my mouth is currently writing checks my ass or my bank account has no way of covering, but that doesn't stop me from signing my name on the bottom. *Memo: Johnathan Ellis Reality Check*

"Maybe I do need a reminder of what a motherfucker you are, but I wouldn't if you had bothered to be present these last four months of our marriage. I wouldn't need to try and remember who my husband is if he wasn't so busy fucking one of my alters, while avoiding me like I gave him a goddamn STD!" His hand was around my throat before I could even take another breath to finish my tirade. Fingers tighten just enough to let me know he held my life in his hand. Just enough to make me feel his power and his control. Just enough to make me realize how he was holding on to his control by a burning string. I stop. I stop fighting him. I stop struggling to take my breaths. I did what he needed me to do in that moment, the only thing I could do in that moment. I completely surrendered to him. I relax my shoulders, allow my head to fall back and accept his dominance.

"Where the hell have you been, lovely?" John's voice is cracked glass and rocks tumbling in a plastic bottle. Broken and hollow. I had no idea he'd been needing his submissive. I've been so busy rebuilding myself after all I learned about me, after losing the child he wanted so badly. I focused my attentions on my alters and me. I forgot we promised to take care of him, too. It looks like Valery was the only one of us who did everything we promised to do in that hospital. *Well shit, I can't be angry with her for doing what we said needed to be done.*

"I've missed you so fucking much. One morning you were there, we were in this together and then out of nowhere… Why? What changed, why did you leave the way you did?" His hand slipped from my throat and wrapped around my left shoulder. He squeezes it. Letting me know how much he missed and needed me. *How the hell had I misinterpreted his behavior?*

"Baby. God! I'm—I am so sorry." The words fall from my mouth like raindrops, if raindrops were made of horrified realization and regret.

"I don't know what happened. I don't have the vocabulary, the skill—I can't make this better because I didn't know how badly I was fucking it up."

"Come on. Let's get inside, lovely. We've got a lot of shit to talk about, okay?"

John removes the keys from the ignition and turns to get out of the car, but my hand juts out from my lap and grabs on to his jacket sleeve.

"Baby, I'm not going anywhere. Sit tight, I'll come around to get you out." His smile is tight, but at least it's his smile. I haven't seen one from him in such a long time, it feels like rays of sun coming through the bedroom curtains.

"Okay." I reluctantly let go of his sleeve and gather my belongings. The door opens and before I can fully turn to step out of the car, his arms are around my waist and his mouth seals over mine and the world narrows down to only John and his lips and his tongue and what he's making me feel with them. *Oh my God, I've missed him and this so much.*

After he pulls his lips away from my own, peppering little pecks across my face, around my jaw, down my neck and on my shoulder; he pulls me from the car and scoops me up in his arms and carries me into the house, like I'm his new bride and straight up the stairs into our en suite.

He hasn't said anything. Even after sitting me on the counter to remove my leopard print, kitten-heel, Manolo Blahnik from my feet. Or when he peeled me out of my 7 For All Mankind jeans. I'm left standing in a basic white tee, my demi-bra, and matching white lace panties. His eyes feast on my long legs, the scars he loves to touch and lick. When he raises his lust-filled gaze up to my breast, I'm basically panting.

Finally, he grants me the privilege to see into him. His pain, anger, love, fear—all of it. He shows me every bit of what he's been keeping to

himself. He may have been fucking Valery, but she didn't get any other part of him. Not his heart, not his soul, and certainly not his love. No, that he saves for me.

"Let's shower. I need to take care of what belongs to me. To know I'm still needed. To feel your lovely, perfectly tight cunt become slick because of my proximity… because you want…no, because you *need* to be owned by me."

"Yes." I don't have enough breath to say anything other than those three letters. My eyes are glued to the tent in his pants and I am indeed wet because he's standing near me. I feel my arousal running down my thighs. The steam from the shower is perfumed with the smell of sex and citrus and spice and John. *God, I love the way he smells*. It tells me how much he wants to destroy me before rebuilding me as a more perfected version of myself. *I wonder if Valery can smell him like this when they are together.*

No! I'm not going to let myself think about that, it's not important. But it's already too late, his eyes are searching my face; I realize I must have shaken my head and even I can feel my brows pulling together forming that little *m* I get when I'm inside my head; overthinking things. I keep forgetting how well John can read me.

"What's that look about, lovely?" His dexterous fingers rest lightly at the hem of my shirt, as he waits for my response. When my face is no longer shrouded in the damp cotton of my clothes, I fix my mouth to answer him.

"I was just thinking about how much I love your smell. How I could always tell how turned on you were by the level of spice in your scent."

"And *that* made the little 'm' form between your brows?"

"No, not that specifically. No."

"Okay, then you want to tell me what, *specifically* made you frown."

147

"No. I don't. Not really, it's not important."

"Let me rephrase this. You're thinking about the times I've fucked Valery. Over the last four months, how I've had at her and haven't laid a finger on you."

No words. Just thick, oil-slick tears coasting down my puffed-out cheeks. I turn to step in the shower in an effort to hide them in the heated water, but I realize I'm still wearing my underwear. I reach behind me with shaky hands to unsnap my bra and unceremoniously throw it on the pile of clothes John has neatly folded and placed on the white marble countertop. Next, I hook my thumbs in the side of my panties and pull them down my thighs, stepping out of them, I leave them on the floor and rush to open the shower door.

"Thanks for usurping the task of undressing you. Even though I was thoroughly enjoying my right to do it myself. Now answer me. I won't repeat myself."

Deep breath. I square my shoulders and I turn to face him. "I was wondering if Valery could smell you like I can. I wondered if the scent I associate with your desire for me no longer belongs to me alone." My voice breaks on the end of my words. Tears mix with the water pouring from the rain shower head. They both land on the chocolate-covered-cherry tips of my breasts. I'm too embarrassed to even look at him. Too scared to hear the answer to my question.

"Nothing I have belongs to Valery. She was here. She was convenient and fucking her was as close as I could get to fucking you when you weren't available to me. She wasn't a substitute for you, she was a distraction for me. Something to keep me from invading your space and causing more damage than I had already caused."

"I'm so sorry, John. These past four months have been… difficult at best and devastating most of the time. I needed you, but I didn't know how to be with you. I don't know how to be me or even who being me is anymore. That's why I started seeing Dr. Kerrigan. He is—a"

"He is a motherfucking corpse if he continues looking at you the way he was looking at you when I stepped into his shitty-ass office. How the fuck did you even find this asshole, Vivian?"

"There were pamphlets in the stuff the hospital sent home with me… with us and I felt like I needed someone to talk with about what I was feeling. I found him and looked him up. Saw where he specialized in PTSD associated with DID and went in for a consultation. I—I like him, John and I'm not going to stop seeing him. He's really amazing"

"Good. I'm glad you *like* him so much. Have the others met him?"

"Yes. Valery actually spoke with him tonight."

"What did she say to him?"

"I don't know. Her session with him is confidential, as are mine. If she gives him permission to speak with me about what they talk about then he will, but if not. I have no way of knowing what they discussed. You sound worried, John."

"Not worried, not really. At least not how you're thinking I am. Valery is a loose cannon on her best days, and I just wondered what she shared with him. With you."

"How much time have you spent inside of Valery, John? You seem to know her as well as you know or *knew* me."

"For fuck's sake, Vivian. She is *you*! What about this don't you fucking understand? That quack of a shrink isn't telling you to think of your alters as aspects of yourself?"

"First of all, he is not a quack. And secondly, I am not the damn original. I am an alter, John! Just like Valery. So, if you want the original, you're going to have to coax Vera's scary ass out of her dark corner."

"Don't you turn away from me, Vivian Anne Ellis."

"My full name. You must be really pissed. Well you know what? Fuck you, John! Don't worry, it's me, Vivian. I can say shit like that, too." I move further into the shower and slam the door. I know he's still completely clothed, so I have a few minutes before he gets in here with me. I'm washing the important parts so fast, I'm not sure I'm actually getting them clean. *I won't fucking be in here when he steps his beautiful, tight ass in to reprimand me.*

"You think you can just walk away from me? The fuck you think this is, Viv?! I'm John Raynard Ellis. Your motherfucking husband. You will not fucking behave like this. Do you understand the goddamned words coming from my mouth?"

"Get your filthy corrupt hands off of me! I know what your fucking name is, you egotistical son-of-a-bitch! You think you're justified in fucking my alter because we share a body?" *He must think I'm crazier than I really am, if he believes I'll go for this shit.* "Nothing is justified. You are a selfish, cheating bastard." I turn in his arms and my fists strike his chest—a chest covered in his bright white tailored shirt—with all the hurt, frustration, guilt, and anger I have boiling in my blood. I'm a crying, snotty mess. I finally stop with my ineffectual hitting and look into his eyes. I see all of me reflected in all of him. He is my mirror and right now, I hate what I see.

23

What a picture we must make. Me, standing naked and soaked in the shower with my fully clothed husband with his hands wrapped around my arms, eyes blazing with a fire born of desperation and fear. Love and frustration? He is the beginning of my destruction and the end of my despair. I'm broken and broke down, but he will not let me go. He just stands there. Eyes locked on my soul. Pulling pieces of me together from parts I don't even have access to.

"Are you done?" His hands leave my arms and start the process of unbuttoning his shirt. I swat them away and take over the task. I start at the bottom and work my way up; it seems fitting to go in this direction. Once I have him out of his shirt, I unbuckle his black leather belt and unbutton his pants. *Why the hell does he have so many buttons on his pants… one on the waistband and two inside.* I go to pull his sodden pants and boxer briefs away from his skin, and I notice he is not aroused. His penis, even flaccid, is impressive and beautiful and causes my mouth to water, but he's not hard for me and my heart stops. Literally, I feel it stutter to a finale and nothing happens after that.

"Vivian?" I hear him, but my heart isn't beating. "Vivian, what's wrong with you? Damnit, Vivian! Take a breath. If you drop dead in this damned shower before we get this shit worked out…I don't know what the fuck I'll do to you, but you won't like it. I can promise you that, lovely. Take a fucking breath for me baby." His heavy hands rubbing roughly between my breast and the edge in his voice cause my heart to jump into action. I'm dizzy and lightheaded.

"Your dick isn't hard." *What the hell am I saying?*

"Why the fuck would I be hard, Viv? My wife is standing here, accusing me of cheating on her… with an alter that resides inside of *her.*

151

And only an hour after I caught her looking at some red-haired-ginger-motherfucker like he hung the moon and stars in the South Carolina sky. My dick isn't hard because my heart is on the verge of shattering. You want my dick, Vivian? You want me to fuck you like I've been fucking Valery?"

"No—I just want you to be... I don't know what I want, but whatever it is that I don't have, it hurts." I turn away from him because my eyes won't stop leaking my resentfulness and the truth is I resent myself and him and every horrible thing that has had a hand in creating who we are to each other in this abysmal moment. Who we are individually and collectively.

And that's when it hits me. One slug in my chest, fragments and spreads its life-giving fire into every part of my solar plexus. *I am not an individual; I am a part of a collective whole. I am a series of experiences, thoughts, and realities that don't originate with me, but are mine all the same.* This is important in my healing, I know it is, but what I don't know, is how. I don't have a way to explain it; I just know I'm not sick. I. Am. Not. Sick. I'm fragmented and need to assimilate the pieces of me, but I'm not sick. *I'm not sick.*

"John? Have you ever had a thought so profound, it left you feeling high... transcendent? I feel like the goddess, Sophrosyne has taken up residence inside my mind... I can't explain it." I vaguely feel myself sliding down the warm tiles as I look up into his face. He wears a persona of fear and worry. I know he thinks I'm cracking up even more than he already believes me to be, but I'm not. I'm so clear in my perception of self. I look into him and smile. This is the first smile I've given him and it's from my whole soul.

And then I feel them, the alters. They're pushing against my mind, asking for co-consciousness and I offer it freely. I want them here. I want

to show them what I see because I know they'll see it, too. I won't have to explain it. I'll show them us, who we are, and why we are.

The Internal House

Where is Vera? She has to be here. She's the beginning of all of us and we need her here to see this.

She doesn't want to come out, Vivian. I've been trying to talk to her for days, but she's so sad about everything. I'm frustrated and scared, and I don't really know what to do. When she was younger, it was easier to help her... to pull her out of her room, but now.

I know, Valeria. You're so used to protecting her, but she's continued to grow, and you eventually needed protection and she couldn't reciprocate. I'll find her, but first—

Oh, so now you gonna be the fearless, fuckin leader over us? Where the fuck you been these past four months, huh, bitch? Where you been?

Valery, I never left you guys. Did I walk away from John, yes and I'll own that, and I'll make it right. But I've been right here working with you guys. You were so busy avoiding me because you were fucking John, but we have more important things to deal with.

Wh-what's all the noise about?

Hi Vera. I'm so glad you decided to come out. How are you?

I'm tired, Vivian, yeah? I'm always so tired, and scared, and lonely. How y'all been doing? What's happening? Something feels different.

I know. That's what I wanted to ask you about. Do the rest of you feel the difference, too?

I don't know if it feels different, but it—my skin feels, I don't know, weird and tight and loose and—I don't know how to describe it. It's like I can feel how the rest of you feel. It feel like little bubbles popping all over my neck and shoulders. What's happening, sisters?

Exactly! Something is happening, and I think it may just be something amazing for us.

How the fuck can loose, tight skin be amazin. Bubbles poppin on your goddamned neck? What the fuck you smokin that got you thinkin you done found some fantasy glue to make us stick? Huh bitch? You gonna super glue our assholes together to keep John from fuckin mine cause your scary ass d—"

Will you please shut the hell up, Valery. This isn't about you, or John are anal sex. And you need to think with more than your clit. I'm saying that I figured something out about us, Val. I mean, maybe—ju"

She means, we ain't broken. We exactly the way we meant to be. It's a reason for us being this way. A purpose, right Vivi?

Exactly. We have a purpose; we have to figure out what each of us is good at. What we feel and how we express our deepest pains and hurt. We have to come clean about what we are most ashamed of and what makes us the happiest. Can we agree to do that and Valery, don't fucking touch John again. Are we clear?

What the fuck you not gonna do is tell me what the fuck to do with my pussy when I'm drivin this body, bitch. If I wanna fuck that cute, little Irishman you see once a week, I will. The fuck you think you talkin to, huh?

Do you really want to test me, Val? You're what… ten months old? I've been here for years and have been in control of this body for longer than any other alter. Do you want to fuck with me when I'm trying to figure shit out?

She has a good point, Val. I mean, even though I'm the first alter, she's so much more stronger than me and even Vera. You don't stand a chance against her if she wanted to—you know—put you away for good.

Fuck all you bitches. We ain't no sisterhood in here. We ain't shit because we ain't real. The only real bitch in here is Vera and she too fucked up to know it.

Okay, fine Valery. Do what you want, but remember you chose to go against us and that means you asked for everything you get.

You seriously threatenin me?

No, I am telling you how things are going to be.

You ain't nobody boss. You silly ass cunt whore. Not my boss. That's for goddamn sure.

I don't want to be anyone's boss, but I do want to figure out what's going on with us and how we are meant to live in this world. You are invited to join in and participate, or…

Or what, Vivian? What will happen to us if we don't participate? Will we have to go away or stop being us?

God, Vera! You're all acting like I'm some kind of god. I don't know what will happen if we don't all work together to figure this out. I only know what I feel and was hoping you all felt, too. That we all feel something and are ready to take our health and sanity into our own care.

Why I gotta stop fuckin John, then?

Because. He's my husband. He fathered a child with—me. He broke and restored—me. Because he's mine, Valery. He belongs to me, and I belong to him. I have never had to share him, and I refuse to do so now… not even with a part of myself. I will learn to do and enjoy his darker proclivities You are not to go near him, when I'm done here—with you all—I'll have a similar talk with him.

I'll make a deal with you, sis. If John don't come for me no more, then I won't go after him again. But, listen. I'm a sexual animal, and I can't go that long without fuckin somebody. So, we gonna have to figure some shit

out, or else, John's magic dick ain't gonna be the only one tappin this magic pussy. Tell him that, for me, huh?

Fine, Val. We'll figure it out. I'll get a journal for us. The journal will be just for us to figure out and record our individual experiences... you know, what each of us excels at. What we do well. What brings us pleasure and makes us feel most alive. What should we call it?

I like the name, Seeking Wonderland.

What the fuck does goddamn wonderland gotta do with us? God, you such a fuckin child.

Why that name, Valeria?

Why not that name. I like it. wonderland don't really exist and whatever we are, probably shouldn't exist either.

Valeria, I like the name a lot. Like how you explain it, yeah?

Thank you, Vera. And I'm not childish. You the one who always talking about sex and having fun and nothing else matters to you. Nothing at all. You the child, Valery.

Fuck you little girl. I've had orgasms that last longer than most of your thoughts.

No thanks, I'm not into women.

Ha! She told you, yeah?

You can shut the fuck up, too. Won't nobody talkin to your slow-movin ass, anyway. Why the hell you even here?

Okay. Ladies, we all have our own opinions and ways of looking at things. Maybe, we can agree on the name of our journal and then agree on what we'll include in our entries.

Thank you little-miss-diplomat. I don't give a fuck what the hell you call it, I just need to know what to put in it and how am I goin to fuck if John's cock is off the table.

All in favor of calling our journal, Seeking Wonderland, say I.

I.

I.

I.

Fuck it, I.

Good. Thank you all for working together on this. Whenever we take a vote on something, it has to be unanimous.

What does that mean, Vivi?

It means we all have to agree, or the vote doesn't pass. .

What if one of us doesn't like something, and we don't want to agree with the rest? I don't want to cause no trouble, yeah?

Then, whatever it is won't get done. It's all or nothing, Vera. We all get a say in what happens to our body, right Vivi?

Precisely. We have to figure out what each of us is created for. What are our strengths and weaknesses. What we love and what we hate. We've already pieced together our life using the journal system. We know about the abuse and neglect and more abuse, and the final act of violence we experienced. Now we have to find a way to make meaning of ourselves as individuals and as a collective whole.

This all sound real kumbaya and shit, but really. What the fuck we know about goddamned collective whole and shit?

I don't know a lot, but I love to go to the library and read about pretty much anything. I can do research and share what I find in our journal.

That's awesome, thanks Valeria. I would start with the collective consciousness and unconsciousness of humanity. Carl J Jung is the best place to start. I remember taking a class in undergrad focused on him and Freud. See what you can find on that. Be sure to let me know when you want to go, I'd like to co-conscious with you if you don't mind.

That's fine. I don't like going out by myself, anyway.

Valery, what are you interested in learning about us or yourself?

Honestly?

Yes, honestly.

I want to know why all I think about is sex and havin a good time. I mean, it gotta be somethin more to me than just fuckin and gettin high. Wouldn't mind findin out what else I'm good at or for.

Have you been getting high?

Once or twice after the baby. But then John caught me and made sure I never went near that shit again.

Is that the morning I woke up with nasty welts from the cane and a sore asshole?

Yep. That was the first time he punished me.

Did you continuously do things to get him to punish you, Val.

Yep. I ain't gonna lie. I loved every minute of it. It's somethin about feelin that much pain and havin it all turn into molten lava under my skin until all the heat settles deep down in my pussy; makin me wet and drip for him. Yeah, I was a fuckin brat.

Ha, we have something in common, then. I would do almost anything to get John to punish me. After an intense scene, and he'd given me aftercare; I had to go and write. I have books and books of poetry I've written after being with John in our playroom. It seemed to be the only way to release the rest of the heat trapped inside of me—you know—to get the rest of it out.

I'm sure I have no idea what you two are talking about. Being hit with a cane, does not appeal to me. I sometimes watch the two of you. When you with him. But everything about him is scary to me. How big his hands

158

are. The size and length of his… you know, his thing. I don't want anything to do with any of it.

Vera, you as old as Vivian and me. Why you act like a fuckin child? Even Lyric ass got more sense than you when it come to shit like sex, dicks and pussies. What the fuck is wrong with your ass.

Valery, you forget that Vera split when she was five. She continued to age and grow, but in her mind—she stuck at age five. And somehow, she's as old as you guys.

Fuck.

All right. Let's agree on what each of us is doing and then we can come back together in a week. Does that work for everyone?

Yes, great master of the fuckin body.

Thank you, Valery.

Yeah, that works for me. Thanks for letting me choose the name of our journal.

You're welcome. Thank you for being so perceptive in coming up with it.

In a week. Okay. I can do that, yeah?

Great! Don't be a stranger, Vera. See you guys later and please remember to respect this body. It belongs to all of us and none of us want STD's and the taste of some woman's pussy on our tongue.

That was only one time, fuck. Give me a fuckin break.

24

I wake up with the mother of all headaches and the heaviness in my chest makes it hard to catch the breath I need to breathe. I'm not sure where I am or how I came to be here. I know if I sit up too quickly, I'm going to throw up all over myself. Mentally, I take stock of my current situation. I have on underwear, at least I have on panties. I'm wearing my sleeping shorts and matching camisole. I'm covered in my favorite chenille blanket. I'm comfortable and I feel safe and cared for.

"Hey, you."

It's John. Okay, I'm home with my husband and I'm fine. "Hi."

"How are you feeling?"

"Like Rip Van Winkle, it hasn't been twenty years has it?" I smile up at his gorgeous concerned face. I hope it reassures him of my lucidity. From the lines around his mouth and the heaviness of his brow, it's going to take more than my smile to make him feel better about whatever he witnessed.

"No, it hasn't been twenty years. Only a couple of hours, but they were a strange couple of hours. What do you remember, lovely?"

"Um. I remember us in the shower. Me losing my shit. Again. About you and Valery. Then, I went inside, and no one came out because we were all there—you know inside my head. What did you see on your end of things?"

"I saw your face crumble in on itself, pain and confusion layered on your skin like fallen leaves on a sidewalk. You know, the way you hold your mouth or the way your eyes were shaped. I didn't know what the fuck was going on and then you just… just dropped like a goddamned stone to the shower floor."

"I guess you saw all of us in there talking, arguing, and figuring shit out. That must be so weird to watch and not be privy to the conversation."

"Fuck yeah, it's weird. But also—it's the most interesting and amazing thing I've ever seen."

"Even more amazing then my spontaneous orgasms?" I see into him and watch as the heaviness falls from his beautiful face. I was hoping to lighten the mood, looks like I did.

"Yes, lovely. Even more amazing then that and anyway, I always knew you were a freaky, weirdo." He lets laughter color his words. The fact we are able to talk about this is what's so interesting and amazing. I try to pull myself up to sitting, but the nausea is so bad, I don't even get my head off the pillow before I'm rolling over to direct my vomit away from our bed. Just as I'm about to let go, John extends the small trashcan under my head.

"Baby. Take it easy." He's holding the trash can with his left hand and rubbing my reality back in to me with his right.

"You okay to get up now?

"Uggh. I feel like roadkill. Are you sure it hasn't been twenty years since I was inside?"

"Lovely. I gave you a hot bath, moisturized your skin, dressed you, and put you to bed. You've only been out for about two hours. What the hell happened in there?"

He helped me stand from our bed. Once he got me safely in our bathroom, I washed my face and brushed my teeth before turning to him with a look of expectation. *God, I'm so hungry; I could eat a cow.*

"John, have you eaten?"

"No, I was waiting on you. We still have a fuck ton of shit to talk about, lovely."

"Yeah, I know. I have so much to tell you. None of it is going to make any sense to you because it doesn't even make sense to me or the girls either, but we're going to figure it out and—oh my God! I've got to call

Dr. Kerrigan—he's going to be so excited about this." I'm turning to try and leave the bathroom to get to the phone when a large hand presses against my flat, firm belly, effectively stopping me from moving forward.

"What the hell, John?" I make to push past his large body and of course, he doesn't even pretend to budge. But he does bend his head low enough to place his full lips against my left ear, sending shivers down my spine and ratcheting up my desire for him from before. He whispers low enough to let me know he's reached a level of pissed I haven't seen in a long time. And fuck me while I'm walking to church, but I'm getting wetter with every heated word blown against my sensitive flesh.

"I don't give a fuck about Dr. Kerrigan's excitement; he will not know what is going on with my fucking wife before I do. Your secret fucking meetings with the good doctor are over. If you continue to see him. If I *allow* you to continue to see him after I go through my background check, we will be seeing him together. Do you understand me, lovely. We do everything together. It is the way it has always been and the only way it will ever be. Right?"

I fix my mouth to protest, but the sound that makes it past my lips is a breathy sigh that probably sounds more like a moan than anything else. I'm shifting my weight from foot to foot, while simultaneously throwing in a little kegel exercise for good measure. I know my summer-sunshine eyes are almost completely eaten up by desire. My lips feel puffy and my nipples are hard and rubbing against the soft material of my cami. *I hate how turned on I am by his possessiveness, his control, and his need for me.* But mostly I hate I haven't had him for more than four months. I need to connect with him before we get into any of what we need to get into.

"John, please fuck me." I don't raise my eyes to look at him. I'm almost ready to drop to the floor and present myself to him as his sub, I want him so much.

"Not now, Vivian. You need to eat, and we need to talk."

I walk from the bathroom over to my dresser and pull the top drawer out. Rummaging through the sixty or so pairs of socks, I find the ones I'm looking for and walk over to the padded bench at the foot of our bed to sit and put them on. My feet are cold. I pull my left foot up to sit my heel on the edge. As I'm getting one of my multicolored, paisley fleece socks on, John takes it from my hands and kneels in front of me. I don't look at him because I'm processing how I feel about his rejection, in light of my conversation with Valery.

"I know what you're thinking, Vivian. Don't." He scrunches one of my socks up and pulls it over my toes. His left-hand crawls up my calf and he pulls it forward, dislodging my foot from the bench. Once he has my leg extended, he pulls my sock up and over my arch, then my heel, and finally my ankle. He places a soft kiss on the inside of my knee and my breath catches in my throat. *Why is he teasing me like this?*

"We are not going to fuck, yet. There's too much between us and I can't have anything between us when I fuck you again. It's been four-long and lonely-months, Vivian!" He's managed to pull my other sock on and to place another kiss on the inside of my right knee.

That's when I look at him. Really look at him and then I see it. The tightly coiled control vibrating through him like a tuning fork. He's more animal than man right now, and I know how barbarous he can be when he wants me this bad. I don't know why I haven't noticed it before, but I guess I would've had to pay attention to more than just myself.

I reach out to him with my right hand, place my palm against his stubble roughened cheek and look into his nut-brown eyes and set my tingling lips against his. No pressure, no movement. Just touching his lips with my own. And for right now, it's enough. It has to be, he won't budge on this just like he wouldn't budge from the bathroom door.

"Let's eat. Everything's already done, we just need to heat it up. You feel like talking tonight or do you want to wait until the morning?"

"I'm good to eat and talk now." He takes my hands and pulls me to my feet. I feel the strength in his arms, but I also feel what his restraint is costing him. He tugs me into the warmth of his loving embrace. This is enough for right now. Really, it's everything.

25

That was the most difficult conversation I'd ever had with John. Even more difficult than any of the ones we had on our first trip to New York. But we had it and he's open to helping me... us, understand who and what we are. It's Friday and we still haven't so much as kissed, yet. I wonder if he and Valery are hooking up behind my back still. My body doesn't feel like he's been using it, but maybe she's just blowing him. *I hate feeling so insecure about this.*

"Mrs. Ellis. I have a Dr. Kerrigan on line two for you."

"Thanks, Tammi. Give me about five minutes and then send him through, all right?

"Yes, ma'am."

I take a minute to get myself together and call John. He wanted to be in on the next phone call with Dr. Kerrigan, no need to give him ammunition against my continuing to see him.

"Hey baby. Are you busy?"

"Lovely, it's the middle of the fucking day. What do you think?"

"Um... all right. I called to let you know I'm getting ready to take a call from Dr. Kerrigan because you wanted to be in on it, but obviously, now is not a good time for you. I'll take the call and let you know how it went, okay?"

"I'm sorry. It's just been very hectic around here. Some smalltime, motherfucker is trying to come for my company. The company I built with my two hands."

"Baby, listen. Take care of what you need to take care of and I'll let you know what we discussed."

"No, the fuck you won't. I'm on the phone now. Add the good doctor, Vivian and we can have this fucking conversation and I can get back to my day."

"Hold on."

"Hi, Dr. Kerrigan. I didn't miss an appointment, did I?"

"No, Vivian. I was honestly calling to check in with you. Your husband seemed overly aggressive and I was concerned for your well-being. Are you all right?"

"John would never hurt me. In fact, he's on the other line and wanted to join us for this conversation. There are no secrets between us, so speak freely. Hold on, I'll connect him."

"John?"

"Yes, lovely. I'm here. Dr. Kerrigan, are you on the line?"

"This is most unusual, I don't normally do this, but Viv asked if it would be all right, and I can't say no to her. I'm sure you know how that is, right mate?"

"Thank you, for joining us. I know how busy your day is. Dr. Kerrigan expressed some concerns about your aggressive behavior towards me last Tuesday, but I—assu…"

"Expressed concern? Listen to me and hear the words I'm saying. You and my wife have a doctor/patient relationship. Nothing about this situation should be flashing friendship or fuck buddy. She's not yours to worry about, you understand that." John's voice blew sheets of ice down the phone line and Dr. Kerrigan probably didn't feel the frostbite, but he would be wise to shut his mouth.

"I assure you, John. I may call you John, I assume."

"You know what they say about assuming, doc? Don't show your ass today and I won't have to kick it, mate. No, you may call me Mr. Ellis."

John is on some other level today. I wonder what's really going on with his company. Dr. Kerrigan continues as if John didn't just hand him his balls on a plate.

"I have every right to inquire as to the safety of my patient. She is my responsibility and if you're not able to care for her in a way she deserves, then I am more than happy to do so."

"Wait, what? Dr. Kerrigan, we don't have that kind of relationship. I value you as a professional, but—I" John didn't let me finish the thought. His heavy inhalation screamed fire down the line and my breath rushed out to replenish his. I knew before the words left his mouth what I would hear, and I couldn't disagree with his call.

"The fuck you said? One. Vivian was, isn't, and will never be your motherfucking responsibility. Two. No one will ever be able to take care of Vivian the way I do. And three. If you contact or come around my wife or any of her alters again, I will hunt your monkey-ass down and send you back to Ireland in small envelopes. Vivian, disconnect from this cocksucker, now."

I heard Dr. Kerrigan trying to say something, but I disconnected the call before he could finish his thought. My breath was coming in little pants and my core was so slick, it saturated my panties. *Holy fucking shit! I can't believe that just happened.*

"John. Please come and fuck me. I need you and I can't wait another day or hour. Please, Sir."

"You are to be naked, except for your panties. On the floor, prostrate with your hands behind your back—elbows clasped in hands—and your forehead touching the carpet. Ass up in the air, showing me all my options. Vivian, I'm not settling for anything less than all of you. Are we clear?"

"Yes, Master." I could hardly get the words out. My body was trembling so fiercely, each syllable bleated out of my throat. He was coming for me and whatever he wanted, I had to be prepared to give him. Could I?

Viv, you can do this. It's john, and he loves you. Don't think about anybody but him. Give him this. Give y'all this. It's time to take your body back from those d-dogs who used and hurt you, yeah?

Yeah, Vera. It's time to take it back. I can do this. I'm going to do this. Not just for him, but for me. And for you, Lyric, and even Valery. Keep everyone in their rooms, I need to be alone for this, all right?

No problem. But if you need us, just let me know. You know, you're never alone. You never have to deal with anything on your own if you don't want to, yeah?

I know. And thank us for that.

26

Le Magnolia Noir closes for lunch between the hours of twelve and two in the afternoon. All of my employees leave and take care of whatever it is they have to take care of. The sun hangs like a golden medallion around the neck of a perfect blue god. There's a soft breeze blowing over the lake, but it did nothing to temper the muggy, sweet stickiness in the warmth of a perfect South Carolina spring day. I waited beside my office door. Just as John commanded me to. On my radio, George Michael's soulful voice lets his lover know there's something deep inside… someone he forgot to be. I humming along and feeling something deep inside of myself opening up. Preparing.

Excitement runs from my slit in a steady trickle. I'm drunk with arousal; the smell of my own sex makes me want to touch myself. Get the first orgasm out of the way, but I know better. He'll know if I did. Part of me—the bratty part, the masochist—wants to do it just to earn John's punishment. *It's Tax Day. He's throat-deep in shit right now and provoking him would not be in my best interest.* Maybe later.

"Lovely. I'm going to fuck you so hard; your soul will orgasm." I had been so deep in thought about the man, I didn't even here him come into the office. I didn't dare look up or respond but seeing his polished Berluti chocolate and cognac oxfords in my limited line of vision made every nerve in my being come alive. This must be what addicts feel like when they need a hit but can't afford it. Willing to do any and everything for just a little of what will calm the nerves jumping all over and under their skin.

One finger. One, thick, callused index finger moves down my spine towards my bare ass cheeks. *My pencil skirt called for thongs, lucky John. Lucky me.* The jumping beans seem to gravitate to wherever his finger touches me. The area becomes hot and cool, sweaty and tight. His slow

descent to my ass has finally reached its destination. My thong does nothing to hide my rosette from him and now that finger is rimming that forbidden place. He's barely touching me. It feels more like a thought than an actual act, but I feel the heat and electricity sparking off his finger and I know he's testing me. I take a deep breath and completely surrender to the moment. Anchor myself in my love for my husband. My best friend. My Dom.

"I want this from you." He puts a little more pressure on my puckered entrance. It flexes, and a gush of thick arousal floods my panties. I hear John take a deep inhale through his nose. I imagine his nostrils flaring wide, like he's scenting the air. Smelling a female who's ready to be mounted. Will he mount me? Or just spread me out on my couch and fuck me into a new, better version of myself?

"How are you feeling, Vivian?"

"I'm feeling... horny, Sir."

"Is that right? What's got you smelling so needy, lovely?"

The way you owned Dr. Kerrigan. When you told him I was yours to take care of. The growl in your voice when you claimed me as your... possession. But I don't say any of that. I can't.

"Uh, your possessiveness, Sir."

"It turns you on to know how much I need to own all of you, Vivian?"

I shake my head as best I can, while keeping my forehead on the carpet. And then I feel him on my left side. The whisper of his warm, minty breath on the shell of my ear. *Damn those jumping nerves.*

"Words, Vivian. I need to hear *you.*"

"Oh. I'm sorry, Sir. Yes. That turns me on. I want to be owned, but only by you, Master." I knew adding that last moniker would solidify a hard, fast ride. It's exactly what I need right now; we can make love later.

Maybe at home, but right now. Right this moment, I need to be taken. Ravaged. Completely torn apart and put back together again. Only my Master can do that. Not my doctors. Not my alters. Most certainly not my husband.

"Are you baiting me, Viv?"

"No, Master."

"What is your safe word, Vivian?"

"Red, Master."

"I can't promise to be gentle with you, Viv. If you need me to slow down and give you a minute, what will you say?"

"Yellow, Master."

"Good girl. When I check in with you and all is good, what is the color?"

"Green, Master."

"Perfect. Are we alone?"

"Yes, Sir."

"Yes *what*?"

"I mean; yes, Master."

"Ah, that's what I thought you meant. Stand up and walk over to the end of the couch farthest away from the door. Stand with your feet shoulder width a part and your hands clasping your wrists at the base of your back. Head down, eyes soft. Go."

I unfold from the floor like a ballerina. Once I'm in position, something like a heavy blanket fresh from the dryer falls over me and I'm the most relaxed I've been in ages. I need his dominance like I need oxygen. He's fumbling around in his satchel at my desk. I've no idea what he has, but all this waiting is weighing heavily in the bottom of my belly. My need for him burns like the red, hot coils found in electric space heaters known for

causing fires. If he doesn't come and fuck me, that's exactly what's going to happen in my office. A five-alarm fire.

Chris Isaak croons about his wicked games and just as he hits a falsetto, John glides his hands up my sides and around my front to cradle my heavy breast. Thumbs and four fingers pull and pinch my demanding nipples. A desperate moan creeps up the back of my throat. I'm rewarded with his teeth biting down in the space between my neck and my shoulder. He soothes the sting with a long, wet slide of his tongue. I whimper because my intimate muscles are trembling and fluttering around nothing.

"I'm going to cuff your elbows together and then I'm going to put the four-foot spreader on your ankles. Straightened out your arms, lovely."

I do what he tells me. And I feel the soft velvet lined leather cuffs wrap around my right, then left elbow. Next, I hear the tell-tell click of the silver connectors that draw my elbows close together and forces my breast to jut up and out. It's not uncomfortable, but I wouldn't want to walk around like this all day, either. He places a slow, soft kiss in the middle of my shoulder blades as he runs his pinky finger under the cuffs making sure they're not too tight. I know he can feel the shiver move down my spine. His lips, still pressed to my sensitive skin, have turned up in—what I'm sure is a beautiful smile.

"How's that, lovely?"

"Fine, Master."

"Good. Thank you for giving me your submission. You know how much I value this gift from you. I don't know if I've earned the right to it, but I promise you I will never abuse it again."

"I know. I trust you, Master."

His breath hitches and my heart fills with love and something I can't even begin to put a name to. I feel his hands move to the top of my

shoulders and down my arms. When he reaches my hands, he squeezes my fingers and then his hands are on my hips.

"Vivian, I want you in the worst kind of way. I want to defile you; and I know you would let me, wouldn't you?"

I don't bother answering him. I would even if it broke me again, I would let him do it. Because I love and need this man.

"Turn around, lovely. I want the first time I sink into you again to be face-to-face. "

"What about the spreader bar, Master?" I was really looking forward to it. His smile is knowing and breathtaking. He's so magnificent and divine when he's like this. My chest hurts and I want to rub my hand over my heart where the pain is the deepest. As if he can feel it, he places his warm hand between my breast and his heat seeps into my skin. The hurt starts to fade as his lips pass softly over mine. He's taking his time with me, and I don't want that.

"Master, may I speak freely?"

"Of course, lovely. What's on your mind?"

"Um, Sir. I need you."

"I'm right here."

"Yes, I know and I'm so grateful, but I need my Master. I need. I need you t-to own me."

"Own you, lovely. I already own you."

"Yes, but I need you to t-take control. I need you…" *God, why is this so hard?* "… don't treat me like I'm broken, Master. I just…" Frustration paints the exasperated huffs of air that fall from my open mouth. Just as I'm gearing up to try again, his command falls like manna from heaven.

"On your knees, Viv."

I sank like a fallen angel in front of him. His hands move to his belt and the clanking of the bronze buckle with the ornate 'B' logo sends a shot of lust so powerful through my blood stream, I'm sure I'll pass out before I get to suck him off. Then the swish of the same supple leather his shoes are made of as he pulls it from the loops of his charcoal gray Savile Row suit pants.

God, he looks so austere and brutal in those bespoke three-piece suits he allows to drape over his enticing body. I hear him roll the belt into a tight coil before he places it on the top of the reclaimed burlwood and cane credenza sitting to the right of where he's standing over me. His suit jacket and vest follow. He folds his jacket and then his vest in half before laying them lengthwise beside his belt. I watch as he removes his shoes from his right, then left foot. His socks are removed in the same methodical manner, revealing the masculine beauty of his sexy feet. My mouth waters and I have to keep myself from bending down to place reverent kisses along his toes.

He's just rolled his socks into a neat ball and placed it into his right shoe, now those shoes and socks join his other articles of clothing on top of the credenza. He's standing in front of me in his suit pants, white shirt— with sleeves rolled up. I'm on my knees, arms bound behind me at the elbows, naked except for my thong. The reality of the situation hits me in the base of my sacrum, heavy and solid, like an anvil. The power exchange I crave is another person in the room. John's formidable body still encased in his impressive clothing. My transmuted body in a submissive pose, mostly naked and waiting for him to do with it as he sees fit. With a deep inhale of my husband's amazing scent and a slow exhale of my own intention; it happens. I accept his will as my own and completely submit to

him; for the first time in our lives together. *This is what he wanted, what he knew I needed from the beginning.*

"You feel that, lovely? I've been waiting for it. I'll always give you what you need. I'll always give it to you, when and how I want you to have it. You said you trust me."

"I do. Master. I just... maybe, I'm having trouble trusting myself."

I hear the hook slide from the bar as he opens the waistband of his trousers, and I swear I can feel him separating me from my inhibitions as he unzips his fly. John makes a meal out of undressing himself, and I'm starving for any scraps he's willing to give. He eases his fine wool over his erection and down his long, well-muscled thighs and legs. First his right, and then his left leg leave the confines of his tailored pants, leaving him standing bare foot in only his black boxer briefs, a white dress shirt and a dark purple necktie. The shirt does nothing to cover the need he has for me that's threatening to tear through his underwear and fall into my willing mouth.

I'm panting and pretty sure I'll orgasm if he so much as blows on me, and his beautiful ass is meticulously folding the last part of his suit before laying it atop his jacket and vest.

"What I'm hearing—" He interrupts himself, to loosen the aforementioned tie and remove it from his neck. As he starts to fold it, he continues. "—is that you're second guessing yourself, but my question is what are you second guessing yourself about, lovely? Are you questioning your need for me? Or are you confused about if you want to revisit the D/s aspect of our relationship?"

His supple fingers are unbuttoning his shirt as he waits for me to answer. I must have blinked out, because when I open my mouth to respond, the smooth, wide head of his dick is resting on my bottom lip and

the man is completely naked. *I guess the talking is over and it's time to play.*

"I feel you smiling around my cockhead, allow me to give you something else to do with those lips. Open your throat for me, I'm going to fuck your mouth. Don't suck me. Don't lick me. Don't you even thing about biting me. Are we clear, Viv?"

I shake my head in the affirmative because I know he wants to hear my words and when he doesn't, he wants to make me say them. His dick leaves my mouth, and he slaps my right and then my left cheek with it, instead. I want to howl at the moon. I love being used by him like this. I used to be ashamed of my need to submit. To be used by my husband, but the more I learn about myself and the alters; the more I learn to accept and love things about my sexuality.

"Open your mouth, use your words, and stop being a fucking brat, Vivian."

"I understand you're going to use my mouth and my throat. Master."

"Open." He slaps me with his cock once more before wrapping his right hand around the back of my head, threading his fingers into my locs, and with his left hand, he strokes—a few times up and down—the most beautiful phallus I've ever seen. I know most would consider the penis an ugly useful tool, but to me; John's dick is a thing of beauty. Seven, maybe eight inches of warm, soft skin the color of perfectly tempered milk chocolate laying protectively over a hot, hard muscle with a few thick veins strategically placed, and capped off with a large, flared head that makes me think about mixed berry jam. *Shit, now I want a chocolate covered frozen banana dipped in jam. Am I drooling?*

27

"You with me, Vivian?"

"Yes, Master." He always knows when I'm floating off somewhere inside my head, but thankfully the girls are giving me some much-needed privacy.

"I felt you drift off, where did you go or who showed up?"

"No one showed up and I didn't drift off. I was contemplating the beauty of your cock, Master." My lips turn in a mischievous smile and I add, "And then I started thinking about chocolate covered, frozen bananas dipped in mixed-berry jam. Master." I deadpan as best I can. I watch as his left-hand falters in its attention and hear the sexy rumble of his chuckle

"Damn it, Vivian!" There's no heat in his voice. Only humor and love. "How the fuck do you expect me to stay in scene when you say shit like that?" I lift my eyes to see his face and the smile gracing his beautiful mouth makes my entire soul light up. He's so fucking gorgeous. I'm baiting him, and I hope he takes it.

"I'm sorry, Master. I was only answering your question. I didn't mean to pull you from our scene, Sir."

"Something tells me you're going for a punishment. Is that what you're doing? Topping from the bottom, lovely."

"I don't think I'm doing that, Master. If I am, I don't mean to."

His right hand leaves my hair and wraps around my throat. Not tight enough to choke me or even restrict the flow of air, but enough to remind me he's in control of me and this scene.

"Stand." He commands me, keeping his hand around my neck, and his left hand around my right arm, he helps me rise to my feet. My nerves are jumping all over the place in anticipation of what he may do to me. I don't have to wait long to know my fate. He kicks my feet apart and grabs the

spreader bar from the couch. After bending down to attach the restraints to my ankles, he locks the bar in place at four feet. He maneuvers me so I'm facing the credenza.

His large hands smooth over my back; as he's moving down toward my ass, he pushes me forward. My breast flattened against the collection of his clothes. While I'm getting use to the feel of his fine wool suit rubbing against my sensitive nipples, I hear my thong rip from my body. A gush of wanton desire floods my core at his aggression. Next, he stuffs my destroyed panties in my mouth and before I'm able to process what's happening, his heavy hand comes down on my naked ass sending lightning and thunder across unsuspecting skin.

"One." Another crack of his hand and garble protests are lost in the soaked crotch of my wet panties currently pressed against my tongue.

"Do you remember your safe signal, lovely? Show me what you do if you need a break. And then if you need me to stop." He moves away from me to watch for the correct signals. I lift my pointer and middle finger and then my first three fingers; indicating a break and stop. He seems happy with that because before I can relax my fingers, his hand comes down like a sunburn on my right cheek. I wince and try to move, but the spreader bar is keeping me immobile. I should be embarrassed by the amount of lust flowing from my swollen cunt, but I can't be bothered to feel anything but gratitude and relief. His hands on me like this. It calms me. Gives me a moment to focus on something other than what's happening inside my head. Something greater than myself.

"That's five, Vivian. I know you have five more in you. Let me know if you're good for five more, Viv." I ball my right hand into a tight fist and pump it back and forth for him. The air whooshing from his lungs reaches and cools my heated ass just before he rains down in quick succession five

licks of feverish pleasure. His breath is harsh as he fumbles behind me. I watch as his shirt is placed beside my head. I hate I'm not able to see him, but I know this is going to be amazing.

"I'm going to fuck you, now. I'm going to fuck your sopping pussy with my dick and I'm going to fuck your perfect asshole with my two fingers. Are you ready, Viv?" I give him the go-ahead with my fist. I take a deep breath and remind myself how much John loves me.

His fingers probe me, collecting my wetness and spreading it over my clit and lips. His fingers go back for more and I know he's getting ready to breach my tight hole. I'm scared, but excited I'm willingly doing this for the first time in my life. *I trust you John; I know you're going to take care of me. I know you love me.* I chant this over and over as he runs his index finger from my clit back to my puckered hole.

"Relax for me. I'm going to make this so fucking good for you, lovely. Trust me to take care of you. Know that I deify and exalt you every time you gift me your submission." He echoes my chant and that alone allows me to give myself over to him.

"If you need me to slow down or stop, let me know. Don't do what you think I want or expect you to do, be honest with yourself and me. I'm not looking to break you again, lovely." The iron in his voice conveys how deadly serious he is about what we're attempting to do, and it further puts my mind at ease. This shit is too important to fuck up." I smile around the gag in my mouth at his choice of words, but I'm as quiet as a church mouse. I'm ready to do this. For him, but mostly for me. I can't move much, but I still manage to wiggle my ass to let him know I'm ready.

Seal's hit, *Kiss from a Rose*, is filtering through the speakers just as John's middle finger pushes against me. I tense a little and he continues to push past my defenses. Past my fears and the bite of pain until he's

completely seated in that dark canal. *Why is he just standing there? Am I not as good at taking this as…*

"Get out of that beautiful head of yours, Viv. I'm only giving you a minute to acclimatize to the feeling of my touch in a place that has always brought you pain." *Well, damn. He always knows. I should be used to his mind-reading ability.*

I take a deep breath through my nose, and push against his intrusion. Only then does he withdraw the solid weight of his middle finger and pushes back into me.

"How are you doing, Viv? I want to add another finger. You're so snug and hot. You feel fucking amazing and you're doing beautifully." His praise means everything to me in this moment. I hear the pride in his voice. I don't know if it's for me or for himself for getting me to do this, but I don't even care. I'm so happy to be doing this for us. For me. I give him the fist pump he needs to see and prepare myself to take another finger in my ass.

"Okay, lovely. I'm going to give you another finger and then I'm going to give your pretty little cunt something to clench down on when you come." John pushes back in with his long, thick index and middle fingers—the burn and stretch is unreal—he doesn't stop until he bottoms out. No time to get used to the heavy fullness back there because his dick finds its home deep inside my slick walls. I'm so fucking full, I can't breathe. It's overwhelming. I can already feel an orgasm building low in my belly. It feels like fire and ice coalescing deep in my core.

The sounds spilling from my throat around my panties in my mouth are more animal than human. I'm drooling and grunting with every push and pull of his fingers and cock. When one pulls out, the other pushes in. I don't know which feels better. My skin is coated in perspiration. I can't

close my legs to absorb the pleasure or lesson the sting of pain. *Oh, my god! He's going to kill me if he keeps rubbing hard, tight circles on my clit.* I'm not going to survive this orgasm. It's going to obliterate me.

Every sound, smell, touch, and feeling is magnified by about a million. Thwacking of pelvic on ass. Course hair rubbing against smooth skin. Pheromones, clean sweat, and sex. He's pistoning into me. Everywhere John and I are connected is infused with so much heat... I know. I just know I'm not going to survive this intact.

"Vivian. God. I am so fucking deep inside you. You are my entire fucking—" He stops speaking and continues fucking me. God I would give anything to see him. I imagine him standing like the god he is behind me. His hands in me, and on me. His tight ass flexing in and out as he uses his lower body muscles to fuck himself deeper into me. I feel his sweat dripping down onto my back, running down the crack of my ass—adding more lubrication for the finger fucking he's gifting me. Hearing the feral grunts and moans clawing their way up from his soul seeking the freedom of air. *I'm going to break for him.* Just then, he pinches my clit. Plunges his dick into me at the same time his fingers bottom out in my ass. And then it happens. I break.

One fine fissure across my surface. Another thrust and pinch and a spiderweb of pleasure spreads from the epicenter of my climax. A hard push forward and one more tight circle over my clit and I'm destroyed. I'm a million different versions of myself at once. I'm all of me and none of me. Everywhere and still anchored here in my office. Connected to the beautiful soul who just fucked me back to my elemental self.

"I love you so fucking much, Vivian." He takes the panties from my mouth. Uncuffs my elbows and rubs life back into my shoulders. Removes the spreader bar from my ankles and rubs them, too. He picks me up—

bride style and carries me to my office en suit to get us both cleaned up. The entire time, he's whispering his love and awe and appreciation for me. John worships every part of me as he bathes me. Tends to my sore ass. Lotions me. Kisses me. Dresses me. There's no wariness in him. No doubt or fear. Just him giving me the aftercare I desperately need.

"How are you feeling, lovely?"

"Loved. Proud. Honored you love and chose me. You want me, Vivian. Not Valery. Not Vera. I'm who you chose to love." I give myself permission to accept the love this man has for me. I smile as I start to hum along with The Spice Girls as they swear to give everything as long as he'll be there. I feel the same way about John.

"Something funny, Viv?"

"Nope. Are you cooking dinner tonight or are we eating out?"

"How about I eat you out. You suck me off. And we'll order dinner in."

"You're the boss." He leans down and kisses my forehead and winks as he caresses my cheek with his thumb.

"Don't forget it. Not for one damn minute, lovely."

28

It's Tuesday and I don't have my normal appointment with Dr. Kerrigan. I realize I miss seeing him. But John was right, he was too attached to me. I don't know how he could've developed feelings for me, but I guess anything is possible. *I mean, I readily admit he is sexy and charming, but there isn't a man on earth or in heaven or hell, for that matter, who could make me leave John.* I'm just packing my bags, getting ready to go, when my phone chimes with a message. I'm expecting it to be John but am totally surprised to see Dr. Kerrigan's number flash across the screen.

I'm pretty sure I'm reading this wrong; he's expecting me to come by for our normal session. He must be confused. I press one on my speed dial. John picks up on the second ring.

"Yes, Vivian."

"Um. I'm sorry to bother you. You sound like you're really busy."

"Yes, I am. But you're not bothering me. What's on your mind, lovely."

"I just received a text from Dr. Kerrigan. He expects me to come in for my appointment this evening. What do you think, should I keep seeing him until I find someone else?"

"How comfortable are you with this motherfucker? I'm not good with you seeing him at all, but I know he was helping you. How would you feel…"

"John, I would feel fine if you were there with me. Do you have—" I realized we were talking at the same time and stopped, trying to hear what he was asking me. Turns out, we were asking the same thing of each other. It's settled. We will meet with Dr. Kerrigan until we can figure something else out or maybe we can continue to work with him.

I'm excited to share what the alters and I have come up with. What we want to try to incorporate into our management plan. I gather my stuff and prepare to walk out of my office as I say goodbye to John. *This is either going to be a complete disaster or maybe a complete breakthrough for all of us.*

***

I'm sitting in one of the four chairs in the waiting area outside of Dr. Kerrigan's office and looking through the notebook the girls and I have been working in over the past week. I can't believe how much work we all put into finding an alternative to total integration. I'm out-of-this-world-glad none of us are eager to have that happen. It's not like we don't all want to survive and live our lives as we see fit. Just as I'm making a small note in the margin, the door opens and awareness skitters down my spine like tiny pin pricks of electricity. I know it's my husband who's coming. I can always feel him when he's near me. It's like he's a part of me on a molecular level. No separation between us… just happened to be born on different days, to different parents and with different upbringings. But in the end, we are the same person.

"Good evening, lovely. Have you been waiting long?" He bends down and gives me a kiss on my right cheek, while he cups the left cheek with a lingering caress. I breathe him in as I lean into the warmth of his touch, turning my face to place a sweet kiss to the center of his palm. I'm rewarded with one of his rare, but beautiful smiles as he sits down beside me, dropping his briefcase to the floor between his spread legs. With a deep inhale, he turns to me expectantly and I remember he asked me a question.

"No. only about ten minutes or so. He's in with another client, our appointment isn't for another fifteen minutes." I finish making my note and

close the journal and for the first time notices the hand drawn wonderland on the cover. It's the most surreal visual I've ever seen. It's a perfect square divided into four perfect squares. Each of the smaller squares are decorated like each of our rooms in the internal house. But it's the circle in the center of the page that has me astonished and a little shocked. I can't tell if it was drawn first or after everything else because parts of the four squares create the common space we share in the internal house, while maintaining the integrity of each of our rooms.

The Internal House

Who drew this? It's absolutely beautiful. This is highly technical in style and talent.

The fuck you goin on about, huh? I thought the damn book needed somethin on the front. It was too plain and borin. Just like the rest of you chicken-heads. Wait... what did you say?

I said it shows a lot of ability and innate talent. I can't draw a stick figure to save my life, but I recognize talent when I see it, and damn, Val. You have some serious skills. With the right training and commitment, you could go very far in the art world. Will you come out and share your thoughts with Dr. Kerrigan about this drawing and can I have co-consciousness when you do?

You fuckin with me right now, Viv? Don't be blowin no sunshine up my ass to make me obey your mothafuckin rule. I said I'd stay away from John's juicy-ass-dick so, shut the fuck up, huh?

What? Valery, I would never blow anything up your ass... you'd enjoy it too much. I meant every word I said. It's beautiful and so insightful. It's how you see us and yourself as a part of and apart from us. I sure as hell could never do anything like this. I love art, but I'm no artist. Apparently, you are, though.

185

Me? A goddamned artist? What the fuck ever! All right. I'll talk to that asshat of a doctor about that silly ass drawin. What the fuck you smilin bout? Get the fuck outta here, call me when I'm up.

You know, Valery. It's perfectly normal to feel pride in what you've done. And it's also perfectly normal to smile when you feel happy. I'm going to go, it's about time for the appointment. I think? I always lose track of time when I'm in here with you guys. See you later… Oh, John will be sitting in on the sessions until we either find a new doctor or Dr. K. gets his personal feelings under control.

Fuck! Whatever, bitch. Get the hell outta my head. Tell John don't come at me wrong. I know shit about him and he knows what I'm talkin about.

***

I refuse to let Valery's parting words affect me or my relationship with John. If he told her something in confidence, then he told her something he needed her to know. *Progress. Slow and steady progress.*

With a few fluttering blinks and a shake of my head, I'm back in the lobby. I look at John and he's looking at me, no doubt trying to figure out if I'm still me or if he's sitting with someone else entirely. Flashing him my signature I've-got-this smile, I watch as his shoulders relax, and his eyes soften.

"Sorry. I noticed something and wondered about it. Of course, I'm never alone in my head, and Val thought it was better to answer me and then we got into a conversation… oh, never mind. I'm good. Is it time to go in?" I'm flustered now, but sometimes it's the most difficult part of having DID. Explaining how my alters and I work.

"Yea. Dr. Irish Arsehole came out about five minutes ago, saw you doing your thing and said to bring you in when you came out. Ready?"

John places his elegant hands on both knees and goes to push himself up to standing, but halts when he feels my hand on his forearm. Turning to look at me with some unreadable emotion filtering through his dark eyes, he waits for me to do or say what I stopped him for. The longer I take, the thinner his patience gets. I feel the tension in his body, and it makes us nervous, that's why I stopped him. Well, that's why Vera had me stop him. She wants to say something to him and whenever Vera wants the lead, I give it to her because she so rarely wants anything to do with this body.

Vera

"Um John? Hi. It's me, Vera, yeah?" As soon as John hears Vera's voice, his eyes soften and he relaxes his shoulders. Making himself as nonthreatening as possible. *How he knows she needs this is beyond me, but I'm glad he does.*

"I wanted to say… to talk with you for a minute, yeah?" I think John has a soft spot for Vera. I'm looking through her eyes and he looks like a little boy who wants to make friends with the shy new kid in his class. *It's the strangest thing.*

"Yeah, Vera. What is it?" His eyes are the softest I've ever seen them, except for when he talked about our baby; before she died. I feel Vera react to my thought and stop thinking to give her the space she needs. I rub her back with firm circles and encourage her to say what she wants to say.

"Um. John. I wanted you to please give Dr. Kerrigan a chance to work with us. He just a man; he can't help how he feel about Vivian no more than you can, yeah?" She dips her head and starts chewing on her bottom lip as she peeks at John from under her thickly lashed lids. It's such a coquettish gesture, I wonder if John thinks it's sexy. But as I look through her eyes at my husband's face, he's considering her request and looking at her with the same need to make her happy. Make her proud. There is no

attraction toward her and I'm even more fascinated by their interaction than I am with him and Valery.

"I guess you have a valid point, Vera. I will do my best to give Dr. Asshole—"She doesn't let him finish his reply. Her face has twisted up in some kind of matronly look of reproach while somehow managing to evoke the hurt, innocence of a child. John's hands come to rest on her shoulders. He squeezes lightly. Once. Twice. And on the third squeeze, he drops his head and speaks so quietly, I have to strain to hear what he says.

"Fine, Vera. You win. Stop with the doe eyes. I'll give him a chance, just the one. *Yeah*?" He mocks her with an indulgent smile and I feel her face split in two as she shakes her head. Nudging me in my ribs, letting me know she's ready to go back to her room.

What's going on with you and John, Vera?

Nothing. He's just a big teddy bear, yeah?

Yes. For you maybe. I've never seen him like that before.

That's cause he in love with you, he just want me to feel safe, yeah? See you later, Vivian.

"Viv?" John's hand on the small of my back helps me recover a little quicker than I normally do after a switch.

"You are a goofy something when talking with Vera." I can't stop the giggles as they color my speculative observation.

"Are you ready, lovely?" His reply is filled with humility. Embarrassment? I don't think I've ever seen or heard him like this. *I love it.*

"Yes, John. Let's get this show on the road." It was hard to keep the joviality from my tone, but I swear I've never seen him like he was with Vera. Wonders never cease, but I think I just fell a little more in love with him. We step into the familiar office and I take my seat on the odd little

chair I always choose and watch as John stands and looks around the space. *I wonder what chair he'll choose to sit in for the next hour.*

Dr. Kerrigan is at his desk typing something in his computer, he doesn't look up when John moves to the large navy-blue wingback directly in front of me. John unbuttons his suit jacket, grabs the front of his pants at the tops of his thighs and jerks the material up to avoid wrinkling them, and takes his seat like he's the psychologist conducting this session. He pulls out his phone and checks his messages as we wait for Dr. Kerrigan to get sorted.

"I'm sorry, Viv. Um, and John. I had something that needed my immediate attention. Thank you for your patience. So, how are you getting on?" I love that he tries to conduct this session as if there isn't a six foot, five inch, 220-pound, brooding elephant in the room. He takes the love seat and settles his recorder on the table as well as his raspberry lavender tea and notebook with pen attached. Waiting for a reply. John looks like he couldn't care less about being here, so I choose to forget he is.

"I'm getting on a little better this week than I was last week. And no. I'm not bullshitting you. Last week was a wake-up call or sorts."

"Oh, how so?" His Tiffany-blue eyes are a x-ray beams—looking through me—seeing what's underneath the skin and meat of my words. I hate when his focus on me is this intense.

"What changed since your husband barged into my office and accosted, threatened, and probably undid most of the work you and I have done?" I look at him for the first time and notice the tight lines around his mouth. The blue flames of his eyes are full of something I've never seen before. John must notice it at the same time, because his phone is no longer holding his interest. He's zeroed in on the good doctor, who seems to be zeroed in on me.

189

"Dr. Kerrigan. I realized last week was not something you are accustomed to dealing with, but in John's defense—"

"John doesn't need you to defend him. We don't have to explain fuck-all to this man, who has obviously lost his professional objectivity when it comes to treating and caring for my wife." John is still sitting in the wingback, his face is the picture of composure, and his voice is as even as Lake Murray on a calm day. I know better than anyone how menacing he is when he's found this calculating space within himself. A coiled black mamba ready to strike, only he doesn't look like he's ready to do much of anything; which is why the results are so catastrophic when he does.

"You know what?" I start while getting up and moving over to John's side. "I think this was a mistake. I'm going to find another therapist, Dr. Kerrigan. I think it's best for all involved." I look to my husband, whose eyes are focused on the doctor. Whose heated gaze is *still* foolishly focused on me. I know if I can't get John out of this office sooner rather than later, there will be bloodshed. *Goodness gracious, why I thought this would work out is beyond me.* Placing my hand on John's shoulders and bending down to put my face in his, I beg him with my eyes to get up and leave with me. But he's not even looking my way. I pull out the big guns and I don't even feel bad about doing it.

"John." I keep my voice low enough so only he can hear what I'm about to say. "You told Vera, you would give him a chance and you have. He doesn't deserve another, so let's go. Let's not upset her. She believes in you." I feel the tension release before he turns his eyes to stare into my own. Honoring me with that same crooked smile he gave me at the door, he stands abruptly and collects his things and mine. Turns and walks towards the door, waiting for me to follow; which I do. Once I'm safely on

the other side of the door, he turns around and speaks his final words to Dr. Kerrigan and they turn my warm blood cold.

"Send the final bill to me. If you ever contact my wife or any of her alters again, I will kill you. We clear, motherfucker?" With that, he shuts the door. *Guess I'll be calling my family doctor for a referral to another therapist who specializes in DID.*

Part Three

"Through the Looking Glass"

"You can't go through the looking glass without cutting

yourself."

--Iris Murdoch; The Sacred and Profane Love Machine

~29~

Four months later

John and I have been so busy at work, we hardly see each other and when we do, it's a mad dash to some unnamed finish line. We still make and find time to connect and reacquaint ourselves intimately but a lot of the time, we end up sharing a meal and checking in with one another. I don't know that I so much as miss him as I'm not used to having this much freedom. Since I've been seeing a new holistic psychologist, John seems to be less involved in my mental health care and is settling into being my husband and Dom.

I've got an installation going in at my gallery and the artist is a temperamental prick, but he's one of the most talented temperamental pricks I've had the misfortune of working with. His work is going to bring in a shit-ton of money for La Magnolia Nior, not to mention the exposure. Not just local either, but this exhibit will put my gallery on the international radar of artists looking to display their talents in more intimate venues such as mine.

"Vivian, Hey. I know you're busy and you have a ton of shit to do, but I really need your help with the lighting. You know the large piece. The one with the broken face and dismembered body parts?" My assistant, Tammi, has the finesse of a bull in a glass house but she's as good as they get at keeping me and the gallery on track. I place my right hand over the mouth piece of the phone and whisper-yell to her to give me a minute. Returning to my call, expecting her to have simply walked away and close the door, when I hear...

"Okay, Vivian. Take your time on the phone. I'll just stand right here holding all these cut up body parts while I wait for you to tell me how you

want me to light them up. You know—make them look maybe not so dead—in the special corner you assigned them to."

I feel my blood rushing through my veins, but all I can hear is the grating voice of my soon-to-be-former assistant as she embarrasses the living-daylights out of me.

"Excuse me, please. I need to place you on hold for one moment. Thank you." I place the phone in the cradle and am up and out from behind my desk before I realize I was planning to move. Tammi is standing there, looking into the middle distance, completely unaware her life is hanging in the clutches of my fraying sanity and my need to get this installation done.

"Tammi, what part of give me a minute, did you not understand?" She turns to me and I see the moment she realizes her little performance was not well received. Giving her no chance to explain herself, I step into her personal space. My nose is almost touching her forehead when I speak through clenched teeth and jaws.

"I tolerate your shit because you are usually amazing at your job, but you should know you are not irreplaceable. I could have ten of you in this office in ten minutes. Now do your fucking job and stop bitching for attention." She has the good sense to look apologetic as she walks off. I don't hesitate to return to my phone call. *What the hell is going on with her lately? She's been a pain in my ass these last few weeks.*

"Thank you for holding, now, where were we?"

***

That phone call should have only taken about twenty minutes, but I ended up staying on it almost two hours. *Needy prick of an artist.* I make my way around the gallery and am pleasantly surprised to see Tammi was able to pull her head out of her ass long enough to do her job. The installation looks exactly the way the design schematic says it should. I'm

walking through the last of the spaces when I hear the door open in the front of the gallery. It's late and I know everyone left already because they stopped by the office one at a time to tell me goodbye.

I make my way toward the front of the gallery, thinking maybe John has dropped by to bring me a late dinner, but my blood stops moving in my veins as I look into the icy blue stare of my former therapist.

Cry Me a River is floating through the surround sound system as he stands just inside the door with his right hand wrapped around the chrome handle of a 45 Smith and Wesson. His face is void of emotion and his body a pillar of hurt and anger. I don't stop in my stride because I need to get to the desk at the front of the store to push the silent alarm. I maintain eye contact with him but I don't speak or allow the thick fear sliding through my body to show on my face or falter my breath. *One foot in front of the other, Vivian. Get to the desk and then…*

"I know you don't think I'll allow you to reach your small desk and push the silent alarm, Vivian? Come now, love. Give me more credit than that, will you?" His perfect Irish accent weaves its way into my ear canal and slithers down my throat, choking the breath from me. His eyes haven't left my own and I can tell he has no plans of either of us leaving this gallery alive tonight.

I make a slight adjustment in my stride and allow my feet to pivot, carrying me straight into his path. No smile or frown. No pout or scowl. Just my face and my eyes, two scared women, and one pissed off twelve-year-old.

What he doing here, Vivi?

Wait… is that a fuckin gun—oh shit! He won't suppose to find out, yet. Fuckin my shit up, Harry. You crazy mothafucker. You really shittin where you put your mouth.

Valery. Please tell me you didn't do anything as stupid as I think you did? Why he here... with a gun?! What have you done? Vera! Get out here. Now!

I have to concentrate to avoid slipping into a conversation with the alters. I want to yell at Valery to shut the hell up, but I can't give into that desire. She and Lyric are going at it now and poor Vera is sitting in the corner rocking and weeping. *I need you all to please be quiet and let me deal with this, please?* They quiet down, but not before Lyric tells me to mess him up and not to let him shoot us when we're finally getting our stuff together. She's not wrong. Our new therapist is amazing and she treats us more like partners than patients. I'm almost lost in the conversation when I hear the click of his gun. *Guess he figured out a way to get my attention.*

"Hello, ladies. Are all of you out and about tonight?" His condescending tone pisses me off and I find I'm tired of whatever game he's playing.

"Dr. Kerrigan. I'm not sure why you're here or why you have a gun pointed at me, but I'm sure you're going to enlighten me." I've come to a stop about two feet in front of him. My heart is hammering in my chest and I'm about two seconds from passing the fuck out, but you'd never know it to look at me. My hands are loosely hanging by my side and my face is the picture of calm, and probably a little tired. *What would John do?*

"Vivian. You look lovely. I have no issue with you, but I would love to speak with that *bitch* Valery." It takes every bit of my self-control not to blench when he spits her name out like it's acid burning out his tongue. *Val, what the hell have you done?*

"I'm sure you know it doesn't work like that, Dr. K. I'm the primary. The alters and I have agreed that I will function as the primary, what is this

about and is the gun really necessary?" His posture hasn't changed at all. The gun is steady in his hand. Slowly, his tired lids close over his azure eyes—showing almost microscopic blue-green veins. Until now, I hadn't noticed the half-moon smudges coloring the olive-tinted skin on either side of his strong nose. I take a moment to study him and I fail to hide the shock as I gaze upon his enervated expression. His lustrous, cinnabar colored hair is dull and greasy; sticking up in all directions in large, unkempt hanks.

"Dr. K? What's going on with you?" My concern is genuine. Even though he may have lost his way as my therapist, he did help me. He got the alters and I on the right track. I don't want any harm to come to him. I feel Valery pull back and slink off to her room and my heart sinks, because I know what ever she's done to this man has cost him dearly.

"You really don't know do you?"

"I'm afraid to ask. I have no idea what's going on, but Valery just left and went to her room. I can't reach her or feel her with the others anymore."

"Vivian. She ruined my whole fecking career. She—" The gun is trembling in his hand; his brogue is thicker than I've ever heard it. When his lids lift, I'm drowning in the Ionian Sea; being tossed in its salty, swirling currents. His anguish pulls me under its seismic shifts and I'm unsteady on my feet. I have to fight against the moving plates of land just to catch my breath. He's so broken. Destroyed.

"What? I don't understand…what are you talking about?" As he is lowering his right arm and the light of sanity starts to seep into his eyes, the door behind him crashes open and I watch in horror as his finger squeezes the trigger in reaction to the loud noise behind him.

The glass explodes; white, angry suffering spreads through my right shoulder. The force knocks me back and I'm stumbling over my Jimmy

Choo's. I watch Tammi's eyes morph into saucers as she pushes past Dr. Kerrigan, making her way to me.

"Don't just stand there, you red-headed fucker! Call for an ambulance. Get some help, she's losing too much blood." She places my head on her lap and whips her shirt over her head, and then a pain that rivals John's backdoor antics, shoots through my shoulder as she presses her shirt into the burning crater of misunderstanding taking up residence on the right side of my body.

"Don't you dare die on me. Open your freaky-ass cat eyes. Do you hear me, goldie. Don't die on me! Your sexy-as-fuck husband will blame me for your death. Open your fucking eyes!

I want to open them, if for no other reason than just to tell Tammi to shut the hell up, but the pull into darkness is much too enticing to ignore. I succumb to its seduction and am rewarded with a reprieve from the pain slicing through my upper torso. I vaguely hear, what sounds like John's voice in the midst of my descent into velvety bliss.

~30~

Someone has taped coins over my eyes. They've been glued shut with sleep, pain, and confusion. *Maybe I'm dead. Didn't the old folk use to tape pennies on the eyes of the dead to keep the souls in until it was ready to go to heaven?* Opening them is of utmost importance, but the moment a sliver of light creeps into my pupils; my lids slam shut again. I'm motionless in the bed, taking stock of my body and how I feel. All ten of my fingers and toes wiggle. I'm able to move my legs without pain or discomfort. I raise my left arm, feeling the restraint of my I-V and other monitors, but no pain. I attempt to raise my right arm, and the pain radiating from my shoulder, has my eyes flinging open and tears leaking down my dry, chapped cheeks.

"Vivian, lovely?! What the hell...? Baby, what are you trying to do? Put your arm down, you've been sh-sh-shot." In all the years I've known John. I've never heard him stutter. I've never heard him sound anything other than perfectly in control of himself, me, and everything else around him. I slide my tear-soaked eyes over to him and my breath whooshes from my lungs. Utter devastation. His soulful, brown eyes are overcast with worry and disquiet. I feel his strong fingers wrap around my left hand, careful not to disturb the I-V stuck in the vein on the back.

"J—J..." I have to clear my throat a few times and my mouth still feels like I've been sucking on moth balls and cotton. He holds a pink, plastic cup with a white lid and bendy straw sticking from the center up to my mouth. I take a deep pull from the room temperature water and I swear it's the sweetest thing I've ever tasted. I try to go back for more, but John pulls it away from me before my lips can make contact with the straw.

"Not too much. You haven't had anything to eat or drink in a while. How are you feeling, lovely?" His tentative question makes me smile, a

199

little. *At least I hope I'm smiling and not grimacing.* He's looking at me. Through me, really, and I know he's trying to figure out what's really going on in my head and if it's me or one of the alters.

"It's me, John. How long have I been out?"

"You always know when I'm not sure who I'm dealing with and it makes me feel like a jerk every time." His unassuming smile betrays his true feelings and I indulge him his privacy as I close my eyes for a moment. When I open them again, he's composed and looking more like the commanding man I've loved and known since my freshman year in college. Using his thumb to rub the underside of my left wrist, he tells me I've been in the hospital for a little over four days. Just as he's getting ready to tell me what's been happening over that time, the door opens and a small, round, bald Asian man floats into the room and lights beside my bed; opposite of John.

Dr. Henry Cho is a living replica of the smiling Buddha statue I have in the corner of my office. His soft, black eyes are pushed into a perfectly round face and there is a sense of joy and peace emanating from them. I am instantly relaxed and comforted as I peer up at him. He is smiling, without showing his teeth, as he looks over my chart and nods his head. Once he's satisfied with whatever he sees, he places it back at the foot of the bed and walks over to stand beside John.

I have to work hard to contain my chuckle. John is in a pair of soft, grey sweat pants, a white tee shirt that stretches across his heavily muscled shoulders and arms. His left arm is crossed over his sternum, while his right hand continues to caress my left one. At 6' 5", John is a formidable sight; however, standing next to Dr. Cho who appears to be reaching towards 5 feet and carries a considerable amount of weight in and through his face and torso…it's just the comic relief I need.

"Mrs. Ellis." He calls my name like it's a question, even though he doesn't use the interrogative inflection. I'm not sure if I should answer him or what, so I wait him out.

"You gave us quite the scare. It was difficult for your husband and I think you owe him an apology for keeping him away from his work while he waited on you to stop being so lazy and wake up." *What the actual fuck?!* John's hand tightens around my wrist and I know he feels the increase in my pulse plus the crazy beeping of the heart monitor confirms what he already knows. I look at the little doctor and prepare to rip him a new one when the laughter in his eyes spills from his full, smiling lips.

"Gotcha!" He barks out as he laughs by himself.

"I love to see what strong-willed women will do when I behave like a pig." He looks at me and realizes I'm not laughing and then he looks at my husband and a cranberry flush crawls up his neck to kiss his cheeks.

"I'm sorry. Maybe it's too soon for a joke. I'm Dr. Cho and I'm your surgeon. Really, how are you feeling?"

I take a deep breath and release my frustration before answering him. "I've felt better, but I don't feel as bad as I could."

"Good answer. Do you recall what happened? How you ended up here at Lex Med?"

"I remember my former therapist pointing a gun at me. The door opening and my assistant, Tammi... Oh my God! Is Tammi all right? He didn't shoot her too, did he?"

"No, Viv. Tammi's fine. She was there trying to stop the bleeding. That asshole only shot you." John's dentist is going to have an ax to pick with him; with the way he's grinding his back molars.

"Oh, thank God. I saw her burst in the door and... I don't think Dr. Kerrigan meant to fire the gun. It looked like he was lowering his arm. I

think Tammi startled him and he just… reacted." I feel John's eyes on me and I know he wants to shake me for saying that out loud. It sounds like I'm defending the man who assaulted me, but I'm not. I'm simply stating facts. Speaking of facts, my mind searches itself for my alters. *Where the hell is Valery and what did she do to that man?*

Dr. Cho clears his throat and looks around the room before turning his eyes back to me. "Yes. Well, Kerrigan shot you in the right shoulder and ordinarily, with gunshot wounds such as those, we find most people experience little down time. Especially if the bullet is lodged in the affected area; however, in your case, he used an FMJ bullet, which tends to over penetrate when shot from point blank range."

I'm having a hard time taking a full breath. I don't know if Dr. Cho is trying to impress us with his knowledge of guns and bullets, but the acerbic agitation snaking up my throat and the black lines wavering in front of my eyes are not impressed. Not at all. He must not notice the tension in the air because he continues on as if everything is as it should be.

"And that means, you ended up with two bullet wounds—a stippled entry and its twin exit wound, leading to massive amounts of blood loss." My stomach lurches at the thought of my blood leaving my body in a mass exodus, but Cho keeps right on talking. I swallow convulsively to keep from throwing up the little bit of water John allowed me to drink,

"Also, you sustained a partial laceration to your subclavian artery… this artery is a major supplier of blood in your arm. Anyway, the angiogram revealed considerable damage, but we were able to use the latest method of repair; a percutaneous endovascular skin graft, which helped to mitigate some of your blood loss. Still ended up needing several pints of blood, though. Subsequently, did you know you have one of the rarest blood types in the world? It's a good thing you do…"

I'm still trying to control my overactive gag-reflex when Dr. Cho pushes into his next round of explanations. I don't need all this information from him, but it's like he has diarrhea of the vocals. *Tell me when I can go home or shut the hell up.*

"So yeah, anyway." *Wait, did I say that out loud?* Judging from the twitch of John's lips and the slight blush on Cho's face, I did. The bullet pretty much shattered your clavicle and left you with pneumothorax. He continues with a little shake of his round head.

"So, there's that. It looks like you're going to be here for at least another two or three days. We need to make sure the skin graft holds, get you set up with physical therapy, and start you on your baby aspirin regiment. Are there any questions?"

John and I look at each other with bemused expressions and I know my husband is like two seconds away from losing his shit with Dr. Cho. I clear my throat and proceed to save what's left of his dignity after my outburst earlier; I don't want John to lay into him as well.

"Okay. Thank you, Dr. Cho. You've been extremely informative. I would love to get out of here sooner rather than later, I have to…" The blood drains from my face as I remember why I was at the gallery so late. My frantic eyes dart back up to John's and for a moment he looks like he's ready to attack whatever is causing my face to look the way it does, and then his features relax.

"Don't worry about it, lovely. Tammi took care of everything. The artist's show was a magnificent success and that *twat*… somehow managed to send you an obnoxious bouquet of black magnolias—don't know how or where he found black magnolias—when he learned what had happened the night before his opening. I'm fucking proud of you."

You run a tight ship over there, baby. Even in your absence; during a traumatic crisis, your staff knew exactly what you wanted done and how to execute it to your standards. The success of that show is a direct reflection on you and what you bring to the world of art." His sensual lips turn up in a beautiful smile, telling me exactly how proud he is of my accomplishments even though he hates the people I work with, sometimes.

Dr. Cho clears his throat again and after a relatively quick run down of what I can expect as a result of the surgery and my physical therapy, he excuses himself for the night. Telling me he'll see me in the morning, and he wants me to get some rest.

"I'm goddamned happy to see those beautiful summer-sunshine eyes looking at me, even if they are bloodshot and swollen." He chuckles and it's gruff with his remaining fear and love for me. I smile at him and pucker my dry, cracked lips for a kiss. I'm sure I look a hot-ass-mess and my breath is probably a potent mix of noxious gasses, but my husband folds himself in half and places the gentlest kiss on my mouth and just like that... my summer sunshine skies open up and rain out all my fears, hurt, and anger.

~31~

It's been a little over two weeks since I walked out of the hospital after being shot by my former therapist. I'm having a hard time reconciling the fact he actually came to my gallery to do me harm—well, not me, but a part of me—harm. I've been chomping at the bit to get to Jessa. She's my new therapist; although she prefers to call herself a guide on the sidelines of my life. I prefer to call her the greatest fucking thing to happen to me since I left my bastard of a father's house.

She is honestly the most centered, positive-without-the-bullshit-platitudes person I know. I had already missed several appointments with her prior to being shot. I got so busy with the show; I kind of let my mental health take a backseat. *Fuck, I honestly let everything take a back-fucking-seat. John. Vera. Lyric. Valery. I can't remember the last time I've been to Wonderland.*

"Hey lovely, are you about ready to go?" John refuses to let me drive myself anywhere. He's probably wise to do so, I can't use my right arm. *Like not at all.* Kerrigan shattered my collar bone and jacked up the artery responsible for supplying blood to my arms and fingers. Until the artery heals and the physical therapist gets me to the point of mobility again, I'm pretty much at his mercy. *Not a bad place to be...not really.*

He also refuses to let me out of his sight because Dr. Kerrigan's whereabouts are unknown. He was arrested but made bail. No one has heard from him and John doesn't know if Valery is still in contact with him because she's not talking to either of us or the others either. Another reason I'm itching to connect with Jessa. I need her to help me connect with Val. I know she's scared, but she can't keep hiding from me and whatever she's done to get us in this horrendous situation.

"I'm coming. Can you help me put this sweater on? I hate not having use of my dominant hand…" I grumble as I make my way down the stairs toward the foyer. I look up and see John waiting at the door with his cell plastered to his left ear. His right shoulder is casually leaning against the jamb, his right ankle crossed over his left one—a sliver of his multihued, cashmere sock peaks out from the tailored hem of his pant leg. I drink him in slowly. His socks drew my attention first, so I make the ascension and am rewarded with the way his strong thighs are encased in the soft, grey wool of his casual slacks.

I lick my lips, unconsciously, because it's been too long since he's been inside of me. He still focused on his phone call, so I take my time to sip him like a cordial of Clasa Azul. His waist is wrapped in his favorite belt… my favorite belt, too. Probably for completely different reasons, or maybe for the same reason. *It leaves the most beautiful marks across my ass.* John is the best-dressed, heterosexual man I know. He's paired his grey pants with a darker grey linen/silk blend, pull-over, V-neck sweater. The tailored lines hug his massive shoulders and draw the eyes up to his smooth neck. The veins standing in relief are the first thing to drag me from my lust-filled haze.

I stop short, about two feet away from him and listen to his voice. It's tense and heavy with a mixture of fear, rage, and systemic control. *What the hell is going on?* I get quiet and listen, trying to hear something… anything to give me a clue as to what has my husband so alert.

"…yes, I understand all of that, but what you need to understand is this. My entire fucking world is being threatened. I will burn this motherfucking city down to the ground if anything happens to her."

Okay. I wasn't expecting to hear that, and my startled gasp betrays as much. It also alerts the pillar of wrath leaning against the door to my presence.

"Listen, do *whateverthefuckyouneed* to do to make shit happen the way *Ifuckingneethemtohappen*. You do not want me to *showthefuckupatyour* building in the middle of the goddamned night, do you? And I will. You know this. Fix this shit and fix it now!" I knew John was good and truly past any point of rational thought because he never allowed the Georgetown vernacular to pass his lips. Unless he'd lost all control, and from the clenching of his jaw and the flat look in his dark eyes... My husband was not in control of himself or the situation that's got him so riled up.

I didn't realize I'd been taking steps away from John until he calls my name and it sounds further away from me than I thought it would. Lifting my head to rest my eyes on his face, I wish I hadn't. A mask of ruthless brutality sits courageously over his beautiful features. His warm, chocolate eyes are frozen over and the chill emanating from them make my nipples hard.

"What's going on, John?"

"Shit. I don't want or need you to worry about any of this, lovely. We need to get you to your appointment. On second thought, do you think Jessa would be willing to come over and conduct your session here at the house? I'll pay her extra." His voice trails off as he finishes his sentence while tapping out a text on his phone, probably to his assistant to tell her to contact Jessa and tell her she's needed at the house. The hairs on the back of my neck become hyper aware of their surroundings and seem to be stretching out in every direction to get the lay of the land.

"Why can't we go to her office? What the hell is going on? And don't give me one of your bullshit answers." He looks at me, and the mask slips for about a second longer than I need, to show me the twisted violence born of fear and desperation. A kaleidoscope of butterflies beat their wings in my chest cavity. The nudging at the center of my forehead is the only warning I get before Valery pushes her way to the front of our consciousness. She doesn't wait for me to relinquish control of the body; she infiltrates my physical space and steals my voice and mannerisms.

"John. Jonathan! Jonathan Raynard Ellis?!" She is screaming at him, but his face is contorted and confused because the body still holds my posture and the eyes are still full of summer sunshine. The voice is filled with my lilting, southern sophistication, but the edge and harshness doesn't belong to me. I can't hijack any of it back from her. She has a hand around my throat and her foot in my stomach. *What the actual fuck is going on with this girl.*

Valery

"Look. Okay, I know you don't know what the fuck goin on. Why I dropped the charges against Harry… but I can't let him go down for somethin he ain't even mean to fuckin do." Vivian squirmed her slick ass away, but she ain't gettin control of this bitch back. Not yet. I got shit to say. John need to hear it from my fuckin mouth, not nobody else's. I see when he recognize me. His face look like a brick wall. All sharp and hard. He probably gonna try and kill me. *I wish the fuck he would.* That be the best thing for all of us. I need to get on with the shit I came here to say. *Maybe he will kill me, my stupid wishful thinkin.*

"He hurtin. I'm the reason he so hurt. I fucked him up and walked away like he ain't even matter. It's me. He went over the ledge. Cause of me. He ain't ever really want to fuck with Viv. He wondered… you know, bout

her, but he wanted me. He wanted to fuck me seven ways to Sunday. And John. Do you know how good it felt to know he wanted *me*? Not your stick-up-the-ass wife? And you *know* how I love fuckin?"

He so tall; and all that damn red hair. His skin look like mothafuckin buttamilk. Can you imagine what my dark skin look like rubbin against his creamy, buttamilk color? I didn't mean to do it, but I—I couldn't *not* do it." I fell for him. Hard and fast and oh gawd!" I take a deep breath cause just thinkin bout his dick make my pussy clench and get all kinda sloppy wet. John face look like thunder now. *Wonder how far I can push this possessive mothafucker?*

"… his dick is magic and so damn long and thick. I kept seein him after Vivian stopped. I made my appointments and we fucked from the time I got to his office til the hour was up. I love him and I *thought* he love me, too." I feel that snooty bitch, Vivian pacin' back and forth somewhere behind me. But she ain't come forward yet, probably tryin to hear everythin I got up to with Harry. *Nosey ass slut.*

I'm glad she can't see John. He look like the devil ridin his asshole. She calmin herself with that funny breathin shit that new shrink been teachin them. Might be workin. She ain't pacin no more. Need to finish this before she push my silly ass back.

"—but he didn't. He said I was a 'interestin subject to observe.' Somethin he could fuck, study, and write a goddamned Nobel-fuckin-Prize winnin book about. He used me! I gave him everythin and he fuckin used me, John!" My damn chest is on fire. I never knew hurt like this. I feel the wetness spill down my face. *What the fuck?! I'm fuckin cryin, again over this mothafucker.* I hope John beat my ass black and blue. I want it. I need all his anger. I snort the snot back up my nose and hurry the fuck up. Need to get to the shitty end.

"—I lied to the girls, to you, hell…I know, I was even lyin to my own damn stupid self."

Vivian on the Inside

My breath has stalled in my chest. Tears clog my throat as the reality of what Val says permeates my brain. I feel the light, tentative touch on my left hand telling me Vera has come out of her room. She smells like cotton candy and dirty bedsheets, but it's not unpleasant, just her. I know she's heard every word Valery poured down John's throat. He has yet to respond. Not a word or a breath. I'm able to see him now and nothing has changed with his features. I'm a little worried about him, but more for this body I share with the alters. They don't know John like I do. When he's calm and seemingly in control, I know he's the most terrifying

There is a preternatural element to his energy. It's like watching a beautiful, black jaguar as it watches its unsuspecting prey. Eyes sharp and focused; ears alert and listening for the exact moment the prey realizes they're already dead. His pink tongue glides over his incisors under his full top lip before coming out to taste his bottom lip and the air around him. I'm mesmerized as his dark, silky eyebrows draw together and his milk chocolate eyes darken to 60% cacao as they narrow. *Poor, stupid Valery doesn't notice any of this as she prattles on and on about how great Harry fucks her asshole.*

I'm stretching my eyes, hoping John can see me behind the crazy that is Valery and remember I'm inside this body, too. It's hard to concentrate on making myself known because Vera is droning on about something but the agitation in her voice finally forces me to pay attention to what she's saying. That, and the incessant pulling on my left thumb. *I fucking hate when she does that shit.* I turn my attention to the shapely, doe-eyed beauty

with big copper curls spilling over her wrinkled forehead and around her concave shoulders and listen.

"She telling the truth. She been having sex with that doctor behind yours and John's back." Not a question. No judgement, just a stating of facts as she understands them.

"She a low-down-dirty bitch—that one is, yeah?" I look over my left shoulder as Vera rubs her warm, moist thumb over the pulse point of my left wrist. Before I can answer her, my heart stops beating when I hear the six words spoken in John's normally smooth whiskey colored voice which is now rolling over a roughen graveled road when he speaks. *I didn't think whiskey was cured in barrels of gravel. Just goes to show what I know.*

"I will destroy you, Valery. Bond." Shit. Shit balls. Shit balls and fire on a fucking stick. *Bond. His word is his bond.*

I feel Valery stumble back into the house we all share. She's crying and grabbing at me, at Vera. I've never seen her so scared or distraught before. Her hands are at my back. Pushing me forward. She wants me to talk to John for her. *Not a fucking chance in hell is that happening.* Vera pulls away from her, leans over and kisses my left cheek before lumbering to her room.

I resume my position of control and look into eyes coated in sadness and betrayal. The tears he only ever lets me see, swim in their depths and before the first one falls I have him gathered in my left arm as he breaks. He's careful of me. Always aware of my needs, even as he takes what I offer to meet his own. I block the others out of my consciousness. This isn't for them. John doesn't want or need them to ever see him like this. Liquid boulders fall on my shoulder. One at a time. Each one heavier than the next, and I know he'd rather not let me see his pain but I'm humbled when he does.

After about thirty seconds or years, his phone buzzes. I caress his damp cheek as he sniffs away the remainder of his devotion for me to answer the call. I trudge into the kitchen to put the kettle on, reach over to my collection of herbal teas and pluck the Ayurveda anti-strain that just showed up in the mail yesterday. Then I make my way over to the bar to get the bottle of his most prized tequila. I know he's going to need it. Hell, I would take some myself, if I wasn't taking these pain meds.

I'm just finishing up his cup, when the slow crawl of awareness moves up my spine to announce his presence in the kitchen.

"Hey. This for me, lovely?" His voice sounds like cumulonimbus clouds just before severe weather breaks across the sky. Zemblanity weaves its ominous desolation from the threads of destruction Valery dumped onto my kitchen floor before fleeing the scene of her crime, and for the first time in a long time, I don't want to look into his eyes.

How can I not look? I know the moment I make contact; I'll be forced to discover the delicate truth I'd rather be ignorant of. I'm trapped in pools of melted chocolate with swirls of honey. Just below the golden hints of his vulnerability, black rage burns brighter than the sun and I think that maybe, this is the first time I'm seeing Jonathan Raynard Ellis in his true form. *He is Exquisite in his noble savagery*

"I'm listening."

"I don't even know where to start, lovely."

"Start with the phone call you were on when I came down stairs."

"Can we start somewhere else. Somewhere a little easier, maybe?"

"No. I'm listening."

"Pain in my ass, is what you are. Stop smiling, this is serious."

"I know. I want to take those dark flames from your eyes, but I am listening. And I'm sorry for being such a brat." The look on his face tells me he knows I'm not sorry. *I've been winding him up for a couple of days now. It's been ages since we've played. And based on his posture, he needs it, too.*

"Forgiven. Nobody knows where the fuck Kerrigan's *cheeky* ass is. He was released and now he's in the wind. I don't trust him not to come after that stupid bitch, Valery again." He places his empty cup on the island and raises his tired eyes to search my face for a reaction, but he doesn't find one. *No need to add to his worry.* The tightness there breaks my heart. *I hate when he's stressed.*

"Okay. I can see how that news caused you to lose your shit. Is Jessa coming over? Wait! You don't think he would go after her, do you?" I've placed my own cup down beside his. I wrap my hand around his forearm, which is crossed over his chest. I don't remember moving, but the need to be closer to him is undeniable.

"I sent Parker to pick her up. He has her and is on the way here. I was thinking the same thing when I made the arrangements to have her come over." He leans down and places a soft kiss on my mouth, silently reminding me to stop chewing on my bottom lip. His left hand reaches up to hold my cheek; I nuzzle into him, needing the comfort. As he continues

speaking, I turn to kiss the inside of his palm before stepping away from him to listen.

"Don't worry about this, Viv. Kerrigan will be found and *dealt* with." The words fall from his mouth like bullets and a shiver races over my body.

"Are you cold, lovely?" His hands lightly rubbing my arms in a way that's meant to provide warmth and arousal, but I'm not thinking with my sex right now. I'm genuinely concerned for and about Dr. Kerrigan and what he may or may not be planning.

"I'm not cold. I'm just—I don't know how the hell we got to this place. Valery crossed a line, John. She took advantage of our trust and abused our body. She placed us at risk, and I don't know if she was careful with it or not. I feel like—I've been, I don't know—raped." I leave the *again* off, but from the way his eyes flair and then turn downwards, I know he hears it all the same.

Tears fill my eyes, but I tilt my head back and look at the tin tiles on the ceiling until I feel them subside. "I'm so pissed at her. At her selfishness. Her recklessness. Her disregard for the rest of us and. And—just. Just… fuck her! Her flagrant disregard for you, John!" I hadn't noticed my fist pounding the marble island counter top until John placed his large hand over it to halt may actions and I feel his soft lips at my ear shushing me. Those tears decide they need to make an appearance, anyway.

"I've got you, lovely. Give me your rage. Use me as your gun, I'll wage war in your name and I promise you, every motherfucker who ever stood against you will be cut down." I feel so impotent in standing next to this giant of a man. He takes every part of me and loves me to wholeness. *God, this man. I love him completely; he's always giving me reasons to fall deeper for him.*

214

Just when my voice finds its way up my throat, the doorbell rings and John pulls away from me with one last squeeze to my left shoulder and a brief kiss to my forehead, and strides towards the front of the house.

I look at what I'm wearing and make my way upstairs to change into my oatmeal colored linen pants and soft, pink cotton tank top. I know Jessa's going to want to do some serious work after hearing everything from John.

***

"Mrs. Ellis, you are not doing well." Not a question. She somehow knows without me having to tell her the state of my whole self. I notice her bare feet as she enters the room we consecrated as a safe and sacred space when I first started seeing her.

"John is losing all of his mind down there. I don't want to talk about any of it. I don't want to hear any of whatever is going on with you and/or the alters. I don't want to know about how you and they are dealing with being shot." She moved further into the room. Lifting her hands and moving them in a clock wise circle as she glides through the space. I notice the white sage bundle in her right hand.

Once she makes her way over to the cedarwood candle burning on the low-lying table and passes the sage through its flames four times. Immediately, the room fills with the pungent aroma of burning negative energy.

"Pray, Vivian." She walks towards me and smudges the space around me as I recite the smudging prayer I've committed to memory.

"Negativity that invades my sacred space, I banish you away with the light of my grace. You have no hold or power here. For I stand and face you with no fear. Be gone forever, for this I will say. This is my sacred space and you will obey."

The prayer is whispered repetitively as Jessa continues to smudge the room and mumble her own prayers into the space. Once she's satisfied the room is free from negativity, she places the burning sage stick into the small soapstone bowl filled with black sea salt to let it burn out safely. I've already taken my seat on one of the floor pillows in the center of the room and watch passively as she walks over and drops into a lotus before resting her almond shaped, moss-green eyes on me. Her long, brown hair is braided in the traditional two braids hanging over her small shoulders. She is extremely proud of her Waccamaw Siouan heritage as confirmed by the intricate beadwork on her bracelets.

"Let's breathe, Vivian. Be sure to invite the ladies to join us. We need all alters on deck tonight. It's been a while and it's obvious we have much work to do." She closes her eyes and leaves me to call my body-mates into co-consciousness with me.

Vera, Lyric, Val. Can you guys come from your rooms and breathe with me. Jessa's here and we have a lot to talk about.

I know y'all don't want my ass to be part of this. You don't have to invite me, Viv. I know I fucked everythin up. I can't even say sorry, cause...

Val, if I didn't want to have you be a part of this, I would have blocked you. Please find a comfortable space and—s..."

"Shut-up, Valery. You've caused enough trouble, yeah? Sit your hot-behind down and do what you told, yeah?"

"I don't care what kinda bullshit I did, you not gonna talk to me like I'm some fuckin child. I'm only doin this cause I got shit I need to get off my chest. So, you can just fuck right off, Vera."

"Could maybe both of you sit down and start breathing. I don't know the last time we've all been together like this. Please, can we—just... just be still for a minute?"

"Hey Lyric. I missed you."

"I missed you, too Vivi."

"Alright, y'all miss everybody except my funky ass. I'm sittin down tryin to breathe. Shut the fuck up and let me do it."

"We just breathing, right now?

"Yeah. Jessa wants us to try and get on one accord. You all right, Lyric?"

"We can talk later, Vivi. I'm good, I think."

"All right, Viv? Who decided to come to the breathing party?" Jessa's monotone voice pulls each of us from our breathing and the alters look to me to answer her.

"We're all here, Jessa."

"Good. Welcome ladies. I hear we have a lot to talk about. Whom shall I start with...?" Valery pushes forward and speaks before Jessa has a chance to call who she wants to speak with, first.

"Jessa. I know I did a lot of shit I had no business doin, but you got to understand where I'm comin from. You know? It was just so... I can't really ex—"

"I'm pretty sure I didn't call your name Valery. But since you decided to take control of this session, how are you doing?" Jessa's tone gives nothin away. I don't know if she's annoyed, excited, bored, or plottin to slit my goddamned throat. *I hate that shit. I need to be able to read the fuckin people I gotta be around. How the hell else I'm gonna stay safe?*

"Do you really care how I'm doin, or you just tryin to get me to open and spill my fuckin guts and shit?" Valery doesn't give Jessa a chance to answer before she steamrolls on with her diatribe.

"I been better. Right now, I feel like the lowest piece a shit walkin the earth. You know what it feel like to let people down who claim they love

217

you? Better yet. You know what it feel like to be let down by the one person who say *he* love you and then you find out he just think you some kind of freak, sex, fucktoy with a lotta fucked-up issues?"

"No, Valery. I can't say I know what any of that feels like. Why don't you share with me and your co-alters?" Jessa makes me want to tear my locs out; one by one. How she can be so calm and indulgent with Val is beyond me. I'm seething and chomping at the bit to tear into her ass, and Jessa simply allows her to just be. I notice Valery has a section of her long, straight, ebony hair wrapped around her index finger. She's been twirling it the entire time she's been talking to Jessa. Her head is tilted to the right as her finger digs deeper into her thick fall of inky hair at the nape of her neck for more hair to twirl.

"I'm gone tell you exactly how this shit feel. It. I—It feel like somebody pullin all my fuckin skin off my body, but they doin it in the most god-awful way possible. You know? Fuck! Like they scaldin it off in the hottest damn bathwater and makin me just sit in there. Goddamn watchin all my skin ripple and burn from the inside out and then, it just peel away from my body. Floating on top of the bloodiest goddamned bathwater."

We are all silent. I don't think Vera or Lyric are breathing and I'm pretty sure even Jessa is stunned. Valery's quick breaths and muffled mumbles are the only sound in the room. *Fuck me, what are we supposed to do with that?*

After what may have only been a couple of seconds or minutes, Jessa clears her throat and gracefully stands from her perfect lotus and silently walks from the room. Leaving three women and a twelve-year-old girl confused and scared as hell. I want to say something. Anything, but honestly. What is there for me to say? I don't understand Valery's rage.

Her pain. I can't get my head around why she, out of all of us, feels as if she endured so much more than we have. I mean really… Vera was here first. She's the original and she's not a vengeful, sadistic bitch.

"Valery, I brought you some holy basil tea. Please drink it slowly, don't say a word until it's all gone. Allow the alters to experience this tea with you. Nod your head if you agree." I watch with passive eyes dancing in solar flares, as Valery accepts the steaming cup of tea from Jessa's small hands and nods her head.

This tea better have some top-notch marijuana steeped in with that holy basil, because I'm quite sure I'm getting ready to lose my shit in this room.

~33~

The tea flows over our pallet and because Valery's eyes are closed, I don't know what Jessa is doing. I hear her moving stuff around the room, and I know she's lighting more candles from the quick sulfuric burn in the air. I'm supposed to be concentrating on this tea and connecting with my alters, but I need to know what Jessa is planning to do about this clusterfuck of a situation that can only be caused by Valery.

"Are you all done with your tea?" I open my eyes to find all the alters looking at me like I have all three of their heads sitting on my shoulders. When I shoot a questioning look their way, Vera tilts her mop of curls towards the Jessa's voice and stretches her eyes into saucer plates before she hunches her shoulders and repeats the entire pantomime again. And that's when it hits me. If all four of us are in the house, there's no one in the driver's seat of the body. *It's not funny, but we're all in here smiling like hyenas after all the lions have gone and left a side of gazelle just for us.*

I blink my eyes and try to ignore the sharp pain in my frontal lobe as the scene before me sends electric shots of confusion skittering down my spine. *What the hell is John doing in here and why am I looking at the side of his favorite Clarks loafers?*

"Valery." The restrained hatred in his voice cracks the air around me.

"No, John. It's me, Viv. What are you doing here and why are you laying on the floor?" My voice sounds a million miles away.

"I'm not the one laying on the floor, lovely. You are." *At least his voice has lost its fury.* He stoops down beside me. When I look up now, I'm met with the sizable bulge seated between his spread thighs. I know he's not hard, just blessed. He places his hands on my left hip and that's when it registers, I'm lying on my right side. On my right shoulder. The shoulder

Kerrigan shot me in two weeks ago. The shoulder still being held together by stiches and glue. And just when I think it's not so bad, the pain hits me so hard I vomit all over my vintage braided rug.

***

When I wake up, it's not in my bed at my home. Peaking from under my lashes at the hulking figure sitting slumped in the small, plastic chair to the left of my hospital bed; my heart breaks for him. He looks shattered. I squeeze his hand before I croak out a greeting.

"Hi."

"Good morning, lovely. How're you feeling?"

"I'm worried about you. You look so tired, baby."

"I'm fine. Your stitches tore a little. Didn't lose much blood, but you went into shock. I suspect it had more to do with what happened before the fall then the pain from the fall itself."

"Always so perceptive. She's so angry, John. Full of piss and vinegar. I don't understand it. Why is she the angriest of all the alters when she endured the least amount of trauma?"

John sits so still and quiet, I think maybe he's dozed off until I feel his thumb brush across my knuckles and hear his deep inhale and slow, methodical exhale just before he opens his beautiful mouth to speak.

"She may have endured the least amount of trauma, but it was trauma dealt by the hand of someone who promised to love, cherish, and honor this body. I raped you, Vivian. You love me. You trust me. You willingly gave me your submission and I betrayed you. Vera was betrayed by her father when she was too young to understand what he was doing to her was wrong. And—V…" I interrupt him because I understand what he's getting at. I never thought about how we all came to be, just accepted that we were. I need to run through our beginnings for myself. In my own words

221

because if he tells me, I won't be able to truly grasp how interconnected we are.

I don't recognize my voice as I tell the rest of our origin story, at least as I understand it. "And that's when Lyric was born…at twelve, she was there to protect Vera from her father's illicit touch." My voice sounds a million miles away when I state how I came to be. "… and when he started using Lyric to pay for his drug habit, when he gave her to a man and told him he could use her for anal if he wanted to. As long as he was willing to give him more crack."

Tears flow in earnest down my cheeks. I never even considered how we all were the result of some traumatizing, cataclysmic event. Like a super nova exploding in the universe and creating a new galaxy. I bring my thoughts back to why I came into being and try to convey it to John.

"They couldn't do it, John. Lyric was only twelve and Vera had already checked out. I couldn't let him do that to a twelve-year-old. At least I was sixteen, not a baby." Tears flow from me but they're not for me or even Lyric. Poor Vera. Her body has never been her own. Never protected or loved by the woman who gave birth to her. Never loved or protected by the man who fathered her. Just a collection of holes to be fucked and abused.

"But you fell in love with me. I fought for and won your love, your trust, your fucking soul… and then I turned around and broke them. I broke every motherfucking part of you. The others were not born because of the acts of someone they loved, trusted, and willingly bent for; Valery was. Valery was born from *your* broken soul and I'm the depraved asshole who shattered it." I can only stare into the storm brewing in his eyes.

It's John's fault that Valery exists, but I can't hate him. I tried and it killed a precious part of me. I'll fight this with forgiveness. Unconditional forgiveness. For me, my sisters, and my husband.

~34~

There still is no word on where Dr. Kerrigan is, and the girls are off in their rooms licking their wounds. I have a large helicopter-husband hovering around me as I go about working from home and trying to get myself together. I'm ready to get back to my gallery but, of course, John would rather fuck the devil's asshole than let that happen. I doubt Kerrigan is going to come after me or Val again, but who the hell knows. What I do know is I'm losing my mind being stuck in this beautiful prison my home has become.

Jessa called to ask after me when I got home from the hospital and wanted to meet with me sooner rather than later, so she'll be over this evening to touch base with me. I can't say I'm looking forward to another round with her, but I'm not inviting any of the others to come out and play. I can't handle another meltdown from one or more of the girls. Although, I am a little worried about Lyric. She's been quiet and spending a lot of time alone. I know she goes to the library because John's been taking her. She knows she's not allowed to go out by herself. There's something going on with her, but she's not ready to tell me or anyone else, that I know of. *I'll ask John if she's said anything to him. He's like a big brother to her.*

Speaking of big brother, I hear my ever-watchful husband coming into my office. He's only been in here five or ten thousand times today.

Smile, Vivian. He love you and he's worried, yeah?

Yes, Vera. I know, but it doesn't make it any easier to be held captive in my own home.

Captive? Shush, Vivian. You sound like a little girl who got everything she wanted on her Christmas letter to Santa except a pony. Be happy that man love you so much, yeah?

I guess so. You're right, Vera. It's all in how you look at it. I guess. I've got to go... he just walked in. Check on Lyric for me, please.

Yeah. Okay. Be nice to John, yeah?

"Lovely.?" My pet name is not quite a question or a statement... a little of both. *What's up with him?*

"Hey you. How's it going?" Keeping my voice upbeat and easy. He seems a little tense.

"I hate to leave you here by yourself, but I have to go into the office. I've missed a lot of time; I know it's my company but—shit. Maybe I can handle it from..."

"John." I interrupt him as I get up from my teal, velvet Queen Ann chair and walk over to him.

"I'm fine to stay on my own. I'm just going to finish a few emails, and reports and then Jessa should be over for our follow-up session." I lift my left hand up to his shoulder and go up on my toes to place a gentle kiss on his supple lips. Before I can drop back to my feet and break the kiss, he encircles my waste with his protective right arm and holds me to him while his left hand goes to the back of my head to tangle in my locs as he takes control of the kiss. His hard dick presses against my belly and I'm pretty sure his zipper isn't going to be able to hold that monster in much longer.

"Fuck, Vivian." How long has it been since I've been inside you?" His words are laced with dark, depraved intent and the muscles in my cleft clench painfully. I'm already dripping into the cotton of my silk panties. *Shit! It's been too long, that's for damn sure.*

"Too long." Apparently, all the blood has rushed from my brain to pound behind my clit, which is pulsing like some kind of tantric drum being played by the most accomplished clit drummer in the histories of clit

drummers. I can't even think beyond the need to have John slice through my wet lips and plunge deeper into my spasming core.

"Have to be inside you, now. Are you... can we fuck, lovely?" *Can we fuck? Will a hooker sweat in church on Sunday morning?*

I immediately fall to my knees; eyes drop to my lap where my left hand is resting palm up. I need to be dominated. Make me feel safe. The room is quiet. I don't even hear his, or my breath. My blood is singing in my veins with anticipation and desire. I should be embarrassed at the state of my panties, but I can't find it within me to care about how wet they are. I feel his hand rub down the back of my head a moment before his warm, cinnamon breath blows on my right ear and kisses my cheek.

"Are you offering your submission, lovely?" His volcanized voice drives a shiver down my spine that's so delicious I'm pretty sure it causes a little micro-orgasm to erupt in my core. I don't answer him. I don't have to. He knows what this position means.

"Answer me, Vivian." I have a mind to be a brat just to see if he'll punish me. I miss the release the flogger or belt or cane gives me.

"Don't fucking push me, lovely. It's been too long and I'm on edge. I don't want to hurt you... well, I do, but not beyond what you can give me considering your injury. Now answer me right fucking now." Although his voice is still low and smoky, he may as well have screamed the words kissed into my ear.

"Yes, Sir. I am offering you my submission. If it would please you."

"It does please me, lovely. On your feet, eyes remain down." I rise from the floor like the Phoenix he makes me. My heart is rushing blood throughout my body at such a fast rate, I'm surprised I haven't passed out. I faintly hear John tell me what a beautiful and obedient girl I am. I feel the

warmth of his approval wash over me, but I can't focus on his words. I'm too keyed up.

"Follow me."

"Yes, Sir."

***

John is pulling my hair up in a high pony while standing behind me. We're standing in the middle of our playroom. My breathing has evened out and a sense of peace and rightness has settled about my shoulders like the mantle of a queen. He's still hard and I'm still dripping my arousal. So much so, my inner thighs are slick with it. I know he smells me, because I smell myself. *Is it sick how much the smell of my silky arousal turns me on?*

"I'm not going to be rough with you, Viv. But I know you need something and as your Dom, I want to give that to you. Don't try to top from the bottom. Do you understand?"

"Yes, Sir."

"Good girl. I'm going to undress you. Tell me if anything "hurts in a way we don't intend for it to."

"Yes, Sir." His nimble fingers unbutton my white oxford shirt. The syncopated rhythm of some Tibetan chant is playing almost soundlessly through the surround sound. He removes my bra and folds it as neatly as he did my shirt, placing both on the vintage dresser painted fifty shades of blue. The richest of the shades is the one gracing the walls of the playroom. Made all the more decadent dressed in admiral blue crushed velvet wallpaper. Makes sense John would choose this color as the dominant one for his playroom; he is always in full command of himself, the space, and me.

"Step out of your pants and panties. Left then right foot. Hold on to me for stability." I want to disobey him but I know he would end this. He's apprehensive, but the heaviness in his cock tells me he needs this as much, if not more than me. I do as he commands me and am rewarded with a soft, slow kiss on my plump wet lips.

"This is the sweetest, most generous pussy I've ever had the privilege of knowing. You're weeping for me, aren't you little pussy? And fuck me; I can't wait until jughead drowns in your salty, sweet tears." My knees are going to give out if he keeps talking to my sex like this. His warm breath is blowing over my wet flesh making it weep even more. *Please touch me, John. A finger. Your tongue. Fuck, I'll settle for the tip of your nose.*

"Spread." I don't say a word. I'm listening and trying not to cringe. Obscene sounds of wet, sticky flesh pulling away from itself add to the sexual soundtrack being played through the speakers. The moment my legs are as wide as possible, I watch an orgulous drop of arousal hit the African blue slate tiles. I stop breathing as I watch John bend forward, snake out his tongue, and take a lazy, filthy lick of the floor. The look on his face when he swallows that drop of my wetness makes everything below my belly clench. Hard. *Oh, my fucking God. He did not just do that.*

"I don't have time, nor do I have the patience to set a scene for us. It's been too fucking long, lovely. I need to be inside you. I'm going to put you on the cross. We'll use the waist and ankle bondages. I'll put your left arm up, as well. I'll start by eating your sloppy, wet pussy first, make you come on my face. Then, I'll fold your sexy ass in half and fuck you deep and hard. Go to the cross and wait for me." I don't hesitate. A faucet of arousal flows between my legs, I'm so embarrassingly wet.

It sounds like I'm walking on wet sponges with every step I take. Once I reach the cross, I turn around in time to see a naked-as-fuck John

prowling towards me. My heartrate kicks up and I hope I don't have a heart attack before he fucks me because holy shit, he's absolutely feral. My mouth waters as drops of pre-cum leak from the broad tip of his fully erect dick. *Fuck, I wish I could crawl on the floor and lick every drop of it up.*

~35~

I'm shackled and helpless. My clit is thumping so hard and fast I'm pretty sure I could come all by myself. He better not try any of this not coming until he says so bullshit. I look down at him on his knees in front of me looking like the best kind of sin. I'm so fucking glad he's my god and he'll absolve me of each transgression I commit.

"Close your eyes, lovely. I don't want to take the time to blindfold you. You come when I say you can. You understand?" *I fucking knew he was going to pull this shit.* I'm slow to answer him because I don't think I'll be able to hold off my orgasm. The spasms are already starting deep in my core from his hot breath blowing over my sensitive flesh.

"Answer me, lovely. I see you're almost there already, but you better not fucking come or I'll spank your pussy raw." *Well shit, that threat isn't going to help me not come.* I'm breathing deeply through my nose and panting from my mouth like a bitch in heat. I'm coming and I'm trying to stop it from happening, but I can't.

He's blowing on me, in attempt to bring me under control, but I can't stop this freight train of release barreling down the tracks of my spine. My limbs and torso are a collection of quaking trembles. My core is pulsating and fluttering around nothing except the idea of being filled by John's beautiful dick.

"I—I can't stop i… it. John!" I realize I'm screaming and crying, but there is nothing I can do about it at this moment. Nothing I want to do about it.

"I've got you, lovely. I'll always give you what you need. But, you better fucking wait for me to slide into your tight, wet cunt before you come." John stands up like a mountain pushing its way through the soil to get to the sun. My legs are hoisted up on his chest and over his shoulders at

the same time, his angry cock slams into my soaked cleft just as the first brutal wave of my orgasm washes over me. He fucks me through the first one and into another one before he finally slows his strokes down and gently wraps my legs around his waist and gives me the slow, measured strokes known to make my back arch to the point of breaking . I'm a mass of noodles and jelly. Boneless and blissed out. My head rests on his shoulders and he's careful of my right arm as he takes his pleasure from my body.

After what feels like hours, his rhythm faulters and his dick gets even harder—bigger, and longer, and so much deeper—and then heat sears my womb and I know. I just know. John just planted our baby inside of me. *Gayle, please guide your sister and help her stay. Thank you, sweetie.*

Life has pretty much returned to normal, except no one has heard from Valery or Kerrigan in the past five weeks. And since I'm still here and so are the others, for that matter, we know she's not with him. We still have security detail, but everything seems to be getting back to the pre-shooting days. Lyric is acting stranger than usual and when I asked her what's going on with her, she just evades the question.

I'm sitting in the doctor's office waiting to be seen. I didn't tell John that I was coming in to have a test performed, I wanted to be sure before I tell him what I suspect will be good news. I'm early, so I have time to think about the conversation Lyric and I had a couple of nights ago.

Vivi? Can I talk to you for a minute. Just us, I don't want anybody else to hear this. Not yet, anyway. Can you come to my room?

The Internal House

Of course, Lyric. What's going on, you seem worried. I follow her into her room and notice the posters are gone from the wall and have been replaced with macabre black and white photos of gravestones. Her walls are no longer the pale pink it's been forever, she's gone with a pristine white with one black accent wall behind her bed. What the fuck is going on with my little Lyric?

I see you've done some redecorating in here. It's… different. Does this new style have anything to do with what you want to talk about?

Yeah. Kinda. Um. Viv, how much do you know about your mother—or… uh, Vera's mom? Our mom? The woman who gave birth to this body?

I only know what you and Vera have been able to tell us; why?

I have questions about her. I mean, what kind of woman would have a baby and then leave her with a monster and not care what happens to it? You know?

I guess, Lyric. But, I mean—why're you so interested in finding out about this woman?

Because. I think she's the key to understanding how we all got here. I don't know what I'm looking for, but I'll know when I find it. Something is leading me to find out about our mother. It's just a feeling I have. We need to know who she is and where she went when she left us.

I'm pretty sure none of the other alters are thinking about this. But, then again, I don't know what the hell Valery is thinking about. Have you seen her?

No, and I don't want to see her. With her stupid self. She so selfish and reckless. We all share this one body and she doesn't stop to think about any of us. Just her own selfish ass.

Whoa, I'm sorry I brought her up. Tell me more about your thoughts on our mother.

I think she's connected to John in some way.

What?!

Have you ever looked at that picture of Violet in his office? Every time I go in there, my feet pull me over to that shelf. There's something about her face. Her eyes. She look so familiar. I know it don't make sense. Like none at all, but I can't shake this feeling.

What feeling?

I think Violet is our mother. Was. Was our mother.

You're right, that makes absolutely no sense. How would she be our mother. And what was she doing with John. Lyric, I think you may be looking for something that shouldn't be found.

No! I'm not, Vivian. Violet is our mother. I know she is; I just can't figure out how to prove it. But I will.

Lyric be careful. A lot has happened in the last few months. You need to spend some time with Jessa. The stress and pressure may be getting to you.

I'm not cracking up. I'm a damn alter. I have one purpose, protect Vera. I know my job, do you remember what your job is, Vivian? Protect me so that I can protect Vera. Remember?

No, I'm not a protector. I'm Vivian Ellis. Wife, art curator, and gallery owner. There is no one to protect Vera or you from, anymore. I'm free to live my life and I suggest you do the same.

***

"Mrs. Ellis, we're ready for you." The nurse's nasally voice pulls me from my reverie. I blink my eyes a few times to clear my mind and stand to follow her into the back. I watch as her curly, black pony tail swings from side to side as she walks. Her peaches and cream skin is such a contrast to her dark hair, but it really works for her. She looks like the girl next door.

"Good morning, how are you doing?" I greet the nurse as she points to the scale on the wall between two examining rooms.

"Good. I can't complain. Wouldn't do any good if I did anyway." She laughs as she moves the masses back and forth until everything balances out.

"158 pounds. You can step down, now. Follow me." I step off the scale and grab the braided handles of my brown and black Fendi handbag from the counter. I kneel down to collect my shoes, my fingers graze the textured brown and black weave of my Chanel pump; and that's when John's Lucca oxfords come into my line of vision. *Fuck! I knew I wouldn't be able to do this without him finding out.*

I accept his proffered hand and stand gracefully to my full height, the shoes dangling from the index and middle fingers of my right hand. Once

John's hand is firmly seated at the small of my back, he lowers his mouth to my left ear and whispers,

"When the fuck were you planning on informing me of your suspicion, Vivian?" He places a soft kiss to my cheek, but the smile he flashes does nothing to soften the hardness. It's barely enough to soften the lines around his sinful lips. I'm having a hard time controlling my breath, but I manage to take a couple of deep inhalations before I attempt to answer him and move towards the nurse at the end of the hall.

Before I make one step, his hand falls to my hip and tightens. Keeping me in place while seemingly steadying me.

"John, can we have this discussion later. I wanted to surprise you if the news is positive." The tension bleeds from his body as he guides me forward.

"Thank you." I mumble just before we get to the door. The nurse gives me a cup, a paper gown, and a sheet as she shows me to the en suite to get changed and provide a urine sample. I'm stepping into the bathroom when I hear her direct John to take a seat and hold my purse and shoes.

While changing, there is a not-so-subtle nudge in the center of my forehead. *This bitch wants to make an appearance now?* I continue to change as I listen to what she's saying. Tears are pouring from her eyes and she looks as on edge as I've ever seen her. When she gets to the last bit of her confession, I drop my folded clothes and the sheet I had covering my nakedness. I can't move. I can't breathe. Black dots encroch from the sides. There's nothing I can do to stop this from happening. With the last bit of strength, I call out for John. I don't know if his name makes it past my dry mouth, but I've already hit the floor by the time I thought to say it.

~37~

The shrill voice in my head is a memory on loop. My body feels weighed down by years of earth. And still, her words run around and over themselves as I try to break through the fog clouding my mind like altocumulus opacus blocking out the sun on a storming day. *Shut the hell up, Valery. Just shut up*! But she doesn't. The words pound against my skull making it impossible to hear my own thoughts.

***

I'm tired of bowin down to all this bullshit psychobabble. We ain't ever gonna be what you... you stuck-up bitch, want us to be. That's why I'm gonna cut your black ass. You feel this blade against your wrist, you fuckin slutpig? I'm gonna cut you, so nobody gonna be able to save your stupid, all-knowin, cock-blockin ass. Not even captain wonder-dick. Right when you bout to find out you for real pregnant. Bleed bitch. This baby probably belong to Harry. I never made him wear no rubber. He fucked me raw.

***

"She's waking up! Her eyes... their blinking open. Get her damned doctor, now!" John's voice is coming from a tunnel. *Why is he so far away?* I feel his fingers on my upper arm, I think those are his fingers. *What the hell happened?*

"Lovely? Hey, Vivian? It's me, John. I'm here. The nurse went to get the doctor. you're going to be all right. I've got you. I've got you." He's cooing these words in my ear as he peppers my face with butterfly kisses. I have no idea what happened, and I refuse to believe Valery actually slit my wrist long-ways, instead of across like most people would.

"Well, hello. Can you open your eyes for me? The lights are dim and shouldn't cause you too much discomfort." I peel my lids back and wince as the low lights pierce my irises. Blinking rapidly to get them to adjust, I

succeed this time in opening both of them. The first face they land on is John's. He looks like someone took a bag of worry and nickels and beat him about the face. I slide my eyes from his and focus on the petite woman standing to the right of my bed. She doesn't look as concerned, but there are definitely some creases in her small forehead.

"How—H…" I cough and clear my throat. John places a bendy straw between my dry lips and only allows me a couple of sips before he pulls it away. I lick my lips before asking the doctor what happened.

"What day is it, dear?"

"Friday, the 5th of October."

"Good. You've been out for about six hours. What's the last thing you remember?"

"I was going into the en suite to change into the paper gown for my exam. I had just peed in the cup and set it in the window, when I felt my alter… I don't know if my husband told you, but I—I" She cuts me off to let me know she's aware of my diagnosis. I continue.

"So, yeah. I felt Valery, one of the more volatile alters pushing for dominance over the body. I didn't want to give it to her, but she just… wrenched it away from me." The sting behind my eyes have nothing to do with the light. I don't want to cry, but I hate being so vulnerable to the whims of my alters.

"Thank you. Do you remember anything else after Valery took over? Were you still conscious?"

"Um. Not really. I heard her talking—inside my head, but I could see or feel what she was doing."

"Okay, so she locked you out of everything except her voice? Where were the others?"

236

"I don't know. It felt like I was very much alone in the house. Um…in my mind"

"You didn't feel either of the other alters then, but are you able to feel them or Valery now?"

I'm right here with you, Vivian. I been walking all over the house, walking grooves in the floor, yeah? Been waiting for you to open them tiger eyes back up, yeah?

Me, too. Vivi. I'm here. I ain't been pacing back and forth like a crazy person, but I been sitting and talking to you the whole time. We don't know where Valery slunk off to, but I promise you if she show her skanky ass up in this house again…I'll kick her ass myself.

No Lyric stay away from her. She's dangerous. And thank you, both. I love you girls so much. Are you all right? Did she come for you guys, too?

"Yes, I'm in touch with Vera and Lyric. They are both doing fine and were really worried about me. Valery isn't in the house, anywhere." I answer her ten minutes after she asked the question. I'm sure John explained to her what was happening. When I chance a look at her, she looks absolutely fascinated and pleased. *Who the hell is this woman?*

"John…um, did anyone confirm what I went to the doctor to have confirmed?" His smile is the sun. It's so bright and beautiful and that's how I know we're pregnant. And this time, our child will be healthy and whole. *Gayle be sure to watch over your sister until it's time for her to be born. Mommy loves you.* I beam a smile in John's direction and feel the faintest touch of cool wind blow across my left cheek. I smile even more. *Gayle.*

"We did confirm your pregnancy, dear. You are such a unique and wonderful creature. I'm Dr. Khara Orinda, and I am so very excited to meet you." She steps closer to me and gently places her right hand over my

237

forehead and then lifts it, only to bring one finger back to draw what feels like a curved line and then a squiggly one beside it. She then places her palm flat against my forehead again and whispers something. I can only make out a few of the words, but something amazing happens as she continues to whisper. A sense of peace falls over me like a cooling mist on a summer day. My mind is calm. I feel a lightness in my soul. My worry and anger fade and I'm filled with gratitude and a sense of rightness.

"How do you feel now, Vivian?" Her almost smile is knowing and innocent at the same time. I look at John and he is wearing a similar smile to hers. When I look back at her, I can't even find a space in my head to worry or stress.

"I am grateful for still being here. I'm happy most of my alters are all right. I'm excited to know John and I are going to be parents, again." I don't have any words to voice the questions running through my mind, but I know she sees them darting around my face and eyes. She's still smiling. I feel like someone shot me up with a hit of the feelgood drugs. Like I popped something really good before she put her hands on me.

"Jonathan. Thank you for reaching out to me. Jessa has done a great job preparing her for this next step and she is ready to embrace the next phase of her treatment." My eyes find John's and he looks just as pleased and happy as Dr. Orinda, but I'm feeling confused and happy and weird as fuck.

"I know, Khara. I told you she was spectacular and would be amazing to work with."

"Okay. Does someone want to tell me what is going on, please?" I can't even find the fire to highlight my concerns. I would like to feel afraid, mistrustful, even angry... but whatever hoodoo she did on me leaves me with this stupid sense of joy. *And did he just call her Khara? What the...?*

38

"Lovely, I've been working with Dr. Orinda since I took you from that facility in Seattle."

"Oh, so it's Dr. Orinda now? Why didn't you tell me about this?"

"Vivian. Don't be like that. I couldn't tell you. It's part of the process. I wanted the best for you, and that treatment center wanted to medicate you. To turn you into a goddamned zombie. When I understood what was going on with you, I immediately put all my efforts and resources towards finding the best professional help I could find for you. Khara is the best. She's a Harvard educated Jungian psychiatrist who has created a wholistic approach to treating mental disturbances. Her specialty is Dissociative Identity Disorder."

"Okay. I get that and thank you for doing this for me. But why all the secrecy?" I bobble my head back and forth between the two of them as I wait for an answer. It's Dr. Orinda who speaks up. Her small, pinched mouth seems too inconsequential to spew such heavy language. I'm not sure of her nationality, but she's not White or Black or Asian. *Maybe Middle Eastern?*

"It's best if you are not aware you're receiving therapy. John was working in tandem with me and my practitioners during the months after bringing you home. He did exactly what he was advised to do, introducing you to yourself as a part of a whole.

"The loss of your baby, Gayle, was unexpected and I'm so sorry it happened. We were unsure how such a huge setback would affect your treatment and then there was John's well-being to consider, also."

My audible surprise at the mention of my daughter's name catches the eye of my husband. I know he can read my thoughts as they pass through my eyes and then the guilt that clouds them over like an overcast day.

Before I'm able to stop myself, words are tumbling from my mouth like vomit.

"I didn't think John cared enough about her life or her death to know what I'd named her. He's never said anything about her or the fact we lost her...I'm not sure how I feel about hearing her name from your mouth when I've never even heard it from his."

The look on his face says a million and one things and none of them are what I need to hear. *He spoke our daughter's name to her, a woman who is a stranger to me.*

I turn my eyes away from his and address Dr. Orinda. "Thank you. Yes, it was devastating but it was also what made me take control of my own healing or at least I thought I was taking control of it. I decided after dealing with my daughter's death, I would become as healthy and whole as possible. I knew I needed to do that if I wanted to have the chance to be a mother to a living child."

John's strong hand wraps around my smaller, shaking one and he squeezes it before rubbing his thumb over my knuckles. I look into his eyes and for the first time since last December, I see it. The profound hurt of loss. Those deep chocolate pools almost drown me in their melancholy. But then his easy smile pulls me out and anchors me to here and now.

"Wait, does Jessa work with you?"

"Yes. Of course, she does. She's my best pupil. My progeny. She's my *daughter.*" The pride in her voice is only trumped by the pride shining from her eyes as she drops that little nugget.

***

I'm resting comfortably in my bed at home and John is once again the doting husband. I'm so over all of this. I can't get Valery to come out and John will not leave me alone. The others have been out, even Vera took

over for a while to give me a break from John's ever watchful eye. The only one who refuses to make an appearance is Valery. I don't know if I really want to see her or if I simply want to reassure myself she's not plotting to destroy our body, again.

It's been a few days since her little murder/suicide attempt. In that time, Harry Kerrigan's body was found swinging from his ceiling rafters. He didn't leave a note, but the police are calling his death a suicide and closing the case. I don't have the energy to be concerned about it, but somewhere in the back of my soul; I know his death was not a suicide. What I don't know is who's responsible for it and why they would go that route.

I'm just about to get up and go down to the kitchen when I hear a loud crash coming from John's office. I jump up and hit the stairs, almost falling on my ass on the way down. When I step through the French doors, John is standing in the middle of his office surrounded by books, papers, his computer, and what looks like the bottle of Macallan I gave him for his birthday. *What the hell is going on in here?*

"Vivian why are you out of bed. I told you if you needed something to let me know and I'd get it for you." He's not really looking at me as much as he's looking in my general direction. I'm not sure what's got him so crazy; based on the look on his thunderous face, I'm not sure I want to know. But like a moth to the flame, I move further into his space and a heaviness envelopes me the closer I get to him.

"I was coming to get a snack. Tired of staying up in our room. I really am feeling fine. I didn't lose that much blood and anyway. I'm going batshit just sitting around. But…" My voice trails off as my eyes wander around his destroyed office before I continue with my question.

"…what the hell are you doing down here?"

"I was looking for an important document and I can't find it anywhere. I know where I left it and now—" I interrupt him with an incredulous lift of my arched brow. He can't even finish whatever he was saying. He finally turns my way and the desperation riding the small creases around his eyes cause my breath to dump from my lungs; landing at his feet.

"What is it, John?"

"I don't want to bother you with this shit. You've been through enough. I'll handle it, lovely. What do you want to eat?"

"No. You don't get to shut me out. I'm your wife. Your partner. Your sub. Now, tell me what's going on."

"Viv, you have enough to deal with. Come on, let me get you something to eat and then we'll—"

"Dammit, John! I'm not so fragile that I can't be here for you. I'm not broken! I may have several fucking people living in my head, but I'm not broken and whatever the hell is going on with you is going on with me, too. Now." I have to take a breath to calm myself down before I continue.

"Tell me what it is and we will figure out how to deal with it. Together."

His warmth wraps around my body and I feel him breathe me in. He dips his face into the crook of my neck and gets lost in my coconut and honey scented locs. I feel him break and I hold him as best I can while he gives his weighted vulnerability to me. I love him as he surrenders this burden to us. To the commitment we've made to each other. Nothing feels more substantial than us in this moment.

"I love you. So goddamned much, lovely. I'd do anything for your happiness. For your peace of mind. Your safety is everything to me. You know that, right?" My heartrate kicks up as his words drip into my ear and

take up residency in my mind. *John, what have you done?* As if he can read my mind, his next words answer my unspoken question.

"I needed to know Kerrigan wouldn't come after you again. He was in the wind and I didn't know where he was. I couldn't find him and none of my guys knew where he was, either." He pauses for a moment and pins me to the spot I'm standing in before he continues.

"I called in a couple of favors from one of my more bellicose clients. I told him I didn't need to know, I just needed you safe."

"Oh god, John. What are you saying? You know what happened with Dr. Kerrigan, don't you?"

"A few days before the authorities found Kerrigan in his apartment, I received a small envelope with a…um, a chunk of red hair with part of the scalp attached and a note card with four words on it. *'She's safe. We're good.'* I didn't want to know, Viv. I tucked the note away after securing the biological evidence."

"Oh. my fucking god! John, who the hell are you working with. What kind of clients do you have who would send you a piece of a man's scalp and call it *good*? What did you do for him that warranted this type of repayment?!" I'm hysterical and I can't find it within me to calm down. John is looking at me like he's never seen me before and I'm sure my look mirrors his own. We're standing in the middle of his destroyed office and he's just shared with me he works with fucking criminals and he put a hit out on my former psychologist. *What the actual hell?!*

39

There are no words in this language, or any of the other languages I speak, to adequately describe what's going through my head in this moment. I'm looking at my husband. The man I've sworn the rest of my life to love, honor, cherish and obey. Right now, I'm one hundred percent sure I don't know anything about who Jonathan Raynard Ellis is. I'm trying not to freak out, not to retreat into myself and let one of the others deal with this shit but fuck me sideways while walking me to be baptized in the lake of fire and brimstone.

"Vivian, I know what you're thinking. And you can't be more wrong than you are in this moment. I. Did. Not. Put. A. Hit out on Kerrigan. If I wanted the fucker dead, I'd have done it myself." He punctuated his words with slow, measured steps towards me. Making me aware of how far away from him I'd retreated. He stops just in front of me. His long, powerful arms hanging loosely at his sides, hands and fingers relaxed. Nothing about his posture is threatening or conveys how truly dangerous he is. But I know enough to know how tightly he's leashing himself as he stands before me. Chaotic energy vibrating through and bouncing off him collides with my own erratic waves; causing microscopic supernovas to explode in the universe we create when we're in each other's presence. *And forgive me, but when he's like this… my panties don't stand a chance in hell of staying dry.*

"Well?" He's waiting for me to say something. To refute his assessment of the thoughts floating through my head. But he already knows. Because he *knows* me.

"Well, John. I kinda thought… yeah, maybe if you know the kind of people who could rip out chunks of scalp from someone's head, and then that someone ends up dead…Yeah, babe. I was thinking you put a *hit* out

on my former therapist." An irreverent giggle bubbles up my throat before I can shut it down. It spills from my full lips and slithers across the floor. *I hope it dies a fast death, but no.*

The giggle crawls up John's wool trouser covered legs and tickles his ribcage and soon we're both laughing like two insane, therapist-killing, lunatics. Until we're not. Until the room is shrouded in a severe silence of acknowledgment that leaves spiders crawling all over our skin. Laying poisonous eggs in our eyes to run like vicious venom as the silence wraps around our throats.

"I didn't order a hit on him. I've only ever killed one person in my life. That motherfucker deserved to die, and I wish every goddamned day for the chance to kill that piece of white-trash cocksucker again. But, I didn't want Kerrigan dead. I was assured by my former client he was alive when they left him at his place." I know John wouldn't lie about this, but why is he so torn up about finding the note if he knows he didn't have anything to do with Kerrigan's death.

"That note, the paper it's written on, has Kerrigan's DNA on it. I know I should have destroyed it, but—I"

"You wanted to keep a *trophy*? Something saying you did what you promised me you'd always do. Protect and take care of me." I watched his face soften and my love for this complicated man doubled and tripled on itself. Multiplying into infinity. *He's as crazy as I am, but oh, how I love him.*

"I knew you'd understand. Because you understand me. Lovely. I didn't want him dead, but someone did because from what my former client told me." He pauses and takes a shuddering breath, letting go of the remnants of lunacy still clinging to him like spiderwebs.

"Kerrigan was a sick fuck who had closets full of videos of him with his clients. Viv. The shit Valery did… with, and for this motherfucker. If I ever see that nasty, depraved, bitch again! I'm going to fucking kill her." His eyes slam down in an effort to reign in his vitriol.

He realizes what he said, and a darkness falls over his handsome face. Killing Valery meant killing all of us. Watching Valery with Kerrigan was watching all of us with him. *Poor John. Poor fucked-up John. Fell in love with a woman who proved to be more broken than he is.*

"John? What exactly are you looking for?"

"I found the envelope with the note in it, I've already burned everything…including the piece of scalp and hair. It stank like rotten pig being barbequed. Almost lost my stomach. But what I can't find is the document written in the hand of Kerrigan admitting to being a fucking perverted predator who took advantage of every client he ever worked with. That's what I wanted from him. I didn't want him dead. I wanted to ruin him and get justice for all of his victims. Even Valery, with her silly ass."

He links his hands behind his head and rests them at the base of his neck. Putting his well-defined biceps on display for me to ogle before he continues with what he was saying. Damn, these pregnancy hormones. *I'm so horny. All I can think about is John giving me what only he can give.*

"Anyway. I had the document in a plain folder, sitting on my desk. It was delivered yesterday, along with all the records he had from his sessions with you and all the recordings from his time with that stupid cunt, Valery."

My hackles came up. He has to know he's talking about all of us when he speaks so harshly about Valery. She's just another aspect of Vera. Just like Lyric. Just like *me*. I knew the exact moment he realized he'd gone too

far with the name calling. His eyes grew slightly in size and his pupils dilated as if he is preparing for a fight or to run away. The tight expression riding the Pharaoh-like lines of his face, is all the contrition I need. I pardon him of his guilt with a slight tilt of my head and an audible release of the breath I was holding.

"I'm sorry, lovely. I know Valery is a part of a whole and that makes her a part of you, but to me. To me, you guys are four different people, who happen to share one body." *Well, that's different from his previous view of my situation. When did he start looking at us that way?*

"I know it's how you see us, but we are more than that. Yes, we all have our own shit and we honestly look nothing alike and our personalities are a different as yours and mine, but we are not four different people. We're one person with four different approaches to living and coping with life."

"Goddamn! Lovely, I don't ever think I've heard DID spoken of in such a cohesive way. I know that's not the work of Jessa because she's from her mother's school of thought. You know, each personality has a right to live their own life with respect to the whole."

"I swear, you sound just like her. Yeah, she's on her democratic approach to living with the alters, but according to our collective journal, Seeking Wonderland; we all decided we're more of an evolution than anything else. And we take what we need from our therapist and from our environment and work together to create something... someone. Altogether new."

"Seeking Wonderland, huh? What is this, a real journal or something you guys have in your *house*?"

"It's real. We keep it in my office... anything we put in there is just for us. No one else is allowed to see the contents—not even your sexy ass."

My heart thumps once. Twice. And then it picks up speed like a thoroughbred, galloping through open grasslands. Holy hell, I know where the document is. Vera. Not able to protect herself, but still trying to protect her *big brother*... I love her, but oh my. She and John have the strangest relationship.

"Why are you smiling like you have a secret?"

"Because I do have a secret. Give me a sec, I'll be right back. Don't follow me, John. I'm going to seek the wisdom of Wonderland." I flounce out the double French doors of his office and push the mahogany antique door to my office open before shutting and locking it. Waltzing over to the large French provincial inspired credenza on the farthest wall from the door, I use the key in the secret hiding place to open the Wonderland drawer. Pulling out the large collection of binders, journals, and notebooks, I find Vera's section and sure enough—the plane folder with a hand-written document, the same one John just tore his office up trying to find.

Vera/Vivian

Vera, come out here, please.

Don't call me out like I'm some child, Vivian. I'm almost as old as you are, yeah?

Yeah, you're only four years younger than me. Why did you take this from John's office, Vera?

I didn't want nothing happening to him because he had that paper in his office. What if somebody found it. What if Valery found it and then took it to the police, yeah?

I know you were trying to protect him, and that's really sweet of you, but he's losing his mind trying to find it. I'm not taking it back to him.

Vivian... don't make me take it back to him. Just tell him Lyric took it or you can tell him I took it—but...

No, Vera! You can't keep doing shit and not taking responsibility for it. This is not what we discussed with Jessa. If you do something, then you are responsible for the fall out. You did this thing...now you have to go tell John why you did it.

You'll come with me, yeah?

Of course, I'll be with you. But it's your show. I'm just going to be in the background. I'm not even driving our body, your show—your drive.

I don't think I like you very much, Vivian, yeah?

I'm all right with that, as long as you take responsibility for your actions. Let's go.

40

I watch from behind Vera's smoky topaz colored gaze as she ambles into John's office. It's hard to believe she's been a part of my or I've been a part of her my entire life and I never knew she existed. The way she moves this body is nothing like the way I move in it. Vera walks around herself, like the size of her thighs and hips require her to make extra effort to take steps. It's the oddest sensation. She never seems to know what to do with her hands. They move independently of each other and the rest of her body. I wonder if John will notice the change.

Vera

"Vivian…urm, Vera?" He notice as soon as I walk into the room. I guess he know when the woman he love leave and the woman he kind to is standing in front of him, yeah?

"It's me, John. Vivian said I had to come and talk with you, yeah?"

"All right. What's on your mind, Vera?" Lord, I hope he don't see my cheeks heating up. He so handsome and so nice. Only man I feel comfortable with. He the only one.

"I—John, you know I don't want any bad things to happen to you, yeah?

"I know that, yes." I love when he smile like that. It make me think of playing on the playground with my friend, Billy. Before my mama left and my daddy… I'm not gone think about that.

"Okay. So. I know what happen with that nasty old doctor. The one Valery was having relations with. Doing all sorts of really sick stuff with, yeah?" I can't bring myself to look up into his eyes. I wish I could stay still and stand tall like Viv, but I just can't do it. He never make me look at him or feel bad about being so weird.

"I know you do. Vera… where is Viv?"

"Uh. She in here with me, but she said she was going to be in the background and not even in control of the body. She make me so sick sometimes, yeah?"

"I guess so, Vere. So, what is it you need to tell and/or give me?"

I hold out the plain folder and when he takes it from my hand. I start playing with the buttons on the bottom of the sweater. I'm sweating under my arms and down my back. *I don't want to disappoint him.* I hear him open up the folder and I know he probably really mad at me. I pick my face up and take a quick look at him. I'm quick to tell him why.

"I took those from your office when they first got here because I knew they was about that nasty doctor. I didn't want nothing of his to be found in your office... you know, if the police came asking about his death, yeah? You know, because he shot Vivian and maybe they would think you had something to do with him dying, yeah?" My heart was beating so fast, it felt like it used to feel just before my daddy would come in my room to read to me... no. *No, I'm not going to think about that now.* I'm scared and nervous, but I know I have to stay here and wait for whatever John's gone say to me.

Vera, calm the hell down. You know John isn't going to yell at you or be upset with you.

I don't know what he's gone to do... please, Vivian. Take the wheel again, yeah?

No! Not until this conversation is over. Get back out there and see what he has to say.

I really hate you sometimes, Vivian. But, I love you mostly, yeah?

Yeah, Vera. I love you mostly, too.

"...think I was going to get in trouble, Vera?"

"What did you say? I kinda went inside for a minute, yeah?"

"I asked why you thought I would get in trouble for having those documents?"

"Because, I know how angry you were with Kerrigan about what he did… you know, when he shot Vivian and what he did with Valery? I thought maybe, you had something to do with him dying, yeah?"

"You thought I was capable of killing him, Vera?"

I don't want to answer him because I don't want him to be mad at me. He's still not looking like he's gone hurt me, but sometimes men don't look like they thinking about hurting you and they still shove themselves inside tiny little slits. I'm going back inside. Damn it to hell and back.

Vivian! Don't you… you better come out here.

No. Vera. You need to take responsibility for your decisions. I didn't make you do what you did. Stand up and face John. Tell him the truth and why you needed to protect him. He'll never hurt you. You know that.

But, he hurt you.

I knew he would. I expected it. I saw it in him the moment my eyes locked with his. But he will never hurt me or any of us again. Trust him.

You promise me you'll come back, yeah?

I'll always protect you, Vera. Always.

Yeah, okay. I'm gone do it. I can do this.

I know you can. You're stronger and braver than you give yourself credit for. You created us to ensure your survival. Strong and brave. I love you.

Thanks, Vivian. Love you too, yeah?

Yeah.

***

I'm not sure what time it is or what happened with John and Vera, but what I do know is John's office is put together and I'm lying on his blue

Chesterfield draped in the cashmere throw I gave him a few years ago for an *I love you* gift. The sun has turned the sky into a pearlescent swirl of coral and gold and orange of a nautilus shell. There is nothing more beautiful than golden hour over Lake Murray.

I amend my thought when my eyes focus on the man sitting at his desk with a tumbler of whiskey in his right hand, black reading glasses perched on his arrogantly arched nose, and a single piece of paper in his left hand. There is nothing more beautiful than golden hour over Lake Murray as a backdrop for my husband as he sits at his desk looking like an sapiosexual fantasy come to life. *Damn, these pregnancy hormones and my love of intelligent men.*

"Vivian, keep eye-fucking me like that and see what happens." I pull my bottom lip between my teeth to keep the smile and sassy retort trapped, but only succeed at keeping my voice silenced; the smirk somehow makes its way across my lips, despite my best efforts.

"John, whatever do you mean?" I go for coy because I don't know what kind of mood he's in. His posture is relaxed, the tone of his voice drips dominance and sheet-clawing sex; but there is something in his eyes… I'm not sure what mine or his next move is going to be. I wait him out.

"You know good and damn well what I mean, lovely. Your eyes have already told me how wet your pussy is. How swollen those beautiful naked lips are—pouting and weeping for my tongue, teeth, fingers, and cock. Will your mouth lie, when your eyes and nipples have already spoken your truth?"

"No. What would be the point in lying, John? You know this body better than I do. You know when I want you. What I don't know or understand is why you haven't made me yours since we made this baby?" His entire face changes. It doesn't last long, but I notice it. *How the hell*

did he forget we were pregnant? The moment he realizes I've seen his tell, he's up from behind his desk. The sexy predator gone, replaced with a man who's in awe with a tiny little hiccup on a screen.

"Fuck! Vivian, how the hell had I forgotten about the reason we were at the hospital the day Valery lost her damn mind? How—is everything, are you and the baby all right. Oh, my god! You haven't eaten all day, are you hungry? Thirsty? Talk to me, Viv. What do you want—or need or, shit."

"Jonathan Raynard Ellis, what's gotten in to you? What are you freaking out about? Have you eaten, today?"

He takes a couple of deep breaths and drops down to his haunches in front of me. His warm hand pulls the throw away from my body to give himself access to my still flat belly. His hand. The same large, powerful hand he uses to spank my ass hot as fire. The same wicked hand he wraps my locs around when he wants to keep me in my place; that hand lays gently across my belly and a peace falls over us. Silence. My breathing and my heartbeat move in simpatico with his.

"I love you, lovely. So much shit has been going on lately, I can't remember the last time It's been just you and me. I miss you. I miss Vivian and John. I'm sorry..."

"Don't ever apologize for telling me how you feel. What you need and want from me, John. I fucking miss us, too. So damn much, it hurts. Here, where I carry you with me, it hurts where my love for you pumps throughout my veins. I want it to be us. Me and you and our baby, but I'm not just me anymore and, fuck if it doesn't make me angrier than being shot by that dick-face, gun-carrying, Irishmen, Kerrigan." I wasn't trying to be funny, but John's bark of laughter was exactly what was needed to diffuse the tension in the air. I joined him with a few snorts of my own before we settled back into each other's eyes.

"I love you. Now, tell me what you need, and I'll do my best to give it to you." I snake my arm out and let my fingers leisurely dance across his soft, but ever-responsive dick. He watches as I taste myself, giving him access to observe the change from the playful summer-sunshine skies he loves, to the sensual summer thunderstorms with flashes of lightening as my lust for him continues to rise to the surface.

The moment he becomes aware of the change, his pupils are blown and all that's left of his beautiful brown eyes, is a slight ring. *Yes, he's going to pound this ache right out of the bottom of my belly. We need this. Really, really fucking need this.*

41

I watch his nostrils flair as he scents the air, checking for any hints of the fresh salty undercurrent of my arousal. He must find what he's looking for because after a beat, he hauls me up and flips me over his shoulder, fireman style, and carts my happy ass upstairs where I know I'll be in for a long and delicious ride.

"You cold, lovely?"

"No."

"I felt a shiver run up and down your spine, if you're not cold then you must be wet as hell right about now."

"Can't wait for you to find out."

The swat on my ass reminds me of the many beautiful things this man can do to my body and how much I treasure every gift he gives me in the form of his dominance and love.

"That's exactly what I intend to do." The door to our bedroom is pushed open and he places me onto our bed, probably the last bit of gentleness I'll receive from him until he's done with me. I observe the fine quintessence of man-flesh that is my husband as he pulls his shirt over his head. Muscles flex and roll under midnight skin that feels like prayers and incantations under my fingertips. *God, I'm a sloppy wet mess between my thighs and I know he's going to love every bit of it.*

"Why are you still wearing clothes, lovely?"

"Waiting on you to tear them from my body like the savage I know you are."

"You better be butt-ass-naked by the time I make it to you, or I'll be tearing more than your clothes off."

My gray and black joggers were on the floor along with my white, long sleeve tee before the words cleared his mouth. Something is riding him,

hard. I don't know exactly what it is, but I know him well enough to know he needed to own me. To tear me a part and put me back together in the image he needs me to be.

Needlepoints of trepidation skitter across my skin as he prowls towards me. His cock, heavy between his thighs, still encased in his black boxer briefs. The curve of his shaft was the most perfect arc in the entire world.

"Keep licking your lips like that, Viv and I'm going give you something much bigger to lick on." I could only watch as he hooked his thumbs in the sides of his underwear and pulled them down his lean hips. The muscles in his ass flexing like he's already deep inside me. Inadvertently, my thighs squeeze together to relieve some of the pressure building in my pounding clit.

"Open." One word. No other directives, just my mouth. Without hesitation, I recline on my back, allowing the mattress to support my neck. My head is between his spread thighs as he leans over me on his knees. Supple fingers skate over scarred skin, raising gooseflesh as they make their way to the wet, warm flesh currently on display for him.

"You know, Viv? The first time I saw these scars on your thighs, breast, and belly." He leans closer, so his cock head bounces off of my chin; still playing with me like we have all the time in the world.

"I wanted to find whoever did this to you. The person who took what wasn't theirs to take. Me. I wanted to be the one to mark you in this artistic, yet primitive way. Does that make you fear me, lovely? Would you let me add to your collection of scars?" I didn't bother answering him because he would do what he wanted with my body, and I would let him. I never wondered who left these scars on my body, until this very moment. *I'll file it away for later. Now is not the time for a head-trip.* I tune back in to what John is saying.

"… I'm going to fuck your throat. I'm going to fuck your cunt. And Vivian, I need it all from you. If you can't give everything, don't give me anything at all."

"Make it good for me, John and you can have all of me. Everything I have."

"Damn it, lovely."

***

Who knew anal could be so amazing? Certainly not me. I'm so glad I'm able to give John what he wants… what he needs. I'm proud of myself for understanding my triggers and working through them. There ought never be anything between a man and a woman in their bedroom. The bedroom is a sacred place where worship and adoration reside. A time for GOD to receive GLORY. When man and woman shed their human pelts and become more and nothing. More of themselves and nothing of their fears or insecurities. More god-like and nothing of the frail human persona. More ethereal and nothing physical. Fucking is the gift of divinity that allows us to ascend and become one with the universe.

I stretch my arms over my head as I come to a full sitting position in the bed. I already know John is not beside me, the man's a furnace and there's no heat radiating from his side of the bed.

***

Fall is my favorite season. Today, I'm wearing a pair of wide-leg Jones New York pants in heather gray, paired with a burnt orange and teal floral silk blouse with a large bow that ties, and sits on my right hip. Shoes and I have a long-standing love affair and today, after creating a shift in cosmic energy with John, I need my power heels. The burnt orange heels from Calvin Klein gives me just enough lift to feel powerful and let me move comfortably throughout my day.

I falter when I see John sitting at the breakfast bar with a coffee in one hand and the New York Times in the other. The scowl on his face, tells me he's not happy about whatever he's reading. Which is why I don't even bother reading any section of the newspaper that isn't the arts.

"Good morning, babe. Why does your face look like you just read your own obituary?"

"Ha! You stay with the jokes, don't you lovely? Morning, baby. How'd you sleep, and more importantly—how are you feeling?"

Leaning over to whisper a kiss over his cheek, I notice he's not clean shaven. I like it. His silence tells me he's waiting for an answer to his questions. The one where I reassure him the rough sex we had last night didn't leave any bloody panties or weird cramps or pangs.

"I slept like whoever's obituary you're reading about. And I feel amazing, thanks for asking. Really, what are you reading that has your face looking so out of sorts this early in the morning?"

Folding the paper and placing it on the counter, he takes a deep sigh and then drums his fingers across the white marble a couple of times before answering.

"I'm trying to figure out how the hell Bush can't seem to find Bin Laden's ass in the fucking desert when the country's got a goddamn satellite that can look into our window and tell them what the fuck we ate for lunch yesterday."

"Okay, and that's got you this upset at..." I check my Patek Philippe for the time."...6:45 in the morning?" Standing behind him, I start to rub his shoulders with enough pressure to alleviate some of the tension, I watch as it evaporates like smoke.

"I don't believe you're this upset over Bush's silly ass. So, what's really got your ire up?"

"Kiss me and tell me what you have planned for today." I do what he asks of me because I know he needs me to. But he knows me well enough to know I'm not letting this go, especially after the shit he told me yesterday. I move to the counter-height stool beside him and wait for him to turn around and face me.

"Now, tell me the truth, Sir."

"You don't play fair, lovely."

"I never promised to, Sir. I only ever promised to play. I'm listening."

"I don't like how this shit with Kerrigan happened and I sure as hell don't like Valery being MIA." Whatever tension I released with my little shoulder rub is back in full force and decided to bring some of his friends along for the ride.

"I know. All of it stinks, but if any of it was going to blow back on you, it would have already. Don't borrow trouble from tomorrow when you don't need to." I slide from my perch to move to the toaster for my bagel. After putting it on a plate with fresh fruit and cottage cheese, I bring it and a glass of orange juice back to the breakfast bar to sit beside John again.

"How the hell do you eat that lumpy shit, Viv?" His face looks like I really do have lumpy shit on my plate. I bark out a laugh and scoop a big fork full of cottage cheese and fruit into my mouth. I hum my pleasure and try not to laugh again at the face John pulls at my over-acting. Once I swallow, I answer him while licking my lips.

"Like that. And don't rain your piss and vinegar on my rainbow, okay? We're fine. Valery will show herself when she's done licking her wounds. Apparently, she caught feelings for Kerrigan, which leads me to a serious question." I pause, because I don't know if I should save this discussion for later when we have more time or just put it out there and agree to talk about it later.

"You're right. I'm sorry, you don't deserve my vinegar and we agreed forever ago there would be no golden showers in our play, so…" He delivers his cheeky apology with such a banality; I almost miss the part about golden showers. That is until his decadent mouth twitches and then breaks into a beautiful smile. I shake my head in admonishment and raise my eyebrow nudging him to continue.

"…and anyway, some of this vinegar *is* for you because why the hell are you torturing our baby with that lumpy, white shit?" He gets up to refill his coffee and grab some fruit before he returns to my side, kissing my cheek as he moves to the other side of the bar. "So, tell me what's on your mind."

"I'm wondering how are we supposed to handle it when one of the alters finds someone their interested in. Someone they want a relationship with? We share this body, but as far as I'm concerned, this body… my body, belongs to you and me. But, obviously that is not a luxury we have. I mean, Valery had an intense relationship with Kerrigan and none of us even knew about it. She said something to me in the hospital before she cut our wrist and it's been bothering me ever since."

"What did she say and why am I only hearing about it now?"

"I'm just telling you about it because this is the first time we've had a moment without the world burning down around us and what she said— was…" I trail off because I don't know how to get the words pass the lump in my throat. The cottage cheese I ate for breakfast is threatening to make a reappearance. I gulp down my water and chew on a piece of dry bagel before I'm able to get the words out.

"…she said she fucked him raw. No condom and this baby could b-be Kerrigan's."

~42~

"*Fuuuuuuuuk!*" I'm a cracked plate. His pain slices through me like a hot knife through butter. I can't look at him. I feel as if I was the one fucking Kerrigan without a condom. I jump a foot in the air as the dishes on the counter rattle and John's coffee cup crashes to the floor, spilling the dregs of his morning joe onto the pristine marble; it looks like an old blood stain. Grainy and dark, full of imperfections.

"Goddammit! Fucking shit! How? How the fuck could she do this to us. To *you*. To all of us. I hate that fucking bitch. I hate I ever fucked *her* behind your back. I hate that it was me. That it was me and my stupid pride who caused the crack that allowed her psychotic, fucked-up ass to slip out. Fuck, Vivian..."

His face dissolves into a mess of brown. Wet with tears, sweat, and snot; a mass of painful, contorted flesh and bone. I look away from his anguish and it's then I notice his left hand is twice as large as his right and I figure he must have hit the countertop with it. He just broke his hand but what he really wants to break is Valery. *Shit, I want to break Valery my damn self.* Maybe I should've waited until after work to spill the T. Now neither of us will be going in today, I've got to get John to the ER to get his hand looked at.

***

After three and a half hours in the ER, John is resting upstairs thanks to the cocktail of pain medicine and anti-anxiety pills the attending physician gave him. I'm downstairs in my sacred space reading through the Seeking Wonderland entries, there's a new one and it's from none other than the ghost, Valery. I'm almost too afraid of what she has to say, to read it but I'm as afraid of not knowing what's going through her mind, not to. God, I

hope she's not dropping more of her caustic truth, but there's only one way to find out. *Deep breath in, blow it out and take a look.*

Seeking Wonderland

OCTOBER 7, 2001

I KNOW Y'ALL DON'T WANT NOTHIN TO DO WITH ME AND TO BE HONEST, I DON'T REALLY WANT NOTHIN TO DO WITH ME EITHA. I FUCKED UP. I KNOW THAT NOW. I'M SO SORRY FOR EVERYTHIN I DID. HARRY MADE ME BELIEVE HE LOVED ME. MADE ME FEEL LIKE SOMETHING ABOUT ME WAS SPECIAL AND IMPORTANT TO HIM. I'M SCARED AND SO FUCKIN LONELY. I DON'T EVEN KNOW WHERE THE FUCK I AM. I WENT SEARCHIN FOR SOME PART OF THE HOUSE WHERE NO ONE COULD FIND ME AND I—I THINK I'M LOST. SOMEHOW, I FOUND MY WAY TO THE SURFACE, BUT IT WASN'T NOBODY IN THE HOUSE WHEN I WENT LOOKIN. I LOOK IN EVERYBODY ROOMS. THEY ALL LOOK THE SAM BUT NOBODY SHOW UP OR COME HOME. IT'S LIKE Y'ALL MOVED HOUSES AND NOBODY TOLD ME ABOUT OUR NEW ADDRESS. I'M SORRY. SO FUCKIN SORRY FOR IT ALL. HARRY, CUTTIN OUR WRIST, BEIN SUCH A MOTHAFUCKIN CUNT TO EVERYONE. I DIDN'T EVEN TRY WITH SHIT. I DIDN'T WANT TO UNDERSTAND WHAT WAS BEIN SAID ABOUT US EVOLVIN AND CONNECTIN TO SOMETHIN BIGGA THAN US... I—I MISS YOU. ALL OF YOU, EVEN VERA AND HER EVIL EYE SHE LOOK AT ME WITH SOMETIMES. FUCK! COME BACK AND GET ME. I'M NOT GOOD BY MYSELF. JUST ME DON'T MAKE A WE... I NEED TO BE PART OF SOMETHIN AND Y'ALL NEED ME TOO. I PROMISE, I'M GONNA BE BETTA AND ACT RIGHT. JUST LET ME KNOW I'M NOT OUT HERE BY MYSELF.

Okay

Valery, Seekin Wonderland

Oh, my fucking God! Where the hell is Valery and why can't I feel her. I need to call Jessa and her weird mom. We've got to get Valery back. Maybe I should write to her, let her know I miss her and want her to come home. *I must have the most fucked mind known to man.*

I mean really, who in the hell exiles a part of her consciousness because she doesn't like what she's done? Apparently, I do. That's who. Vivian Bruno Ellis...I'll write her back and let her know I'm coming to get her.

She's not alone and forgiven, unconditionally. *First I'll write her back, then I'll call the mom and daughter team, and then I'll tell John.*

Part Four

"Use the World Around [you] as a Mirror"

"Warriors know every aspect of their being most intimately; even their

laten tendencies, and most especially their hidden potential. To achieve this

warriors use the world around them as a mirror, for in that mirror all stands

revealed."

–Théun Mares, Cry of the Eagle: The Toltec Teachings—Volume 2

~43~

It's been nine days since finding Valery's entry in our shared journals. Nine days since calling Dr. Orinda and Jessa to come over, only to have their service inform me both women were out of the country doing some sort of research. Nine baffling days since telling John what I'd found and listening to him rage about how he hopes *the bitch never finds her way back this way again.* Nine days since I wrote back to Valery with no answer. And finally, as I sit in my sacred room pretending to read *Mercy* by Julie Garwood, I hear the doorbell ring and John's deep rumble of a voice invites the good doctors in. *It's about damn time!*

"...she sounded absolutely frantic on the phone, John. Did you take her through all the exercises..." Dr. Orinda's whisper-soft voice trails off as she steps into my sanctuary for the first time and stares at me, wearily. I'm sitting on one of my extra-large floor pillows with the paperback in my hand, looking every bit as calm as I feel. *What did she think she would find when she got here, today?*

"Vivian?" I'm still focused on the door, waiting for Jessa to walk through, but the lilliputian woman is the only one to traipse into my space with her disenchanted eyes. Questions mark her face like someone forgot to blend her foundation before sending her out onto the stage to perform her role as a world-renown-psychiatrist.

"Yes, Dr. Orinda. How are you? I'm so glad you could make it. I didn't realize both you and Jessa were out of the country. Speaking of, where is she? Jessa's, not with you?"

"Um. Oh, yes. Jessa decided to stay behind and give me some time to work with you one-on-one. She felt it was best for your care to be turned over to me."

"Is that so?"

"Well… yes, of course. She knows things have become more complicated with you in recent months and with the missing alter—"

"Valery. Her name is, Valery and she's not missing. She's lost and scared and completely ashamed of her behavior. I would much prefer to talk with Jessa. We, the girls, and I, have a relationship with her already. No offence, but I—we. We don't know you and haven't had the opportunity to establish enough trust in your motives."

"None taken, really. I understand how you feel and why you feel the way you do; however, Jessa is great to talk to, but she is a psychologist. *I*, on the other hand, am a *psychiatrist*. I understand if you're not able to comprehend the…"

"John!" I call for my husband to get this woman out of my room and get Jessa on the phone immediately before I lose my shit and Tombstone her tiny ass. I've been trying to stay calm for myself, the girls, and the baby but this woman is trying my patience.

"Viv, what's wrong? Are you all right?"

"I really appreciate Dr. Khara Orinda coming all this way to see me—to see us, but I much prefer her daughter and you were aware of that, right?"

"Yes, but Vivian. Jessa is busy with her research and—"

"And she told me she'd drop everything the moment we needed her. When I spoke with her yesterday. She assured me she had some possible ways to pull Val back from the darkness and I want her here right this minute or as soon as is possible."

John looks at the esteemed Dr. Orinda and shakes his head slightly as he holds the door open for her to walk through.

"Jessa's on her way; I called her as soon as I heard the tone in your voice. We'll talk about this later, okay?"

I'm left to my own devices while I wait for Jessa to show up. *I don't know what the hell John was thinking, but we will certainly talk about this later.* I've since put the book I'd been pretending to read down and turned on the radio to 104.7, hoping to find some music to take my mind off everything that's going on. Just as my favorite morning DJ introduces Jennifer Lopez s hit song, *I'm Real*; the door to my space swings open and in walks my therapist, Jessa.

"Turn that vile music off and get something a little more Gregorian on, please." I'm quick to oblige my friend and mental coach. My mind-bender because I'm so happy to see her. I have a sinking feeling, John and Khara were up to no good. *The road to hell and all that.* Once Jessa's happy with the music, smudging the space, and lighting three new candles she pulled from her Mary Poppins bag of goodies; she invites me to sit on the antique Turkish kilim chair which sits atop a beautiful Moroccan Kilim carpet in a subtle tones of chocolate, rust, and deep shades of cream.

I've settled in. Automatically, my eyes are closed, lulled into an almost meditative state by the acrid notes of burnt sage and the subtle undertones of the Melissa, neroli, and ylang ylang oils burning in the diffuser on the small table under the window. Which must be slightly ajar because I notice a cool breeze passing over my face. I'm feeling all sorts of calm and less angry or agitated than I was when Jessa's mother was here earlier. *Don't think about her right now, Vivian. Calm, peaceful thoughts. Only positive vibes.*

I breath deep and even but am also aware of my surrounding. Even in this stressful moment, there is peace.. Jessa speaks softly, lifting the vibrations in the room; we're in for some heavy work. I know that, and I'm doing my part to prepare this body and share with the girls what they can expect.

Vera. Lyric. We are getting ready to retrieve Valery. I need to know you're both on board with doing this. We all have to want to bring her home.

Why, Vivi? She don't love us; I don't care what she wrote in our journal. She just scared right now. If we bring her back, who know what her crazy behind gonna do to us. What harm she'll do to our body.

I don't want to leave her where she is, but like Valeria just said; what if she don't really mean us any good, yeah? We don't want to take that kind of risk. At least... I don't want to, yeah?

I know it's hard to trust Valery right now, especially right now. But she is a part of us and in this moment—she's apart from us. You... I feel like a fourth of me is missing. I'm not really complete without her, are you guys? Are you complete with Valery missing?

I guess—I mean, I don't know what complete feels like, and really neither do you. How can we ever feel complete when none of us are whole, Vivi?

Yeah...I don't know, Vivian. I don't really know much about Valery, yeah? She showed up such a short while ago, and then ever since she got here, the house been a hot-stinking-mess, yeah?

I know. I know, but Vera. Listen—Valery came to my rescue when I couldn't deal with what John was doing to me. It's like when Lyric came to your rescue when you were five years old and then I came to her rescue when she couldn't handle being passed on to those bad men...

I get that, Vivian. All right?! I get she another protector, but she also a vicious, tormenting bitch. I hate how she abuse our body, yeah?

Me, too. I hate how I never know what she done with it. Who she give it to. I always feel scared I'm going to come into some kind of diseased,

sore-covered body that smells like old toilet water. I'm twelve years old! I don't want to deal with burning. And itching down there. Have you seen pictures of STDs, Vivi? Have you?

Okay. I know Valery is an unpredictable, loose cannon and she has never shown any regard for the body or mind or life we share, but she is still a part of us—a

No! Vivian. She a part of you. The part of you who like nasty butt-sex but too shame to admit it, yeah?

Vera! I—um… I don't even know what to say. I have fully accepted how much I enjoy anal with John. But, some of the darker sex is not something I'm ever going to want to visit, again. I had enough of it when your father passed me around to every drug dealer he could whore me out to for a little piece of crack-rock!

You think you had it worse than me, Vivi?! I was the one her daddy groomed to do what her whore of a mother refused to. The only one who really got out of this unharmed is the biggest damn baby in the house. Right, Vera?

Valeria! That's not fair. Vera is not untouched. If she were; you, Valery, nor I would be here. Vera's mind—mo. Her entire soul has been broken up into all these shards just so she can make it through the day.

But is she making it through the day? Hell no! You didn't even know about us, until John broke you. Vera been dormant so long, I almost forgot about her until you and John started making sexy time and she crawled out from the rock she been hiding under. Why so quiet, Vera?

Shut the hell up, Valeria! You shut your stupid, big, little-girl mouth, right now. You don't know what you think you know about me or what or how I live with anything, yeah? You think I wasn't there when my daddy

did what he did to me? You think I don't remember what it was like to have a mama before she got tired of being his wife?

I still smell her. Like soft, petals from the yellow jessamine she grew outside the kitchen window of the big house we all lived in… before. She said the scent come from the fancy powder she dust on after her bath. She always remind me that the flowers was poison if someone ate them. She said, 'If someone mess with you, you could kill them with them yella flowas out under the kitchen winduh.'

The powder-puff was big and soft. The way it glided over her lighter than a brown-paper-bag colored skin—so smooth and pretty. Then, she look at me with them honey-dipped-purple eyes and ask me why my face so damn black and why my eyes look like fire burning in a pile of snow.

Vera? Do you remember your mama's name? What your daddy called her?

Why does it matter now, Vivi? We trying to decide if—

Lyric! It matters, okay? Just… it matters.

Yeah. Of course, I know my own mama's name. Who could ever forget their own mama's name, yeah? My daddy sang this silly song when she was in a smiling mood. Della. 'Della-Della, skin so yella. Went and got 'yoself a blue-black fella'.

"John! Oh, my God! John! You've got to get in here!" I'm up from my chair, almost faceplanting in Jessa's lap before catching myself and running toward John's heavy footfalls. The alters are shouting and begging me to come back to the house, but I can't. A part of my soul—Lyric—has suspected this, and now it has been confirmed.

John burst into the room and looks from Jessa, who—to her credit—is as calm as a cucumber on a hot summer day. Still sitting in a perfect lotus a few feet from the chair I just tumbled out of. "Vivian, what the hell's the matter with you?"

I'm pretty sure I look like I've gone several rounds with a rabid raccoon... and lost, badly. I'm not even a little bit concerned about how crazy I look. Not now. Not that I've made *this* discovery, one in hindsight should've been shared with my alters before sharing it with John.

I take a couple of deep breaths, and quickly tell the alters to pipe down and listen in, so I only have to say it once. Then I tell Vera to be ready to talk to John and Jessa once I'm done. Once everybody is quiet and Jessa is standing beside me, while facing John. I stretch out my right hand to him as an anchor for myself, or maybe it's for him. *Jesus H. Christ of Nazarene on a donkey holding two palm fronds! Who knew this would be so damned hard?*

"I was having a conversation with Vera and Lyric about going in and trying to bring Valery back. We got a little off topic and ventured into some weird gray areas and then Vera started talking about her mother. The woman who left her and condemned her to the depravity of her father." The frogs climbing up from my throat as I try to say the words, make me sound like I've smoked a pack of no-filter cigarettes every day of my life.

Vera, please describe your mother to John and tell him what your father used to call her... what he used to sing to her. Please. It's important.

Okay, it don't bother me none to talk about her, yeah?

Let me tell him what's going to happen. Lyric and I will be right here, if you need us. Thanks, Vera.

Okay. Why are you acting so strange, Vivian?

Just tell him. And then... then you'll understand.

I open my eyes to the most beautiful, melted chocolate pools I've ever dared to dip myself into. The slight up-turn of the right corner of his lip and the sharp angles of his handsome face, gives him a bemused, yet intelligent expression. The look he gives me when he realizes we're all in the house having conversations. I love his acceptance of this craziness, but I don't know how he's going to react to what Vera is about to tell him.

"John? Vera has something to tell you about her mother. I need you to listen and save your reaction for when I'm back in the driver's seat. Okay?"

"Okay, Viv." He's wearing a curious half-smile that betrays his espérance about what he's going to hear. I can't say or do anything about anything, right now. I give up control and sit back with Lyric while Vera gets into the driver's seat and takes the wheel. *Oh, sweet, baby Jesus rocking in a manger.* I feel sick to my stomach; maybe it's the baby. No, it's what's about to come out of Vera's mouth and how John will react to it that's making my stomach crawl up my throat.

Vera

"Hey, John. You look like you hope I got some good news for you, yeah?"

273

"Vera, that's because you always have good news for me. " He always smile with his whole face. Like he seeing his baby sister or favorite cousin when he look at me. It make me feel so safe. I never knew a grown man could be safe to be around. But John. He so different from the ones I knew. He's really going to be a good daddy. *Not like my nasty one, was.* He still looking at me with that smile. *Oh, yeah. I got to tell him about mama.*

"So, we was all talking—inside the house—and things got pretty hot, yeah? Vivian is the only one who want to bring Valery and her nasty ways back to our house and you know how Vivian can be when she set herself to doing a thing… and well. Anyway, I got to talking about my mama. I don't think I ever told you or anybody, really anything about her, yeah?" He scrunch up his thick eyebrows and his face look like a puppy when you talk to it in a weird voice and it don't know why. But he still look and sound kind when he answer me. So, I don't mind his puppy-dog face so much.

"Can't say you have, Vera. Why don't we go over to the small sofa and sit down while you tell me all about her." John put his bigger than life hand around my sweaty one and give me a little squeeze. It don't hurt none. It make me feel like he don't want me to hurt no more, so I squeeze his big hand right back. Because I don't want him to hurt no more either.

Now we both sitting on the little sofa. My body feel too big to sit so close to him. I try to squeeze my thighs together to make them smaller, but his knee still touch my knee. I wrap my arms around my soft, round belly and hope my titties don't look as big as they are. John don't ever look at me like he look at Vivian. I'm glad about that.

After I take a deep breath and nod my head at Vivian and Valeria when they tell me to tell him; I look at John's sweet puppy-dog face. A face too

pretty to be on a man, but not like a woman. Like a *pretty man. Is that a thing. Can a man be pretty? Come on, Vera. Let's get it over with, yeah?*

"So—um… about my mom. She was the color of one of those brown paper bags you get from Piggly Wiggly. Not even that brown, but not really buttermilk color either, yeah?"

"I know the color well. My own mother looked like a slice of skillet cornbread… so a little lighter than your mama."

"Then how the world you get to be so black?"

"Same way you did, I guess? My father. Although I never met the man, was obviously dark as midnight." John laughed and it sound like thunder playing with the clouds. It make me want to laugh. But I don't laugh or smile too wide. Too much attention. But my lips pull up on each side like somebody got two strings hooked into the corners of my mouth and pulling just enough to show John that I think he funny.

Never show my teeth. Teeth make grown men think about biting you in places where teeth don't suppose to bite little girls. I feel all right to smile a little with John. He don't ever show his teeth like he want to pull my underclothes down and bite me between my legs where daddy put his banana in Valeria. *Enough of those thoughts, yeah? Get back to the telling, Vera.*

"I see. My daddy was so black, I could only see his teeth and eyes when he would come in my room at night, yeah?" John face don't have a smile anymore. *I forgot he know what my daddy did to us when he came in my room. Need to finish.*

Oh, uh. Um, yeah. Anyway. Vivian want me to tell you about how my daddy use to sing this song to my mama when she was in a smiling mood, yeah?"

"Oh, yeah?" John's voice sound like it come through a long pipe filled with wind and rain and summer storms. *He still thinking about what my daddy did to us. Vera, hurry up, yeah?*

"You're going to sing it for me, Vera?" He did smile, then. A little. But his whole face didn't. And his eyes didn't smile, either. Not this time. But I still bent my head because he made my chubby cheeks go hot and I smiled with some teeth showing.

"Yeah. I sang it for Vivian and Valeria just a while ago and that's what sent Vivian yelling for you. She sure love yelling out your name, *yeah?*" Now John look like his scruffy cheeks feel a little hot and that make me chuckle a little more. But I don't open my mouth. *Go on, Vera. Sing the man the song, yeah?*

"He only ever sang when she smile at him and me. 'Della-Della, skin so yella. Went and got yoself a blue-black fella'. He thought it was smart. I remember when she smile at him and how happy he was about her smile. But her smile never last long and when they went away... nobody smiled."

"What is—was. What was your mother's name, Vera? All of it. The entire name." I knew I didn't have to be scared of John, but right now. He look like somebody waiting to hear something they *don't* want to know but can't stand not knowing it, either. The look he giving me is burning a hole right through my face.

Valeria? I don't want to be out here by myself. Please. Come out here and I'll tell you what to tell him.

Vera. You can do this. John's not going to hurt you. You know he won't. Tell him what he ask you and then come back inside.

I'm right here with you, Vera. You're not alone. Just. Just tell him your mama's whole name and I'll take over after you say the words. All right?

276

You won't make me answer anymore of his questions by myself, yeah? You going to be the one to talk with him. Even if I have to give you answers, yeah?

Yes. Vera. I'm so freaking proud of you! You are doing a great job. And I know you can complete this conversation. You ready?

No. But, I will finish what I started, yeah? And Vivian?

Yes, Vera.

Thank you.

"Her name was Della R. Bruno. I don't know what the R stood for, but she and my daddy was married. So her last name was the same as ours, yeah?"

***

Thanks, Vera. I got it from here. You were incredible.

Yeah? Why you want me to tell John about my mama? He don't look so good. What's wrong with him, Viv?

Vera, I need control, please. You and Lyric need to stay and listen so you understand what just happened, but John needs me now and I need to be there for him. Please come back.

Okay. You didn't make me say something to hurt him, yeah? John is the only man who never hurt me. I never want to hurt him, yeah?

He's knows that and no, you didn't say anything to hurt him. I would never manipulate you like that. Stay quiet and listen.

~45~

John's face is as flat as a super model's ass. There is no denying he's made the connection; the same connection I made when I heard Vera sing that damn song. I'm waiting for him to speak. To move. Something, anything to let me know he's all right or at least he will be.

From my peripheral I see Jessa edge up behind John, but I don't take my gaze from the turbulence in his brown eyes because I don't know when or if he's going to have a reaction. And then... like the lethal, predator I know him to be; his hands are around my throat and I'm pushed up against the wall as he squeezes the air from my lungs and bares his teeth. Mágoa in the form saliva and foam slip and slide between his lips and gums, while his chocolate iris fades to black with his hurt and heartache expands his pupil. His features contort with such unmistakable loss of control; it makes me do the one thing I know he needs.

After taking a deep breath, I relax my shoulders and drop my head into his care and show him my eyes. Jessa's on the phone, probably calling the police and ambulance. Vera and Lyric are spazzing out jumping and yelling about the baby. But me? I'm as calm as a springtime breeze. I feel it the moment he realizes what he's doing and who he's doing it to. His hands drop from around my neck. Beautiful brown eyes gain focus and clarity, just before he grabs his keys and bolts from the door through the kitchen leading to the garage.

Moments later, I hear his black on black Toyota 4 Runner peel out the driveway and screech away from our home. From the pain that just lodged itself into the recesses of his soul.

My butt hits the large floor pillow, as I'm gulping air and holding my bruised neck. I allow the first tear to carve a path down my cheek and rest

in the corner of my downturned mouth. *Maybe I should have approached this differently, but I didn't expect him to react so viscerally.*

***

After explaining to the police and ambulance there was a misunderstanding on the part of my therapist and sending Jessa home with more concern than I was comfortable with. I found myself sitting in a warm, jasmine scented bath surrounded by votive candles and the soft sounds of Kenny G's *Songbird,* floating through the surround sound speakers on the wall.

I know he's home. I feel him as a sensation crawling up my spine. The door to the bathroom opens. He steps beside the bathtub. His back facing me, but I can see his haunted expression in the mirror. The shirt, then pants and briefs hit the floor. He must've taken his shoes and socks off before coming in. I scoot up to make room for his big body.

The water rises as he slides in behind me. His long legs encase my own as his fingers move over the scars on the tops of my thighs—like each raised piece of flesh is a word written in braille. My honey-cinnamon colored locs are twisted up in a high messy bun, so the light bruising around my neck is more than visible.

His solid chest expands on an inhalation that he holds for the longest time before finally exhaling. The sound is heavy and filled with contrition. Tiny kisses of apologies pepper the right side of my neck. He moves his sweet expression of regret just below my ear, and my breath catches as he smooths his warm, wet tongue along the worse of the abrasions. The answering shudder rolling through my body makes his dick jump and dig into my lower back.

"Lovely."

"I love you, John. I'm sorry. I—I"

"Don't ever apologize for your honesty. I needed to know that shit. I should be apologizing to you, lovely. Look at your motherfucking neck."

"It's not as bad as it looks, I didn't know if I was right about what I thought... but I had to let you hear it from her."

"What does this mean for us? Is Auntie... is Violet? Is she your mother?"

"Not my mother—not really, John. She's Vera's mom. Maybe that's why you have such a soft spot for her."

"Yeah, maybe. But it doesn't make any sense. Why the hell would she leave her baby with such a sick fucker? The woman I knew, Viv. She was so loving and protective. She gave me everything and even when she couldn't be with me anymore...oh shit! Does Vera know? Who—who her mother is? I mean, who she is... I mean was." He takes a calming breath and then much slower, he asks. "Who she was to me?"

"No, I don't think so. They're both tired and in the bed. You scared the hell out of them, John. They were concerned for me and for the baby."

His hands rest on my flat belly; the weight of them is more comforting than the warm water we're submerged in. He's not even breathing anymore.

"We're fine. Jessa called the ambulance, and I checked out fine."

"Vivian, you give me too much credit. Too much leeway with you. With your body. You know how fucked up I am. Yet you trust me with your life, and the life of our unborn child. Forgive me, Viv." He pauses and as he continues to speak, I recognize my favorite verse from Pablo Neruda's poem.

"*I love you without knowing how, or when, or from where. I love you straightforwardly, without complexities or pride; so I love you because I know no other way*"

"Show me. Show me just how sorry you are and then we'll deal with everything else in the morning."

"I'm yours, lovely. Whatever you need."

"I just need you, John. Nothing more and nothing less. Can you wash my back before you make me lose my mind with the three or four orgasms you're sure to give me?" He chuckles softly behind me as he rubs strong, sudsy circles all over my back. On a huff of air he jokes.

"Oh, yeah, Viv? How many of those will it take to earn your forgiveness?"

I feel his smile on the back of my neck as he pours warm water over my skin from a ladle formed with his large hands. A small pinch to my right side makes me laugh and that's how I know we're going to get through this clusterfuck like we get through everything else. Together.

~46~

I'm tucked tight against John wrapped in the safety of his arms after he made good on giving me those three orgasms plus one. My right-hand rests over his heart. Its blessedly quiet. Only our combined breaths and the occasional sigh or exhale breaks the somnolent haze floating around and through us. That is until John's sex roughened voice rumbles through the small slice of space between us.

"Do you think Auntie knew what was happening to you—I mean to Vera? You know, she told me all about her first husband and how she left her child with him when she was five. She said, something about never wanting to be a wife or a mother. How her people made her marry a man she only wanted to play around with.

"At the time. I didn't think anything about what she was saying. I mean, I was, what? Sixteen going on seventeen years old. I honestly didn't give a shit about her life before me… I just wanted what we had, you know? Just her and me."

The juvenile words falling from his lips in his grown man's voice does something to me… and not in a good way. The hand resting over his heart, flexes of its own desire. My nails dig into the warm skin and nothing I tell myself can stop me from needing to draw blood. I want him to pull my hand away from him, but he's lost in the memory of a pedophile who didn't care enough about the baby she carried for nine months to stay around for or take with her.

I feel him take a breath like he's preparing to say something else. Some other nice thing about *his Auntie*. Before he can open his mouth, words I don't expect to hear fly out of mine.

"How? In, the hell could you fall in love with *that* woman and then with *me*. With the same heart currently beating in your chest? She is a monster.

A monster who married a monster; only to leave her innocent child to be devoured by the very monster she ran away from. Fuck her, John. And fuck you for loving Della R. Bruno. Fuck you, her, and the fucking horse she rode in on!"

There is no room in my heart to contain the impotent cries of a little girl who needed her mother. No space in my jars to catch the forgotten dreams and hopes of a teenager whose childhood was a joke. Even though she never got the punchline. Probably because she was too busy getting punched. Never able to find the line that would have secured the benefits of her sacrifice.

It's not until I feel John's hands around my wrists that I realize I've been hitting him in his face and on his chest. He pulls my taut body into his and wraps me in his warmth. My head is thrashing side to side. My heart hurts so bad, I can't even remember what breathing feels like.

John whispers calming words in my ear, while rubbing his hands up and down my back. I'm aware of all this happening, but it doesn't feel like it's happening to me. Everything is getting dark, and I feel like a heavy, oil-soaked blanket is thrown over my soul.

The Internal House

What's happening to me. I'm so scared. John? Mama? What's happening?

Viv? Is that you? What's wrong? How the fuck you find me? I been hopin somebody was gonna come for me...I always knew it would be your stubborn needy ass.

Valery...? Oh, my god! Val! How did you get back? Wait, you are back aren't you?

How the fuck am I suppose to know? I mean, I ain't where I fuckin was before. That place don't have a smell, or sound, or anythin. It was like bein in a picture of my life... or our life. But knowin it ain't for real. You know?

Is this different? For you, I mean. Does this feel real?

Fuck yeah, it feel real. For one thin, I ain't by my damn self. I can smell Vera and Valeria. And you. I smell the sex on you. John kinky ass done somethin you ain't with? Is that what happen, Viv? You were sinkin into some dark shit... what the hell goin on?

I—so much has happened since you went away...

Valery? Val, it is you! How'd you get back here and what'd you do to Vivi, this time?

I ain't do nothin to her. She's upset because—wait. Why you so fucked up, anyway?

It's so much going on. You guys. Vera and Valeria, after John left the house and I got checked out. You guys know he didn't mean to hurt us, right?

Wait one fuckin minute. That upidity mothafucka hurt you and... and that's what pulled me from where I was. You needed me... I came back for you.

Hell has frozen over if you think we believe that lie, Valery. You tried to slice her vein, yeah?

Vera, shut the fuck up. Your simple ass can't understand any of this. I said I was sorry, I meant it. But Vivian need me—us. So if you wanna stand around and shoot the shit, fine. Or we can figure out what the fuck John crazy, sadistic ass done to our girl.

I already know what's going on with her. She figure out John lover, Auntie, is the same woman who gave birth to Vera and then left her with the man who raped her. And pimped her out to drug dealers. I'm right, Vivi.

Yes. Lyric, you had a feeling all along. And thanks, Val for coming back when I needed you. I didn't realize I was spiraling until I heard your voice. Talk later… if it's all right with everyone.

Vivian, I don't care much about why she come running back here like some kind of captain-save-the-alters, but I want to know more about what Valeria said about my mama, yeah?

Vera. The woman John believes made him the man he is, is the same woman who gave birth to you and then left you. I thought I was fine with it. But I'm really fucking angry with her. How the hell do you walk away from your own child. Only to take up with somebody else's child and love him. Give him everything while your child is being torn in pieces. Living off what-ifs, I-thought-I-understoods, and what-the-fuck-just-happeneds?! I don't understand how he could have been in love with her and still be the man who claims to be in love with me.

Vivian, you saying John's 'Auntie' was my mama.

Well fuck me when I'm walkin on my hands! That old ass piece of pussy John fucked back when he was like, what—fuckin 16 and just gettin his dick wet—is the woman who gave birth to this goddamned body?

285

Jesus H. Christ on a cheese cracker! Valery, why you always so crude?! We just finding out who 'mama' is, but Vera always knew who she was. But finding out she left her and took care of John. This is hard for her.

Why the fuck this so fuckin hard, Vera? You ain't even the one losin your shit about this. Vivian was the one meltin down like a goddamned ice cream cone in the middle of mothafuckin July in downtown Columbia. Vera, your silly ass ain't look like nothin new happen since I been gone. What the fuck, Viv.

I'm not melting like a damn ice cream cone, Val. I'm processing what this means. I'm trying to wrap my mind around the fact John and our birthmother were lovers. That she loved and cared for him. Left him enough money and resources to make him a multi-millionaire by the time he was seventeen. How we were eating whatever we could get from school and neighbors. Or the goddamned food bank!

I'm trying to reconcile the woman John waxed poetic about with the same sociopathic, evil, bitch who left an innocent five-year-old baby with a man who broke her—not once, but twice.

What is more fucked-up is how one of those goddamned broken pieces found Mr. Sexy-Multimillionaire at that shitty ass college she went to. The same sexy millionaire that Vera mama loved, and that silly slutpig whore… gave him permission to break her a-fuckin-gain.

Well, damn.

Wow.

It feel like she left me so daddy could make Vivian. Then she went to made John for her, yeah?

Yep.

Yes.

This shit is a fuckin hot ass, stankin mess.

All four of us stand in the living room of our internal house, holding hands and staring into eyes that all vary slightly in shades of amber, blue, grey, and green. There is no way this can work out for any of us, especially not for me and John.

But if she hadn't left, there would be no me. There would only be Vera. And John would never have known Della. He would never have come into his own, and his step father would have killed him just like he killed his mom.

Della R. Bruno. What did you know that led you to make the choices you made? Did you know what would happen to your little girl at the hands of her father? Did you know I would be the result of the sodomy at the hands of that drug dealer, Junior Eli.

Wait, his name wasn't Junior, it was J.R.; daddy called him J. R. He said he didn't like people calling his given name, yeah?

***

I jerk awake and realize I'm in our bed. John is wrapped around me like my favorite blanket; breathing easier now that I've calmed down. I'll let him sleep and tomorrow we'll talk.

But there is something niggling me. Something about the first drug dealer to have me. He never wanted to share me. He told Vera's father I was only for him. Nobody else could fuck my ass. He was tall and broad. I remember thinking how handsome he was and trying to figure out why he wanted to hurt me. *What the hell was that man's name? There something about him. Something vaguely familiar.* I'm tired and need to rest. I told John, we'd deal with everything in the morning and we will.

47

It's too early for either of us to be awake, after the night we had but I hear John moving around the bedroom. He's being as quiet as possible. I don't know why because he is as connected to me as the girls; I feel him as a part of myself.

"John? It's eight in the morning... not as early I as thought it was, but still early. Where are you sneaking off to?"

"Not sneaking, Viv. I need to go into the office. I have a lot of shit to do and missing as many days as I have is costing me a fuck-ton of money." He walks into the closet and I hear the drawers open and shut. *I wonder if he'll where my favorite tie.*

"I know and I'm sorry you've missed so much time because of me and... I just thought we'd have some time to talk before you left. I should get up, too. It's been a long while since I've been in my own gallery and Tammi says there's so much to do. She's getting ready to hire another boss lady to replace her old one." I smile as I throw my legs over the side of the bed; the slight ache deep inside my core reminds me where my husband's been. I miss him already. *Does that make me stupid—missing his dick— knowing if I wanted it again, right now, he'd give it to me.* I decide it doesn't and walk into the closet, where I take my sleep shirt off and notice his nostrils flare at my nakedness.

"You need something this morning, lovely?"

"Do you have something to give me, Sir?"

"You know... if you make me late for work because I'm fucking you, I'll have to punish you."

"I can't make you stay and fuck me, Sir. I haven't even asked you to." His eyes are drawn to my long fingers as they slide through my slick, swollen lips. I walk over to him, feigning my need to discard my shirt into

the rattan hamper; I lift my wet fingers and paint his bottom lip with my sweet, musky essence.

He captures my fingers between his teeth, biting on the fleshy pad, sending electricity shooting straight through the bottom of my belly to pool at the apex of my thighs. The little squeak that leaves my mouth is a little embarrassing, but whatever. If it gets me bent over the closet island and fucked to within an inch of my life; I'll squeak like a chipmunk.

"What's got this beautiful cunt so horny this morning, lovely? You went bat-shit on my ass last night and then you checked the fuck out. Didn't wake up. Look at me, Vivian." He thinks I'm someone else. *Who else would try to fuck him, except for...*

"Valery... oh, my God!"

"Valery?!" John's hands are like a vice grip around my naked shoulders. His eyes bore into my own, trying to ferret out if it's me or if Valery has somehow made a sneak appearance and is trying to destroy us. Again.

"It's me, John. I just remembered...Valery came back. Last night, she came back when I—I went *bat-shit*. Said she thought I was in trouble. Felt like I needed her to protect me from... *you*." I know I sound even more crazy then normal, but the words are coming faster than my mouth can process them. He's looking at me as if he can see four separate faces sprouting from my neck at the same time.

"The fuck you just say?"

"Valery. She came back last night during my freak-out because she thought I was in trouble again with you because she said I smelled like sex and she felt me diving or something like that, but the point is—she found her way back and we all had to fill her in on what happened with Violet or Auntie or mama...and then Vera was there and when she finally got the

gist of things I think she kind of went still—but then we all came to one big, crazy conclusion about *your* Violet and our mama. But we can talk about that later. Can you please just bend me over this marble countertop and take what belongs to you, Sir?"

Nothing. That's what I hear when I peel my eyes from the deflated bulge in his pants. Nothing is what he does when I reach out to him. Nothing is what I see in his eyes when he looks at me.

Until something flickers in the back of his melted gaze; something that looks a lot like fury. He slowly removes his arms from my shoulders. Smooths the flat of his right palm down the navy-blue tie; ensuring the little dolphin are all as perfect as he wants them to be. *At least he's wearing my favorite tie.*

"I'm going to work."

"John?"

"Not now, Vivian. I can't be near you knowing that hateful bitch is sharing your headspace on top of all the other vile shit floating around my head with…" He cuts his words off before he says something that would further destroy whatever this latest revelation seems to have broken between us. With a slash of his right hand, he moves to leave the closet… and me.

As his shiny oxfords carry him away from me, his voice rings out and I know he's really done. "I can't with any of this fucking bullshit right now. I'll see you later this evening. I may have to work late, if so, eat without me. I—I'll try to *tend* to you later."

He breezes out the closet door and the mouthwatering sillage lingers in my nostrils and just like that; I'm hot as fish grease.

***

290

Today has been one hot mess after the next. Every time the phone rang, I thought it was John. *It never was.* I was not going to call him because I'd done nothing to deserve his ire. I'm sitting in my office, with my confused head in my hands when I hear someone walk into my space. I know for a fact, I should be alone, but my addled brain can only deal with what's in front of me.

Lifting my leaden head, I find myself staring into the most beautiful pair of gray eyes, I've ever seen. Not just gray. These eyes are an empyreal phenomenon—the planet Mercury in retrograde. *Fuck, but he's as gorgeous as his eyes.* I wait him out, because I'm sure I wasn't expecting him. I'm not expecting anyone. I'm waiting for the alarm bells to ring inside my mind. For the girls to be up in arms about a stranger showing up at the gallery after what happened with Kerrigan, but no. Nothing.

I level him with my I-take-no-bullshit face and tilt my head slightly to the right. His energy is a moving, writhing thing in the space between us, if he doesn't say something within the next five seconds, I'll be pushing this silent alarm. *Five, four, three…*

"Um…I'm sorry—I think. I apologize for comin' on ye withit an appointment." My lips twitch before I'm able to pull them back into their severe pinched state. His voice; it sounds like he may be humming behind his words while he speaks them. I've never heard anything like it before, it's extremely satisfying to listen to.

I realize now, I'm the one staring blankly into his eyes as if I don't speak the same language as he does. *You don't speak the same language, Viv.* The downward tilt of his head and the slight clearing of his throat brings me back to the moment.

"Excuse me?"

"Um… I said, I'm sorry for comin' to ye withit an appointment but I've been waitin' for like four hours an' th' lass told me to sit down an' bide until ye came out your office to get me. Walked it th' door about ten minutes ago. She didn't tell me to leave… so, I thought I'd check in wi' ye. Ye can, see if I shoulds leave ye and try again in tha' morn. Night." I vaguely understand some of what he's saying. Enough to know that this poor guy has been waiting for me for hours. He has the most lyrical way of speaking. When he says words with the 'or'-sounds, it sounds like he says them with the 'ur'-sound. And then there's that humming sound at the back of every word

I am going to murder Tammi! Right after I fire her slack ass. "I'm sorry, did you say you've been waiting outside my office for *four* hours? And my *former* assistant Tammi told you to do so?"

"Aye. She said ye were thrang as buck an'…" I cut him off because I know I have no idea what the hell he just said. I wear my confusion on my face like I'm proud of it. He notices and flashes me a smile that probably could leave me pregnant if I weren't already carrying a child. *Holy fucking shit, but the man is gorgeous!*

I find my voice and tip my mouth up in a rueful smile of my own and incline my head in question. Raising my right eyebrow for good measure.

"Mind telling me what thrang as buck means before you continue?" I broaden my smile, so he knows I'm amused but not making fun of his beautiful, lyrical speech patterns.

"Aye. Sometimes I forget I'm not at home. Carolina is as bonny as Auld Reekie, that'd be Old Smokey to ye. I hail from Edinburgh, Scotland.

"That explains your beautiful tongue… I—I mean, the beautiful way you speak." I shake my head and feel the warmth grow in my cheeks at my Freudian slip. I chance a look at him and see an enchanting bemused

twinkle in those ethereal eyes. Like stars dancing just for the joy of being able to do so.

"Aye. So, to clarify what I said. It means to be busy. Extremely busy. She—Tammi said ye probably wooldn't have time for my; an' I quote, 'raggedy, white-trash ass'." His forced American accent is a thing of hilarity, but what the hell was Tammi thinking?

"For the love of all stupid people. I'm so sorry you were treated like that. And in my gallery, too! I'm Vivian Ellis, owner of La Magnolia Nior. It's really late, and I was getting ready to lock it up and head home, but since you've been waiting all this time—how about I order dinner and we sit and chat a while?" He looks as if he wants to jump across the desk and kiss me. I hope he doesn't, he's too pretty and I'm still too angry at my husband to stop him if he tries.

48

It's after 12:30 am when I walk into the kitchen from the garage. The only illumination is coming from the three hand-blown pendulum lights we had custom made at One Eared Cow in downtown Columbia. I don't hear anything, not even my own breathing and then I realize I'm holding my breath. I let it out slowly and shake off the weird feelings buzzing under my skin.

"John, I'm home." I walk into the breakfast nook situated just off the kitchen, looking for any sign of life. Not finding any, I head towards his office through the family room, but before I can move into the hallway, a hand grabs me around my neck from behind. I feel his big body press against my back and smell the Macallan riding his warm, humid breath as he breathes words, slurred and heavy, against my goose flesh skin.

"So, you are. *Lovely-mine.* So. You. Are." He smells like he's been drinking all day and all night; for every day he's been alive. The weight of him as he holds himself up using my back is too much, I move to side step but his hand tightens over my windpipe.

"Where have you been, *lovely-mine*? Surely you didn't have people wantin' to pur-ch-ase art at this late clock time." His words and breath are so heavy, they sound like led encased in cement. If we were under water, each soft syllable spoken would drag us further into the murky depths of his anguish. *What's got him in such a mood?*

"No, not a customer, John. An artist who had been told to wait outside my office until I came to get him… it's a long story; I felt horrible for him having to wait for over four hours, so I took the time to chat with him over dinner at the gallery. I called and left several messages. I even texted you a few times. You never responded… so—"

"So, you what, lovely? You thought it… that I was f-f—okay wid you stayin' out by yo-self when we still can't find that fucker, doc-Ha-wee-mothafuckin'-Kerrigan? Is tha' what you thought, *Vivan?*" His sloppy, wet lips are pressed against the back of my neck, making the yummy vegetable lo mein noodles I had for diner, crawl up my throat. I swallow convulsively in an attempt to keep the bile down, but I'm not going to win this battle. Between the pregnancy hormones, his sour breath, and the nasty feel of his mouth on my neck; I'm pretty sure I'm going to vomit all over the floor.

And that's exactly what I do. In college-girl-after-a-kegger fashion; I leave everything on the hardwood floor in the doorway between the family room and the hallway leading to his office.

"Wha' the eva-lovin fuck, Viv?!" His hand leaves my neck and he's jumping back like my vomit is radioactive and able to disintegrate his sorry ass if it touches him.

"You stink like drunk and filthy men who do vile and nasty things to little girls! And your mouth. So sloppy and wet on my skin, you make me sick. Your rancid smell and soft, careless lips…" The tears are flowing in earnest, now and I know exactly why I'm crying. I also know, they won't stop. I stomp over the mess I made and run up the stairs to our bedroom, slam and lock the door before I go into the bathroom. I lock that door for good measure before starting the process of disrobing and turning the shower on.

"Fuck you! Fuck you, Jonathan Raynard Ellis!" I scream to the top of my lungs and cry from the depths of my shattered soul. *I really, really hate him right now.*

There's a single path of dappled light streaking across the bed at an angle so perfect, it makes me want to get a picture of it. I run my hand

through the band of diffused moonbeam because it looks so warm against the gray bedding I'm snuggled in... alone. I'm wrapped in my 8000 thread count sheets all by myself because my drunk, asshat of a husband is a... well, an asshat.

***

Sleep finds me with tears in my eyes and a heaviness in my chest because right now, my heart is breaking. I can't believe he would do what he did tonight. Knowing what I endured at the hands of the men my father gave me to. The drug dealers who used me over and over again for their own filthy and depraved pleasure. He knows my triggers. What they do to me and still... he would approach me the way he did.

***

"Damn, Bobby! you didn't lie when you said that she is worth a week of crack."

"Daddy, what's going on—who is this Daddy? Daddy don't let him touch me. Help me...Daddy."

Once he was naked, he grabbed his dick. It's too big...even in his giant man-hands. He's going to hurt me with it.

"Come over here and put them juicy little-girl-lips around my fat dick and let me shoot my hot come straight down your throat."

I didn't know what to do, so he stood up and punched me in the face. Marching me out to the front room where my daddy was sitting; sucking on a pipe...

"Bobby. Show this little bitch you gave me how to suck a dick.

Daddy puts his crack pipe down and kneels on the floor in front of the man and wraps his lips around the other man's dick. He works his jaws like when he makes fish lips at me, then he moves his head back and forth, like a chicken.

The man grabs daddy's head and won't let him move it anymore. Then he squeezes my daddy's jaw and they fall open. The man starts to pump himself into my daddy's mouth like my daddy pumps into Valeria when he think he pumping into Vera. He comes. The man. He sounds like a lion. Looks like some kind of king. His skin was the darkest I'd ever seen. Even darker than my daddy. He was so tall and broad. Even I thought he was handsome. Why is he doing the things he does. He could be somebody important. Have any woman he wanted. Why hurt me. I'm only 16. Better me than Valeria. Better me than Vera. Better me than my daddy.

"I'm gone to take this little slut into that room and fuck her asshole. Bobby. Bobby!" Daddy looks up with the man's come dangling from his used lips and nods his head.

"You sure nobody ever had her asshole before."

"Nobody ever had her pussy but me. And nobody ever had her asshole. I was going to take it, but then.."

"Come with me. Time to pay for your daddy crack habit, little-juicy-virgin-asshole-having-girl. Listen..." His voice trails off until we get into my bedroom. "Don't you ever touch drugs. Don't you ever touch liquor. Don't you ever let your daddy or anybody else touch your asshole. That's just for me. Bobby got it bad, he gone to pass that sweet pussy you got around to every drug dealer he can. But I'll let all these fuckers know—you and your asshole belong to me, J.R. Ellis. You got that? Now bend over, time to break this gorgeous backdoor in.

He shoved his giant middle finger inside of me, after spitting on it, and then licking and spitting inside my butthole. He said it needed to be a little wet, and the next time he'd bring something called lube. It hurts. Nothing has ever gone inside of me, back there.

After he stuck two more fingers inside me, he slapped me hard on each of my butt cheeks. He didn't care if I was crying and screaming my head off. He just kept right on pumping in and out of me.

"You startin to bleed. That's good...mean you'll be slick enough for this fat dick to push inside." He took his fingers out and wiped them on my naked butt. I thought he was done, but I felt something bigger than his fingers poking at my gaping backside. Pain. White, hot like lightening cracking open the sky. No rain to diffuse the electricity and make it something beautiful. Just more white, hot lightening cracking me open.

He started to move in and out, tearing skin and abusing tissue... he pumped hard and fast. My bowels poured from me and all over him, and there was nothing I could do to stop it. It stank so bad but I was in too much pain to be embarrassed. I hoped he would stop. Would think it was as gross as I did.

"Fuck yeah. Now you giving us something to work with. I can't get enough of this sweet little asshole. Blood, shit, and tears. I'm hard as fuck."

He was more excited after I lost my bowels than before. When he finishes and wipes himself down he throws my sheet over my destroyed body. I'm still covered in filth and urine, his come, and my blood. When he stands over me and tells me, "You gone have to give me that sweet little asshole and your mouth once a week. I'm gone to keep your daddy high enough to not touch you again. If you tell anybody what happens here...I'll kill you, your daddy, and I'll find that high-yellow whore of a mama and kill her, too.

***

298

I wake up shaking and covered in the coldest sweat I've ever felt on my skin. I run from the bed to the bathroom and throw up just before I reach the toilet. Luckily, the trashcan catches most of it.

After a quick shower, I dress for work and try to shake off the nightmare that John's antics brought on, as I scan the room to make sure I didn't forget anything I need for the day.

The house is pleasantly fragranced when I make my way into the kitchen. There is no sign of what took place only seven and a half hours earlier. I only threw up twice before coming down stairs, I guess morning sickness is starting. I tell myself that to avoid dealing with my nightmare. I grab my favorite travel tea-press mug and put the kettle on. After placing my nettle, ginger, and mint loose-leaf tea in the steeping basket, I set it in my mug while I wait for the kettle to blow.

I mess around the kitchen looking for something to eat that won't make me pray to the porcelain goddess, again. My head is stuck in the pantry, I have my hands around a pack of cheese crackers, when the warmth of possession seeps into my left hip. A slight squeeze and I know he's ready to apologize and possibly talk about what happened yesterday and last night. *Too fucking bad, I have a busy morning and he'll have to wait.*

"Lovely. I'm so damned sorry about. Everything." I back out of the pantry with my mouth full of crackers. *Oh, my God... these are the best damned crackers I've ever eaten. In my entire life. This is the last pack. Add them to the grocery list.* I scoot around him and turn the eye off, pour the steaming water into my travel mug, push the press down and screw it on the top. After swallowing down the knot of crackers lodged in my throat, I look up at him. I just stare into what looks like those nasty chocolate covered cherries with the red syrup inside...he is a beautiful

tragedy. My beautiful tragedy. I flash him a tired smile and give him a minute to accept the olive branch extended in good faith.

"Thank you, Viv. I'm an asshole of epic proportion and you put up with me. Why? Why do you put up with me?" He looks so confused and lost, I drop my beloved pack of cheese crackers on the island beside everything else I need for the day and go to him.

Wrapping my arms around his trim waist, I whisper into his neck, "Because I love you. Because I know when you're hurting and scared, you don't know how to handle it. Because I know you, John." I back away, grab my pack of crackers, my cup of tea, and my satchel. I turn to leave; his hand reaches out for me like he doesn't want me to go, but they fall back to his side. He looks so ruined. I turn the doorknob and walk to my car. He has to learn to deal with his own shit in more constructive ways.

~49~

Seven days ago, I left a broken and dismantled John standing in our kitchen. I left him to deal with his shit in a more constructive manner. I hugged him and told him I loved him. That I knew him. Then I grabbed my shit and walked away from him. While his entire sense of self was breaking into a million tiny pieces. I. Fucking. Left. Him. To deal with this shit in a more constructive way!

Vivian, it a mothafuckin thing you or nobody else coulda done to keep John in this goddamned house with us. Why you keep beatin yourself up bout it? He a grown ass fuckin man, if he don't wanna be here...let his funky actin ass go. It ain't like you need him to take care of you and the baby.

Valery! Please? Just... leave me alone. Get out of my head and let me work my way through the fact that the soul made to mirror my own just up and walked out of my life. No note. Nothing. He's just gone.

Well, first off—it ain't just your mothafuckin head! It belong to three goddamned other people; did you forget about the bitches inside this crowed head?

How in the hell could I forget about you all? Stop being stupid, Val. I just—d-don't feel like. Talking about this.

You seem plenty fuckin alright to talk bout it with Mr. Collin-I can't speak no English, but I can eye-fuck you in all the languages-Duguid.

Are you fucking kidding me, right now?! Collin is a client. I'm working to help him get established as an artist, and why the hell am I explaining any of this to you. Leave me alone, Valery.

***

I open my eyes and realize I've been standing in my closet for the last however many minutes or hours having a stupid conversation with a stupid alter, all while thinking about where the fuck my stupid asshat of a husband

is. The ringing of the doorbell jerks me into action and I somehow find myself moving towards the stairs. *God, I hope this is Jessa. I need her like manna.*

"Still no word." This is how I'm greeted as I open the front door of my home and wait for Jessa to come in. She's one of the earth elements; draped in burnt orange and deep maroon. She looks like the perfect fall day, bright and crisp, but still warm and inviting. Like a hug. A warm hug. As soon as she crosses the threshold, I fall into her arms and soak up some of her Fall warmth.

She wraps her arms around me and continues to envelop me in her love and serenity. In her arms I find what I need to keep the break from happening. I will not let Jonathan Raynard Ellis break me. Not again, never again.

"I've got you and you've got you, too." Jessa coos into my ever-growing breasts as she rubs firm withershins circles in the center of my back. Somehow; her voice and counter clockwise ministrations ease the tension that's been riding me like I'm some kind of work mule. I take my first real breath since John's disappearing act. I continue to breath her in and just let myself be. Be cracked. Be hurt. Be angry. Be scared. Be alone. Be supported. Be loved. Be me.

"That's it, Vivian. Be exactly what you are and don't try to be anything else in this moment." I just keep right on breathing, focusing on the sound of Jessa's voice and the feeling of her hand on my back and my breath. I focus on my breath; how it expands my entire ribcage and then brings it all back together again. I like the feeling of being filled up with air—so full, there's no room for anything other than me.

"Take another cleansing breath for me and hold it this time while I loosen up your energy some, okay?"

"Yes." That's pretty much all I'm able to get past my lips before I'm taking the deepest breath I've ever taken in my life and holding onto it like it's the only thing giving me *life*. Jessa cups her hands over my forehead, covering both my eyes and nose and part of my mouth.

Heat is radiating from her fingers as they hover just above my skin, not touching but still in contact with me. I'm not sure how long I've been holding my breath, but I have this warm feeling floating over and through my body. Like someone is blowing warm air in my nose and into my bloodstream.

I'm breathing, but it's not like any breathing I've ever done before. The breaths I'm taking are full and complete. Each one bringing with it a sense of peace and calm. Like everything is already alright. Like the path I'm embarking on may not be the one I saw for myself, but it's the one I need. The one we all need. Wherever John is, it's exactly where he needs to be. Right now. Right at this moment, his place is not with me and this child growing in my belly.

***

"I send you love and peace and balance, Jonathan Raynard Ellis. I'll love you always, you are as much a part of me as my alters. We are as entwined and fated as Baucis and Philemon. If I don't get to love you again in this form, I'll love you in whatever form we take the next time we meet." I speak these words aloud as if I'm having a conversation with John because for some reason I know he feels what I'm feeling. Jessa encourages me to continue to speak my truth to my husband as if she believes he hearing it, too.

"John. I see what we are, what we always were. All this time, I thought my soul had been broken and destroyed by moments and circumstances too difficult for me to bear. Loving you. Sacrificing myself to you—to your need

303

for me; showed me the truth of myself and the truth of you, too. John. Sir. Master. You house the soul that mirrors my own. Both shattered by love and lies and secrets. Created to devastate the other. Who knew we would fall so deeply in love?" I smile thinking about the irony of our union. How unbelievably inexplicably John and this body are mirror reflections of each other. A soul so dynamic and complicated, he required four souls to show him the truths he hid from himself.

"Is there more you want or need to say to John, Vivian?" Jessa's soft voice brings me from my ruminations and I nod my head in the affirmative.

"You knew, didn't you, John? Why you were so drawn to me? Why you had to have me? Until recently, I had no idea why I reacted so instinctively to you. Didn't understand how I could acquiesce to your demands for my obedience; my submission; but we were inevitable, John."

"Vivian, what are you talking about. What do you mean, you were inevitable?" I ignored Jessa and kept right on talking to John as if he were standing in front of me. I can see him looking down at me with the sweetest, most obsessive gaze known to man. His full bottom lip pouting slightly, while the sculpted top lip rest patiently to either smile or scowl. The second most beautiful man I've ever seen.

" I knew exactly why I was drawn to you in the beginning. I'm finally letting myself see what I never wanted to see before. You are the spitting image of your father, the man who pulled me into existence. The man Vera's father turned loose on his twelve-year-old daughter to further abused her body. The demon who supplied her father with all the drugs he could ever want as long as he got to have filthy, depraved sex with his only daughter." I hear Jessa gasp in the background. The girls are clawing inside my head for my attention but I know if I don't get all of this out right now, I'll completely lose my mind. So, I continue speaking to John.

" He made me call him Junior Ellis. I thought his name was Junior. He was using his initials. Didn't want me to be able identify him if I ever got bold enough to tell someone what was happening to me. To Vera. To Valeria. But his name wasn't Junior Ellis. His name was Jonny Raymond Ellis. Turns out, you're not the first Ellis man to covet my ass for your selfish desires. We were made for each other, John. Della created the perfect Dom in you; and your father created the perfect sub in me." Silence. Not even the girls are saying anything. I don't want to look over and see what I know is on Jessa's beautiful face, so I finish telling him the last of what I need to say before I lose my nerve.

"Mirrored souls. We were created in the bowels of depravity, greed, and shame. I don't know if we were fated to love, hate, or destroy each other but it doesn't matter one way or the other; does it? We reflect the best parts of you and you reflect the best parts of us. When you're not with us, our light ceases to shing and the same is true for you… with us. How else is a soul to know every facet of itself if there is no suitable mirror to shine light into the depths of its hidden truths?" *I love you through infinity and even further than that. If you don't come back to me in this life, I'll see you in the next one. Don't be late.*

THE END

Epilogue

I never thought I would come back to this god-forsaken place. I pay taxes on both houses. Pay some company to maintain the yards. Pay another company to come in twice a week to keep the homes in pristine condition, reporting any maintenance issues to a dummy number I established to get messages and handle any problems. The home... house my mother and step father died in is still beautifully updated and as empty as it always was. The—the house where Auntie spoon-fed me my manhood is as beautiful and magically destructive as it always was.

What the fuck am I even doing here? I have a beautiful, pregnant, but fucked-up wife back at home. She has no idea where I am or why I left. I had every plan to be waiting for her when she came home from work after gifting me with her forgiveness and walking out the door. I'd stayed up all night. Cleaning the floor and the rest of the house.

I knew exactly what being drunk and sloppy with her would trigger. I wanted to hurt her because the revelation Vera laid at my feet fucked my head up. I blamed Vivian for making her tell me. *Stupid fucking asshole.*

It's been fifteen motherfucking days since I've slept in my house, and sixteen since being inside my wife, but nothing inside me will allow me to drive back home. I can't face her because if she asks me the question she did in the bathtub—before she beat the shit out of me—again, I don't have an answer for her.

I need to be able to answer that damned question. To do that, I need to figure out why the fuck Auntie would do what she did. Why would she leave an innocent little girl and go off to live her life. Only to settle down in our neck of the woods and take care of someone else's child. Because that's what I was; a child. Sixteen and subbing for a thirty-eight-year-old

306

woman who had a twelve-year-old daughter who was being passed around to drug dealers and coping the only way she could.

I open the door leading into Auntie's house. I still smell her sweet jessamine scent. I only close the screen door as I place my keys on the desk. I watch the autumn leaves dance with such vim, I wish I could join them. Feel as energetic and lively as they do. Just as I turn to sit at the desk, the tinkling of windchimes draws my eyes to the side of the porch. They sound just like Auntie's and Vivian's laughter. My breath dies in my chest. My heart refuses to beat. And for one eternal moment I see them all together. Della R. Bruno holding a chubby little girl she named Vera Anne Bruno. A man stands behind the chair with his hands draped over the shoulders of the woman he loves and the child he adores. He's handsome and kind. Della turns her arrogant chin up to look into his doting eyes and she mouths the words that seals the fate of all of us.

I don't want to belong to you or her anymore. I break my ties with both of you. If that means both of you break, so be it. Break. But you will do it without me.

I'm sitting at the desk when the image fades away and the tinkling is no longer making a sound. I feel her moving through the rooms. Taunting me. Teasing my senses with her scent. With her energy.

Della. Auntie. Violet, what did you do? What the fuck did you do?

I pull the pen from the mason jar sitting on the upper right corner and find some writing paper in the drawer. *Exactly where she always kept her fancy stationary. I can't have Viv worrying after me.* I need to find answers and I can't do that here. She'll understand because she understands me. We are exactly what she said we were. Our souls aren't mated… they're mirrored. When I return to her and our child, our souls will be consecrated.

THE END

307

Excerpt from Consecrated Souls

I can't believe it's already November. Time flies when you're too busy to give a damn about days of the week. But here it is. November 3, 2002, and I'm sitting in the doctor's office waiting to be seen. I'm a little over thirteen weeks pregnant and already in my second trimester. I haven't heard a word from John since the day he left. I'm doing all I can to stay centered and focused on what's in front of me. No need to look back, I'm not going that way.

Jessa and the girls are so supportive. Even Valery seems to have gotten her shit together. At least for now, she's behaving. Maybe John is like catnip to her. Maybe having him around made her a little—okay, a lot bit crazy. Jessa says that make sense because it was John who wrenched her from my soul. I don't see Jessa's mother, in fact I fired her as soon as I realized John was no longer here to guide me in this journey. I miss him. Lord, I miss that man but if he needs to be out there doing whatever he's out there doing. Wherever he's out there doing it…I hope it's working for him.

"Vivian Ellis, we're ready for you. Come on back."

"Hi. You need to get my weight, right?"

"Yes ma'am, we do. If you'll just remove your shoes and place your belongings on the counter. We'll get it over with."

"Okay." I walk over to the scales and step on. Immediately I close my eyes. I haven't been eating all that well, and I'm sure I'm not at the weight I should be. I've got to do better. At least the morning-last-all-day-sickness seems to be fading some.

"Alrighty then. You're at 162 pounds. Only gained four pounds since your last visit, Hmmmmmm. How's the morning sickness?"

"It's actually getting a little better. I haven't thrown up in the last two days. I'm keeping my fingers crossed that it's over. I haven't been able to eat anything except celery and wheat crackers. Oh, and bless the ginger ale gods because they save me." I chuckle as I walk toward the examining room.

"Will Mr. Ellis be joining us today?" The nurse asks as she hands me the requisite paper gown and sheet. My heart stops, sputters, and starts again. Even it's with a strange rhythm.

"No. He won't be able to join us today." I don't offer an explanation. I don't owe her or anybody else one.

"All right. Well, if you'll get changed, your doctor will be with you shortly. See you soon."

That was not fun. Not at all, but I got through it and I'll get through everything. *I am not alone.*

Even if you wanna be the fuck alone you can't. So what's the point in sayin shit like, I am not alone. Bitch, please. Take your ass in that room and change. No, I ain't here for no trouble. Just heard your silly ass mumbling and came to check on you. You good?

Yes, Val. I'm good. Thank you.

Whatever, bitch. I'm gonna go back to my fuckin room and finish this sketch I been workin on. Hey Viv, you think you can look at it. Tell me what you think?

Uh... um, yes. Of course. I didn't know you were still into art.

Bitch. You don't know everythin about me. Go on. Get naked and put them legs up in them straps. Let the doctor see what your pussy look like and how it feel.

You are not funny so, stop laughing. Stay in your room during my appointment. Nobody needs you trying to squeeze an orgasm out of a pelvic exam.

Ha-ha-ha! You funny as fuck, you know that? But for real, it been like a while since I fucked. Getting backed up over here.

Put all that sexual energy into your art. See what you come up with. I dare you to channel your sex drive into your work.

Channel my sexual energy? You mean mastabate and use my cum to paint or some shit like that?

Valery! What the hell are you thinking. No, don't masturbate and smear your... no. Just no. I mean if you're sexually frustrated because you're not having sex, use that frustration and create something artistic with it.

Oh! Okay. That make sense. I was about to say, damn. Vivian, you a bigga freak than me. Her laughter follows her back into her room, and I find my shoulders shaking with quiet chortles as I change into my fancy paper ensemble. I turn the nob and open the door to walk into the examining room and stop before my foot touches the floor. There's a hum of awareness under my skin. I develop an acute onset of diaphoresis; the paper gown is sticking to my sweat covered body. *How in the hell is he here?*

"Lovely. You've already opened the door. All you have to do is walk through it, now."

Acknowledgments

There is no shortage of people I want to acknowledge in the writing of this second book in the Broken Souls series but I have to start with my husband and three daughters. My husband has been my biggest supporter, sharing me with all the hot, sexy men in my head and not even caring when I compare him to them, lol. Thank you, babe. I love you the most. Oh, and he gifted me with my Writing Cottage during the COVID-quarantine!

To my three girls, you are all rock stars and I love you through infinity. I know I spend a crazy amount of time talking to people you can't see and can't read about...and you still introduce me to your friends. That means a lot to me.

To my beta readers, turned great friends, Thank you so much for your feedback, support, and suggestions. Larissa Trapp, you are so helpful and your support led to some really great opportunities. Somehow we have almost everything in common and we still haven't had a proper coffee together. Love you. Tina Caldwell, your friendship and support mean more to me than I can say. Thank you for being my best cheerleader, I love you. James Davis, what can I say. I love you like a brother...ha-ha! Thank you for being in my corner and reading everything I write... even the sucky first drafts.

To my editor, Vickey Brown of Brownstone WES Consulting Group, LLC... What can I say. I gave you over one hundred thousand words and you gave me a sharp knife and made me bleed my manuscript. Thank you for your tough-get-shit-done approach to editing. And for the red wine at the end. You make my stories readable.

Last because you are the most important ones on my list of thank yous. The readers who continue to take a chance on an independent writer committed to sharing stories featuring Black characters with dignity, style, and grace. Thank you for reading, leaving reviews, and recommending my books. You willingness to do so inspires me.

About the Author

I knew I wanted to be a writer from the young age of ten or eleven. I'd just finish reading Flowers for Algernon and had completely fallen in love with words; how easily they swept me away to places I never even knew existed. I decided then and there that I wanted to be a magician and use words to create different worlds where other people could travel and discover new parts of themselves.

But then I grew up and accepted the notion that magic wasn't real and I traded in my dreams for a steady paycheck and summers off. Thankfully, the Universe saw fit to release me from my poor decision and gave me the freedom and time to pursue my first love of writing again.

In 2013 I was diagnosed with systemic lupus as well as a host of other autoimmune disease. I won't lie and say it's easy living in a body hell bent on attacking and destroying healthy organs, tissue, and systems but it did change my perspective on what it means to truly be alive.

After getting a handle on managing my health and assembling some of the best doctors in the Southeastern USA and making some difficult lifestyle changes, I was free to write the books I wanted to read, but couldn't find.

It's because of the love and devotion of my best friend and soul mate, that I'm able to stay at home and do what I love instead of what I have to. Together we have three beautiful daughters who constantly inspire me to strive to be the highest version of myself and live my most intentional life as I embrace my sacred womanhood..

Made in the USA
Middletown, DE
11 June 2023

32083866R00175